PERSONAL
DAYS

< *ED PARK* >

Random House Trade Paperbacks   New York

PERSONAL DAYS

A NOVEL

A Random House Trade Paperback Original

Copyright © 2008 by Ed Park

All rights reserved.

Published in the United States by Random House Trade Paperbacks, an imprint of The Random House Publishing Group, a division of Random House, Inc., New York.

RANDOM HOUSE TRADE PAPERBACKS and colophon are trademarks of Random House, Inc.

Grateful acknowledgment is made to Alfred Publishing Co., Inc., and Hal Leonard Corporation for permission to reprint an excerpt from "Run," words and music by Peter Hook, Gillian Gilbert, Stephen Morris, Bernard Sumner, and John Denver, copyright © 1989 by Vitalturn Co. Ltd. and Cherry Lane Music. All rights on behalf of Vitalturn Co. Ltd administered by Warner Chappell Music Ltd. All rights reserved. Used by permission of Alfred Publishing Co., Inc., and Hal Leonard Corporation.

Library of Congress Cataloging-in-Publication Data

Park, Ed.
Personal days: a novel/Ed Park.
p.   cm.
ISBN 978-0-8129-7857-5
1. Offices—Fiction.   2. Interpersonal relations—Fiction.
3. Office politics—Fiction.   4. Corporate reorganizations—
Fiction.   5. Satire.   I. Title.
PS3616 .A7432P47   2008
813'.6—dc22   2007040834

www.atrandom.com

Design by Liz Cosgrove

147028622

For my parents

Well you don't get a town like this for nothing
So here's what you've got to do
You work your way to the top of the world
Then you break your life in two.

< NEW ORDER >

< *CONTENTS* >

< **/** >

C A N ' T

U N D O

< **1** >

Who died?

On the surface, it's relaxed. There was a time when we all dressed crisply, but something's changed this summer. Now while the weather lasts we wear loose pants, canvas sneakers, clogs. Pru slips on flip-flops under her desk. It's so hot out and thus every day is potentially casual Friday. We have carte blanche to wear T-shirts featuring the comical logos of exterminating companies, advertising slogans from the early '80s. *Where's the beef?* We dress like we don't make much money, which is true for at least half of us. The trick is figuring out which half. We go out for drinks together one or two nights a week, sometimes three, *to take the edge off.* Three is too much. We make careful note of who buys a round, who sits back and lets the booze magically appear. It's possible we can't stand each other but at this point we're helpless in the company of outsiders. Sometimes one of the guys will come to work in a coat and tie, just to freak the others out. On these days the guard in the lobby will joke, *Who died?* And we will laugh or pretend to laugh.

The Sprout

In summer the Sprout, our boss, suggests we form a softball team. His name is actually Russell. We refer to him as the Sprout, because

Russell → Brussels → brussels sprouts → *the Sprout*.

No one knows who came up with the name first.

We're incredibly mature.

Also once in a while he has a bit of comb-proof hair sprouting from his scalp's left rear quadrant.

Jonah says it's hard to take the Sprout seriously because he's always using *i.e.* and *e.g.* in his sentences, vigorously but interchangeably, a mark of weak character.

He sometimes gives us little salutes when he sees us in the hall. Lately he's been flashing the peace sign. Sixty-five percent of the time he acts like he's our friend but we should remember the saying: *Friends don't fire friends.*

Sticks and carrots

Sixty-five percent of the time is what the Sprout would call a *guesstimate*. He's always breaking things down into precise percentages. He used to be almost normal to talk to, but now he'll ask if we're *on the same page* and say something is a *no-brainer*, all in a single sentence.

It's not just the frequency of these expressions but their haphazard use. Last week he told Laars to *think outside the box*. They were talking about which size manila folders worked best. Afterward he said, *Keep me in the loop and let's touch base next week.*

Pru has wondered if the Sprout, a proud native of Canada, is taking a class in annoying American English. His new thing is a variation on *I gave you a carrot, but I also need to show you the stick*. So far this month, he's said it to Pru, to Jack II, to Laars.

So show us already, Pru complains to Lizzie.

The Sprout understands that it sounds a little sadistic, and lets us know he recognizes this menacing aspect, at the same time wanting us to understand that he doesn't actually mean it in that way. Jonah's take on it is that he *must* mean it in that way, or else he'd use another phrase.

A league record

Softball is a morale-boosting carrot that the Sprout most likely has read about in a handbook or learned at that seminar he goes to every March. Morale has been low since the Firings began last year. Pru says *morale* is a word thrown around only in the context of its absence. You never look at a hot young thing and say, *Check out that spring chicken*, but only use it to describe your great-aunt: *She's no spring chicken*.

Pru has a point. We tend to trust her, with her serious eyebrows and inevitable skeptical *hmmm*. She went to graduate school. We think it was in art history, but maybe it was regular history, the kind without the art.

We decide to give softball a shot. There are eight of us. In decreasing order of height: Laars, Jack II, Lizzie, Jonah, Jenny, Crease, Pru, Jill. We need a ninth, and Jack II happens to bump into Otto, who used to be in IT. He is now working somewhere in midtown and clearly has too much time on his hands.

It might be nice to rejuvenate our comically untoned bodies. Too many of us have been eating bagels at our desks, too many mornings in a row. We look like we've been squeezed out of a tube and haven't quite solidified. Everyone has issues with posture except Lizzie, a corseter's dream.

Laars and Jenny are the only ones who have ever played softball before—Laars at his last job, Jenny as a seven-year-old. The concept: You try to hit the ball hard but without so much upward arc that someone can catch it. Then you run in a square, or more properly a diamond, making sure to step on each base and not get tagged by someone bearing the ball. There are other rules that we never quite iron out.

Lizzie is having trouble seeing the carrot aspect of the game.

We buy mitts, glove oil, cleats. Laars buys two aluminum bats and two wooden ones. He buys a third kind of bat, a titanium hybrid that looks like a nuclear warhead. Laars can be seen doing push-ups near the storage area, counting off under his breath.

We have jerseys and caps printed with our emblem, a buxom elf winking and holding a pool cue. Jill found it on some Finnish clip-art site.

We prematurely end our season after losing the first game 17–0, said to be a league record. What's left of our morale seeps away. We never see Otto again. All the gear gets returned, except the jerseys and caps. Autumn approaches, the air too cool for the jerseys, but we still wear the hats sometimes.

The cult of Maxine

Maxine never officially joined the softball team but bought a jersey from Jill, cutting the collar to create a plunging V. She still wears it on occasion, even as the weather turns nippy.

Maxine towers over us in her medium heels. She makes us feel like hobbit-folk, with our stained teeth and ragamuffin outfits. With the exception of Laars, we have zero upper body strength. We are moderately proud of our youthful haircuts and overpriced rectangular eyeglasses but that's about it.

She smells great and we are all basically obsessed with her. *It has to seriously stop,* Lizzie says. Crease calls her *aggressively hypnotic* and can hardly bear to be within a twenty-yard radius. He sometimes crosses himself after she passes.

Her hair! Jack II will e-mail, out of the blue. Everyone knows whose hair he's talking about.

Sharing an elevator ride alone with Maxine can be intensely disorienting. We try to avoid it. Several times of late, while waiting for the elevator at the end of the day, Crease has sensed Maxine's approach, her distinctive shoe-clack sending him darting in the other direction. In similar situations, Jenny has been known to mumble to herself, giving the impression that she's forgotten something at her desk. Jenny likes boys but sometimes when Maxine is in the room she's not so sure.

Laars says Maxine smells like the exquisite blossom of a rare hybrid fruit that you can only find at this one stall in a market in Kuala Lumpur.

The worst is when you turn the corner and you see her and you want to say *Hi* in a normal way but all that happens is your mouth opens and you make a little croaking sound or make no noise at all. It was Jules, no longer among us, who first identified this phenomenon.

There is so much to take in. Not just her clothes or lack of clothes, not just her amazing hair, but her entire philosophy of being. You can detect an aspect of the beauty queen in her looks and high-gloss appearance, her attention-yanking laugh and borderline moronic statements. But Pru has argued, in the landmark case *Pru* v. *Jonah,* that she's not only not stupid but definitely more accomplished than the rest of us. We don't know what's on that résumé, but it doesn't matter—she's got that magic, that *spark*, utterly unclouded by self-doubt.

Maxine is on a different track than the rest of us. She entered the office at a higher level and we'll never catch up. By the time we reach her current position—in the event we haven't burned out, drifted away—she'll have scaled even greater heights, afloat on a cloud of boundless confidence and even more tantalizing scents. All of this should be illustrated in the manner of a medieval vision of the afterlife.

Lizzie is lying

Empirically speaking, Maxine's not so hot, according to Lizzie, the nicest of us. This is what passes for dissent in our little group. *I seriously don't see the appeal.*

In time Lizzie comes to share our fascination, albeit in a different way. For Lizzie what's interesting is the phenomenon of Maxine worship, rather than her actual qualities. She compares it to when we all obsessed over that reality show in which ambitious people our age backstabbed and slept with each other in order to become chefs at an exclusive French restaurant, and then the restaurant turned out not to exist.

Let's not and say we did

Maxine's latest e-mail bears the subject line *Let's Talk About SEX.*

No, moans Pru, dreading yet another sexual-harassment seminar. We never had one before Maxine came to the company. The seminars produce the opposite of the intended effect, making us feel like sex maniacs, but at least they're better than the mental health seminars the Sprout used to hold. *Those* made us depressed, even violent—Laars once punched the wall by the bulletin board so hard that his hand has never been the same. He blames this injury for his subpar softball performance.

Today Maxine makes wanton eye contact with the seminar leader, a lawyer named George. She's wearing a sheer shirt known commonly as *that shirt*. Pru knows the brand and everything.

George looks like he's just come back from vacation and is about to go on another one. His relaxed manner is exhausting to contemplate. All of us secretly wonder why we didn't go to law school, and also whether it's too late.

It is.

The gist of the meeting is that you should never date anyone in the office, ever. You should also be extremely careful about what you say to someone of the opposite or indeed the same sex. Many seemingly harmless sentences, phrases, even words, and actually individual *letters* can be construed as harassing. Never say anything about what somebody's wearing. Also, just to be safe, don't wear anything too revealing.

We all frown and gaze at Maxine in her flesh-colored mesh number. The hypocrisy, the *everything,* is too much.

Jonah says, *Don't we need eros in order for commerce to happen?* in that affected pensive tone he sometimes adopts, a pause every two words.

Do we? Admittedly, it's a stumper. None of us really knows. He sits up straight, strokes his chin in agitation. The tips of his ears go scarlet with rage. He should have been a philosophy professor or a union organizer for sooty paperboys. He says that, by the logic of the seminar, the subject line of Maxine's e-mail constitutes sexual harassment of sorts. He slaps the table—case closed!

The rest of us don't say anything, partly because we're afraid the Sprout is taking notes and will fire us, but mostly because we are getting hungry and have lost the will to fight. Usually at these meetings there's a stack of sandwiches and coffee—what the Sprout would call a *carrot*—and sometimes actual, literal carrots. But not today.

Lizzie nudges Pru. The Sprout is in the corner, eyes narrowed in concentration, chin planted in chest. Jonah's remarks have sent him deep into thought, so deep that he's actually sleeping.

The outside world

As we're filing out, George, the lawyer, asks Maxine, *Grab lunch?*

Just like that.

Two words.

She beams at the prospect. Our jaws fall off their hinges and Crease mimes shooting himself in the head.

Lizzie goes foraging for Claritin and Red Bull. *Does anyone want anything from the outside world?* she asks.

On the way to the drugstore she spies George and Maxine sliding into his car, a silver BMW.

Maxine is gone for the rest of the day. We have all been monitoring the situation intently. Laars says something critical of BMWs, German engineering, the legal profession as a whole. Laars rides his bike to work when he can. Today he wears a faded long-sleeved T advertising a New Jersey swimming pool company, the white letters nearly washed away, a recent flea market find. What could Maxine possibly see in

George? Pru points out that George wears a clean shirt, the kind with buttons.

Us/them

Is Maxine one of us? One of them? For the first few months we were under the misapprehension that she was someone's secretary, but then we started getting memos from her, some with a distinctly shape-up/ship-out undercurrent.

She might even outrank the Sprout. The subject merits closer, more fanatical observation. Could it be that the Sprout reports to *her*?

Pru tells us how all of the Sprout's issues about working for such a practically mythological creature as Maxine get inflicted on *us*. His lust for her leads to his hatred of us, roughly. His fear of her makes him want us to fear *him*.

As Pru talks, she flowcharts it on a pad, little multidirectional arrows and *FEAR* in huge letters.

The cc game

Against the advisement of George, Maxine will sometimes compliment us on our hair or other aspects of our scruffy appearance. The next day, or even later the same day, she'll send an all-caps e-mail asking why a certain form is not on her desk. This will prompt a peppy reply, one barely stifling a howl of fear:

> Hey Maxine!
> The document you want was actually put in your in-box yesterday around lunchtime. I also e-mailed it to you and Russell. Let me know if you can't find it!
> Thanks!
> Laars
>
> P.S. I'm also attaching it again as a Word doc, just in case.

There's so much wrong here: the fake-vague *around lunchtime*, the nonsensical *Thanks*, the quasi-casual postscript. The exclamation points look downright psychotic. Laars plays what he calls the cc game, sending the e-mail to the Sprout as well. You should always rope in an outside witness in order to prove your competence or innocence. On the other hand, this could be seen as whining.

Maxine never writes back. The Sprout will not get around to Laars's e-mail for a week. He doesn't like to deal with the petty stuff, though it could also be argued that he doesn't like to deal with the big stuff, either.

He will study the e-mail for a few seconds, frown, and then delete it.

Stalling

Despite Maxine's scatterbrained management style and seeming incompetence, we can't help but be caught in her spell. We realize that this is bad. It makes her incompetence seem like brashness, her haphazard ways a calculated line of attack. The more she does everything wrong, the more she can do no wrong.

Lizzie still can't use the bathroom if Maxine's in there. If Lizzie happens to see her by the sink, she'll head into a stall and sit in excruciating, faucet-drip-counting silence.

< *2* >

Jackrub!

Everybody needs a routine. Jack II's thing these days is to drop
by your cubicle between two and three every afternoon and
say *Who needs a backrub?* Even if you don't exactly raise your
hand he latches his mitts onto your shoulders and starts working away. It was nice at first and then it was funny but now it's
out of control. His stress-release technique is itself stressful.
At the sound of Jack II's voice we automatically tilt to face
him so that he can't sneak up and get a grip.

Jackrub! Pru will shout-hiss, a warning signal to all in the
vicinity.

Today, to everyone's surprise, Lizzie accepts a Jackrub. She
says she did something awful with a calculator: She punched
in the Net Pay from her paycheck and multiplied it by 26. The
total was so low she was sure she'd dropped a digit, like maybe
she had multiplied by 6. *I have to economize,* she says, *but I've
already been economizing.*

Except for the shoes, says Pru.

Lizzie needs a new job, but for now she'll take that Jackrub. *Lots of tension in this room*, says Jack II, cracking his knuckles.

The Original Jack

We call him Jack II because there was a Jack before him, now known as the Original Jack. He was let go during the Firings a year ago and no one's stayed in touch. This nickname-after-the-fact makes us think of him as a whimsical chap, always ready with a wisecrack or droll observation. Actually he was on the dull side and could be a total asshole.

People drop off the radar once they leave the office. Week after week, you form these intense bonds without quite realizing it. All that time together adds up: muttering at the fax machine, making coffee runs. The elevator rides. The bitching about the speed of the elevator. The endlessly reprised joke, as it hits every floor: *Making local stops.*

You see co-workers more than you see your so-called friends, even more than you see your significant others, your spouses if you have them. None of us do at the moment, though there are reports that Jenny's on the verge.

Lizzie has a hunch that Crease was once married. *He has that I Was Married look*, she says. *The blank stare.*

We know each other well but only to a point.

Instant folklore

Laars looks gaunt these days, his floppy hair hanging limp around his temples. More and more he lies for a spell on the pungent but very comfortable maroon sofa he inherited from Jason. *I just need to close my eyes.* He confesses to spending his evenings nursing Scotch before his computer at home,

Googling himself until the wee hours. There's a person out there who shares the same name, incredibly enough. Person or persons. He's found himself in Appalachian hiking e-gazettes, antique typewriter societies, and University of Alaska alumni newsletters. *I must destroy them*, he says.

Worse is when he Googles former girlfriends, high school crushes, drunken flings from his semester abroad. There are more of all of these than you would imagine—indeed, than *he* imagined.

He's good-looking but not that *good-looking*, says Pru. Lizzie thinks he gets a lot of mileage out of the floppy hair.

Laars's innumerable past dalliances trouble him and he publicly declares a vow of chastity. We could be imagining things but for a second Lizzie's eyes droop with sadness as he says this.

Alas, Laars is powerless to stop the hunt for figures from his past. He tries to devise searches that will sniff out maiden names and the like. But some people are gone for good, they have vanished, and the string of words he puts into the engine returns the most hilariously useless links: midwestern college soccer squads, science fair runners-up, family trees dipping into the eighteenth century.

He does this all day at work now, too, in between complaining about the pencil sharpener and complaining about the air-conditioning. He's found out a lot about his cousin's ex-girlfriend from Spain. No doubt he's Googled everyone in the office, uncovering secrets nestled in the thirty-fifth screen of results.

Jack II says that when you feel a tingling in your fingers, it means someone's Googling you. We take to this bit of instant folklore immediately.

Friendship

Jonah's e-mail sign-off used to read *Sincerely,* then *Sincerely Yours,* then *Cheers.* He disapproves of Lizzie's *Best,* let alone Jenny's *Warm best.* He says it's important to set the right tone with your tagline. For a while he used *Thank you in advance for your cooperation.* Lately every e-mail ends: *Your friend, Jonah.*

What if you're not their friend? asks Pru.

< **3** >

The Californians!

Our company was once its own thing, founded long ago by men with mustaches. After several decades it wound up, to its surprise, as the easternmost arm of an Omaha-based octopus. The tentacles eventually detached, or strangled each other, a few of them joining forces, most dying out altogether.

Over time the name shrunk and mutated, changes captured in reams of old letterhead in the closet by Jonah's office. The stationery reads like the fossil record. Syllables disappeared. Ampersands were added and later removed. In the mid-'90s everything was consolidated into a set of five initials, two of which don't actually stand for anything. The vowelless result defies easy pronunciation, even by longtime employees. You say it a different way every time. This quality lends it a daunting preverbal power.

Lately we hear that some Californians want to make us *their* easternmost outpost. We base this conjecture on an opaquely worded one-inch paragraph on the fifth business page of the *Times* that appeared last month.

Think positive, we tell ourselves. There's no reason to believe that a new owner will be any worse than the current one. But when have things ever gotten better?

We know that the Firings were just a taste of what's in store, and like morbid climatologists tracking twisters, we anticipate their return. If something ominous happens—nasty memo, Coke machine empty two days in a row—we see it as a sign of our new owners' impending arrival.

At these times Pru likes to shriek, *The Californians!*

Jack II thinks the best thing would be for them to come in and clean house, install their own people. He says it's unlikely any of us will survive. *Their mentality is totally different out west*, he says. *I mean, I should know.* He lived in San Diego for about a year after college, trying to be a comedy writer, despite the fact that he is neither outwardly funny nor humorous on the printed page.

You are here

Our office is located on what must be the least populated semi-wide street in all of Manhattan, a no-man's-land just far enough from two fashionable neighborhoods to be considered part of neither. Wind gets stuck here. At twilight, crumpled newspapers scuttle across the pavement like giant crabs. Plastic bags advance in tumbleweed fashion. Sometimes it feels like the edge of the world.

We occupy the middle three floors of a nine-floor building, at the uneasy intersection of two quasi-avenues, which merge without clear signage. Further complicating matters is the abundance of honorary street names for people you've never heard of. Rabbi S. Blankman Street? "Mama" O'Sullivan Road? Who were these colorful figures of yesteryear?

Cabbies throw their hands up and think of turning in their medallions.

The Starbucks just down the road, uncomfortably situated on a corner between a boarded-up bar and a boarded-up locksmith, looks like a bordello. We call it the Bad Starbucks for its low-impact saxophone music and an absence of natural light combined with doomed, possibly improvised original drinks like the Pimm's cup chai.

The Good Starbucks, two blocks farther in the opposite direction, also looks like a house of ill repute, but with better ventilation and more freebies, little paper cups of cake.

We're within five minutes of two subway stops, but at such illogical angles to them that we have difficulty instructing people how to get here: *You go left and then cut across the second parking lot, not the one that says PARK.*

To make it easier we tell them we'll meet up by the newsstand right outside the subway station three blocks away. We ask them beforehand, *What will you be wearing?* We describe ourselves: *Glasses, dark shirt.* This could be anybody.

Slice of life

The Bad Starbucks is where Jenny sees her life coach every Thursday at 4. She doesn't think we know, but we know.

Laars wonders what the difference between a therapist and a life coach is.

A life coach doesn't have an office and isn't accredited, says Lizzie.

Lizzie has been out of sorts these days, slumping at her desk, leg hopping like a jackhammer. She is between therapists right now. She used to see one way uptown. He was good but the commute was killing her. She'd get there late and then they would spend half the remaining time discussing the reasons behind her lateness.

The real reason she stopped going, though, is because the pizzeria around the corner from his office had raised its prices by a quarter. Her therapist used pizza as an inflation barometer, and set his fee at one hundred times the price of a slice, which was now at two bucks, exclusive of toppings.

Jenny later concludes that her life coach uses bagel prices to set her fee.

The grand tour

Sometimes one of us will have a visitor. If it's his or her first time to the building, we'll say, *Do you want the grand tour?* like it's our new apartment. Actually, it's always the guest's first time. No one ever comes back if they can help it, possibly due to overhearing someone like Laars shouting *You are not going to believe the size of this roach.*

After braving or ignoring a sermon from the Holy Roller security guard, and taking the leisurely elevator up, the visitor walks straight into the middle of a labyrinth. Without a reliable guide, he or she can wander vast tracts of lunar workscape before seeing a window. Lizzie remembers her first day on the job: Stepping into this feng-shui-proof layout, heading straight to the bathroom, and crying.

Most of us spend our days at a desk in one of the two archipelagoes of cubicle clusters. The desks have not been at capacity for over a year now, and so we let our stuff sprawl, colonizing adjacent work spaces, hanging a satchel in one, a jacket in another.

A few of us have our own little rooms. Even though everybody could probably snag one at this point, given that staff is dwindling, the Sprout gets very agitated at any such request. *That doesn't work with my comfort level right now.* Better to play it safe. Some of these rooms look out on the back of another office building. We wave to the workers there if our gazes happen to meet, and they wave back. That's as far as it goes.

Jonah has a room with a *door*, but no window. Crease has two desks, on opposite ends of the floor.

The college of noncompetitive running

People put too many things on the bulletin board. Bizarre newspaper items, notices for group shows exhibiting the disgruntled visual expressions of friends of friends, ironically saucy or inscrutable postcards. *Wish you were beer.*

Laars polices this corkboard commotion, giving everything a week before tearing it down. Schedules, announcements, responsibilities: These weigh on his spirit. When Laars started with us—six months, nine months, a year ago?—he was full of pep, but we managed to squeeze it out of him.

Laars occasionally gives off an Ivy League vibe, but he actually went to a small liberal arts college called Aorta or something. None of us have heard of it, a school in the Pacific Northwest that doesn't have grades or even pass-fail. It emphasizes feelings rather than performance. On the website you see pictures of a guy with the eraser tip of his pencil resting on his lip, two girls running noncompetitively—one's wearing jeans—on a weedy-looking track, a white guy with an Afro reading under a tree.

Multiple-desk syndrome

I've got it down to under a minute, says Crease, and as with a lot of what he says, we need a moment to figure out what he's re-

ferring to. *Forty-seven seconds.* He means the traveling time between his two desks. In his mind, everyone is always thinking
about him, worrying over Crease minutiae.

Last year Jason got fired, right in the middle of a project.
No one saw it coming. Crease, who was not on the same team,
was told to take over—*Step up to the plate,* per the Sprout—
but was never told exactly what needed to be done. He had to
figure it out on the fly. *Baptism by fire,* as the Sprout, and later
Crease himself, put it.

With no time to move all of Jason's folders and meticulously organized report bins to his own desk, Crease com-
muted from one side of the office to the other, doing the Jason
work until 2 and his own until he left at 7, at 8, at 9.

When the project was over he started moving his own stuff
from his original desk to Jason's—the same model, but with
better-greased drawers. Jason had vividly colored Post-its from
Japan, exquisite semicircles that he bought on a trip. Crease
loved them but used them sparingly because once they were
gone, that was it.

After his initial burst of nesting, Crease soon discovered he
had more old files than he could easily move, and found himself drifting back to his original home for certain tasks. Now
he keeps his Creasedom divided, flitting between the desks
several times a day. Each desk has a computer. He logs in as
Jason on one, as himself on the other. The commute has become his major form of exercise. He also thinks the division is
a good survival strategy: If they try to fire him when he's not
at one desk, they might lose interest before they find him at
his second home.

< *4* >

It's OK to relax

A while back, the Sprout handed out self-evaluation forms and said, *Help me help you*. We just needed to be as honest as possible. The evaluations would remain anonymous. Some of us, actually all of us, didn't take it seriously enough, writing things like *I enjoy ice cream and unprotected sex*, in a crazy-person scrawl. That was when the Sprout had a sense of humor. Jules, when Jules was here, answered entirely in Spanish.

We thought the Sprout had abandoned this exercise but today there's another round. Everyone gets a golf pencil and a three-page packet. This time he wants our names printed at the top. Maxine strolls the conference room perimeter like a strict but hot schoolteacher, like we imagine teachers are in California.

We put a number to everything, 1 to 6, to reflect the strength of our feeling. The statements have a North Korean vibe, affectless yet intense.

I am happy with the way I am treated.
As the workday ends, it's OK to relax.

Jonah is sure there's a law against this sort of interrogation.

We all respond the way we think the Californians want us to respond, except Jenny, who misheard Maxine's directions and thought that 1 indicated Strongly Agree.

I feel there are other opportunities for me here.

It's not OK

The self-evaluation ends with an essay section. Maxine encourages us to *be creative.*

A flutter of panic turns into a full-fledged spiritual crisis. We all want to get out of there but no one wants to be the first to leave. All of us except Jill wind up staying for ninety soul-searching minutes, crafting epic texts of dashed hope and toxic cynicism. It doesn't occur to us that this is a bad idea until we put down our pencils, fingers sore from using such antique devices.

Jill leaves her sheet blank and flees before everyone else.

Maybe it was an 8

A month ago Maxine e-mailed us elaborate charts that none of us could decipher. The words were cryptic: *Release, Objective, Orient.* Was this information meant for us? She used five different colors, a rainbow of anxious strategy. She used fonts we'd never even seen, fonts so powerful most of our computers crashed.

Our latest theory is that she's a consultant in deep cover, looking to increase profits by 20 percent before the company is sold to the Californians. We base this knowledge on the fact that Laars saw a pie chart in the Sprout's office, with a green wedge that said 20. We're trying to decide whether this means she wants the profit margin to expand to 20 percent, or that the current margin should increase by 20 percent of itself.

Some of us are not so good at math. This might in fact be *why* we were hired.

It should also be noted that later Laars thinks maybe the 2 was a 3. He didn't get a clear view. *Maybe it was an 8?*

The not-so-funny part of our Maxine theory, based on something Pru overheard: She's going to fire three of us by the end of the year, or possibly the end of the month. Pru stood outside the Sprout's office for a whole minute, listening to Maxine complain about us.

On the human-interest side of the ledger, Jenny reports that she's seen Maxine with the sexual-harassment lawyer guy, George, jogging lustily in the park.

Emotional rescue

Jenny says she's heard the Sprout sobbing, the door to his office only partially closed. Jonah accused her of trying to humanize the enemy.

Maybe he was laughing, says Laars. But we all know that the Sprout's laughing doesn't sound like crying. It sounds like this:

Hoo-hoo!

Security issues

Crease thinks that everyone is out to steal his limited-edition Japanese Post-its, the magenta and olive and mandarin orange stickies that he inherited from Jason. We like them, but we're not thieves. On the other hand, why should *he* get to keep them all? He and Jason were never particularly close. Crease's desk has no locks and he doesn't feel that his supply is safe. Sometimes he puts them in his satchel when he leaves the building for lunch.

< **5** >

Because

Whenever we sniff a layoff coming, which is always, each one of us thinks, *It can't be me because* _____.

Because I have *too much work to do*.

Because I'm *exploited as it is*.

Because, really, how much money would they save by getting rid of me versus what untold profits my labor/hard-earned know-how brings in?

I mean I'm joking but seriously.

Realistically, no *way* can it be me.

And then, all of a sudden, it is.

Stay the course

Beware of compliments. You don't want your stock to rise. You want to stay the course. Someone's stock rises and we all feel envious for a couple weeks. Then that person gets axed, or is made so miserable that there's no option but to quit.

It happened to the Original Jack, with his dogged work

ethic. It happened to Jason, with his complex yet elegant system of Post-it notation. It happened to Jules.

Jonah thinks the preliminary praise is unconscious on the Sprout's part, like a poker player's tell.

The departed send us e-mails after they leave and we forget to write back forever.

Dead letter

Has anyone noticed that the names all begin with J? Pru writes. *All the fired people.*

Jonah should be very nervous right around now. Same with Jack II. Management will not touch Jenny, because then everything would fall apart. She wound up absorbing the Original Jack's duties, then Jules's. She got a bump in title but her salary stayed the same, and she never left work before 7.

She calls it a *deprotion*, which is a promotion that shares most of the hallmarks of a demotion. Jenny and Pru and also Lizzie and sometimes Crease like to think up terms for things that happen in the office. *It could make a good book someday*, says Pru.

Jenny is safe in theory. But we shall see.

No effect

We often forget about Jill, who makes it easy. She is shy around most of us, and when she does speak it's usually to compliment someone else: Lizzie for her outfits, Pru for her smarts, Jenny for her organizational skills.

My problem is I have a quiet voice, she once confided to Jenny.

What?

She wants to try therapy but is too shy to call for an appointment.

Jill is worried enough as it is, about life, about everything—quiet voice, limp hair, zero boyfriend prospect, the impossibility of therapy—and so this *J* conspiracy theory does not noticeably disturb her.

Red alert

Waiting for the microwave to finish, Jonah sees a sleek figure gliding across the far end of the hall, tossing something into a wastebasket as she passes. The microwave beeps. An hour later, en route to the photocopier, he notices a glint in the trash. He picks out five broken pieces of computer disc, careful not to smudge the words in thick black Sharpie.

At his desk the pieces fit together quickly, and the mock-grandiose title snaps into view: MAXINE'S TOP SECRET FILES FOR WORLD DOMINATION. Penned beneath, in smaller letters, is the name of our former colleague, Jason.

Jonah is so perplexed by this discovery he closes his door and takes a nap.

< **6** >

Greek tragedy

Long ago, in another life, Crease taught English and social studies at an all-girls' school on the Upper East Side. He left because he felt he was in a rut. Why he thought a fresh start at our office would be even marginally more interesting is not known. Everyone can make a bad career decision but we wonder if there's something he's not telling us.

He's called Crease instead of Chris because last year an ex-student, part of a wealthy Greek kitchen-counter-manufacturing family, began stalking him, saying *Crease, I love you, nonstop.* Perhaps he did not remember her so well? But she had been able to think of nothing but *Crease* for the past seven years. She had returned to Athens to be with her family but was now back, to study communications at NYU but really to be closer to him. *Nonstop.* It had the makings of classical tragedy. She would stand in the lobby, telling her story to anyone who would listen, including the Sprout, while Crease snuck in through a side door and took the freight elevator up.

One afternoon Laars saw her chasing our hero down the street, shouting, *Crease, Crease!* collapsing in sobs at the corner as he jumped into a cab. Pru began taking an interest in Crease. She'd hardly noticed him before the stalking started.

Apostasy

Of course, Crease was already a Maxine worshiper by then. But now he's announced that he's breaking away from the pack.

Laars says that in feudal Japan they would suspend Jesuit missionaries by their feet and dangle them in pits of offal. The people in charge would cut little notches behind the ears so that blood would get in their eyes and noses until they broke down and renounced their faith.

Laars thinks this is what must have happened to Crease, Crease who once showed us a sonnet he wrote that used the letters of Maxine's name to head each line.

Crease reports that those days are over, finis. Yesterday he took the elevator up with the most beautiful woman in the world. He felt extremely self-conscious because of his allergies. He had just concluded a prolonged sequence of sneezing, nose blowing, and eyedrop application. There was the uncomfortable sensation that all his head orifices were leaking in assorted unspeakable ways.

He wanted to say something but couldn't think of the words. All air had left his lungs. He looked at her profile for one second. Then he looked at the ground. It was just too much beauty in too small a space.

She hit 7.

The seventh floor is shared by a small ad agency, a nonprofit dedicated to giving pets to the homeless elderly, and a vaguely menacing telemarketing concern called Robodial Unlimited or something.

Crease blithely ignores the last option and deduces that she's therefore either a creative type or a saint.

I think I've seen her before, says Jonah. *She's sort of average height, skinny?*

Thin, says Crease. *Thin and tall. And Eurasian, do people still say Eurasian?*

Thin and tall is Crease's type, though he himself is on the short side and skews endomorphic. *And she has this amazing British accent.*

Apparently she had asked him to *hold the lift.*

Is she the one with a lot of makeup? asks Pru.

Pru might have a crush on Crease. Some days it's clear that she does. Other times, not so much. She is thin but not terribly tall. She might have a chance if she lost the nose ring, but the rest of us are not sure that a chance with Crease is the key to happiness. In the past some of us thought we detected *sparks* between them. But the days of possible reciprocation seem to have come to an end.

I can't stop thinking about Half Asian British Accent Woman, he e-mails Laars at 3 in the morning. Laars forwards the message to all of us.

The haunted résumé

Pru says, *I have this phantom line-space dilemma and it's driving me nuts.* She's working on her résumé but the computer keeps giving her a double line space in certain sections, though she only wants a single. There's no way around it. She's tried copying the text, scrubbing it with the freebie scrubbing application she's downloaded, and pasting it into a fresh document.

She's tried changing the font, bolding it, shrinking it. She's tried rebooting. She's tried e-mailing it to her home computer and then re-e-mailing it to herself at work, hoping the bugs will fly off in transit.

Twice Pru has simply started new documents, new résumés, typing everything in as if for the first time, and as soon as she tries to save it, the double line spaces pop up. It's as if the computer loves her and doesn't want her to leave. The computer wants her to stay in her cubicle within earshot of the vending machines and be miserable for three more years, for five, for ten.

Pru doesn't want to call the IT guy, because then he'll know she's planning to leave and can blackmail her. His name is Giles and none of us trust him. There's a newer IT guy, Robb with two *b*s, but we're not sure about him, either. Some of us bonded with Otto, others avoided him. We've only unanimously liked Lisa, but that was four IT people ago.

Jenny, who knows something about everything, takes a look at the document and says the problem might be a sequence of letters somewhere in the résumé that's being read as a command by the word-processing program, causing it to throw in the unwanted extra line space.

In other words maybe it's her name that's messing things up. Maybe P-R-U launches some sort of word-processing monkey wrench.

This is possible, since we use an obscure program called Microsoft Word.

Pru says she's not going to change her name just so she can have a clean résumé. But all of us think that maybe she will. Or at least use her full name, Prudence, which she hates and which would only get her a job at a library in a nunnery on Nova Scotia.

The point

For the past three months Pru's been saying, *I have to get out of this place.* Lizzie started muttering similar sentiments two weeks ago. Jonah has been saying *Time to leave* for six months now. We have all been saying it, in some fashion, at assorted volumes, without quite realizing it. Perhaps we've all been saying it ever since we started here, in our dreams, in our strained and silent thoughts, the right brain murmuring it to the left, or is it the other way around.

Laars has a different mantra. You can hear him say it as he slices through his junk mail every morning with an old butter knife: *What is the point?*

Long-term strategies

It can't be stressed enough: You never want the Sprout to call you in and tell you what a terrific job you're doing. The Original Jack and Jason and Jules all had these meetings, and then were gone inside a month.

The Sprout calls you in, intercoms invisible bigwigs, chortles about fantastic results and brilliant numbers. He praises you to the skies, says your work is *fabulous.* Where did that come from? We all hate that word and want to kill it.

The speakerphone static is so bad that only the Sprout can understand what they're saying. He laughs at what you imagine are jokes, turns serious at what might be grim statements of purpose, pulls a face in inscrutable fake alliance with you when the entities on the other end say something ludicrous.

But of course you can't make out a word. That room is tor-ture. You smile and stare out the window, hallucinating insane methods of escape.

Lizzie has survived two such meetings this year but knows she won't make it through another. She has started backing up various work files by e-mailing them home, in case she needs to look for other employment. She does it surreptitiously. Her résumé is all typed up and suffers no double line spaces, though Laars has noticed that most of it is in Baskerville ex-cept for two lines that are in Baskerville Old Face. He was going to mention this to her but she'd already made a hundred copies on expensive heavy bond.

Ideally such a job hunt will be superfluous. Lizzie's long-term strategy is to marry a handsome Swedish baron or win the lottery. Pru also wouldn't mind marrying a baron, though she has never specified a country of origin. Maybe they'll fight over the same one—a slumming baron looking to get fixed up with a bitter but peppy American girl in a faded Almond Joy T-shirt, a girl with her hair in a ponytail. Laars says that's a rec-ognized fetish in some parts of the world.

The Original Jack used to express interest in dating a so-cialite. *A socialite or a Rockette,* was his line. We wonder what he's up to these days.

The lottery

We all play the lottery. We buy our tickets individually be-cause we don't want to have to divvy up all that loot in case the numbers come up right.

Another plan

Laars says, *I want to be a househusband.*

The wording

Lizzie and Crease are on the elevator with three people who are going up to seven, Starbucks in hand. Crease is on the verge of asking if they know his half-Asian mystery woman. He's working on the wording, figuring out how to be charming rather than creepy, but there's no way. *I am a lonely man*, he might begin.

Lizzie and Crease reach our floor. He casts a wounded-sheepdog look as the door shuts and the carriage continues its ascent into paradise.

< *7* >

Don't forget the files for the thing

Upon initial acquaintance, the Sprout displays the ingratiating optimism characteristic of all Canadians. Twice a year, on Canada Day and at the holiday party, he wears his maple-leaf tie. We think he'd like it if one of us were from Ottawa or wherever, to talk about forgotten hockey teams and spell *colour* with a *u*.

Baking-soda-white teeth glint behind thin, disturbingly kissable lips. He has a superb, full head of hair, sleek, except when that famously unruly sprig is driven to express itself.

He doesn't have a mustache, but possesses the sort of meaty upper-lip real estate that suggests a mustache once thrived there and might return.

Some of us have noticed that he smells very nice—a faint clean soap smell basically but also something else. He and Maxine should form a rare-good-smell club. The Sprout is not conventionally handsome but not ugly, which for men of his age means handsome. He went to a community college, transferred to Hamilton, then to Cornell. Or possibly he's from

Hamilton, Ontario? Jules used to think the school was *Colgate*, but that was because of the teeth. The community college thing also came from Jules, who said he got it from Emma, the former receptionist who supposedly had a crush on the Sprout. None of this is necessarily true.

Passing his office we often hear him say, *Memorandum*, then start talking, a stream of numbers and abbreviations, with very little in the way of actual sentences made up of words. Other times we've heard him call his home phone and leave a message for himself: *Hey Russell, it's Russell, don't forget to bring the files for the thing.*

It's possible he wants us to hear how casual he is: The files for the *thing.*

Sometimes he leaves messages for himself that are just scattered words: *showerhead* or *onions* or *Napoleon thing at nine.*

We've deduced that the Sprout's cell phone plays Pachelbel's Canon when Sheila calls. It plays Chopsticks when his kid calls.

He has an MBA that he got through distance learning. At least three times a year he is sent to a management seminar in some place like Syracuse. Last year he went to Australia all by himself. Nobody knows why.

Don't start liking the Sprout too much

Jules was there when the Sprout fired Emma. She was in the middle of answering a call and he told her to put the phone down and come into his office. It was over in less than a minute. She was never replaced, and for a while the Sprout actually handled the switchboard calls from his desk. Most historians consider this episode part of the Firings, even though it happened several weeks before the real slaughter began.

The Fates

The Sprout lives with his wife, Sheila, and their kid, out in a leafy suburb that recently split off from a longer-standing one. Sheila is taller and older than him, a very attractive redhead we've glimpsed exactly once, at a holiday party. She is a VP at an investment bank and additionally has family money, according to Jules.

We wonder if Maxine has a disc on *her*.

Right out of college Sheila acted in a B movie, *Tempting Fate*, that we haven't been able to get our hands on. We *think* it's the same Sheila. She plays Angie Fate, the skeptical younger sister of the hot astrologer heroine, Linda Fate. Both Jack II and Laars have plugged *Tempting Fate* into their eBay alert lists but the movie is not available on videocassette let alone DVD and never will be.

Jules claims he saw it as a teenager, though admits this could be a false memory implanted by his last therapist. He thinks there was a nude scene, not at all impossible given the genre, light teen sex comedy. That it should involve horses, horseshoe crabs, or a hearse—Jules can't quite remember which—is altogether less likely.

The syllabus

Books on the Sprout's shelf:

The Art of War, by Sun Tzu

Analects, by Confucius

The Prince, by Niccolò Machiavelli

Prophecies, by Nostradamus

Something called *How to Sell Yourself Every Time*

Webster's New Collegiate Dictionary, 9th edition

The American Heritage Dictionary, 4th edition

Roget's Thesaurus
Complete Idiot's Guide to Microsoft PowerPoint 2000

The inventory

Other items in or atop the Sprout's bookcase include a framed photo of Sheila, a battered candleholder without a candle, an unidentified liqueur, a plastic ukulele, and the White Pages from two years ago with the shrinkwrap still on.

A shorter Maxine

We imagine that the Sprout has a mistress. This is a regular topic over drinks. We drink and visualize a shorter Maxine, someone with eyes like Sheila's, someone much younger or fifteen years his senior. The mistress wears her sunglasses on top of her head.

All of us have imagined the Sprout having sex. This just must be the way it is everywhere, an occupational hazard for Sprouts in offices nationwide: You become a permanent installation in your underlings' minds. Every night the odds are that at least one of them dreams of you.

All of us have imagined him with Maxine. Some of us have imagined ourselves with Sheila. Even Pru—especially Pru. For Pru it's a fantasy that culminates in her inheriting all of Sheila's old family money. The Sprout is demoted to groundskeeper and occasional sex slave.

Pru would never tell her therapist this but she's happy to give us the details.

Mathemating

Laars says there's a mating rule: You can go out with someone half your age, plus seven years—that's your lower limit. By the same formula, your upper limit would be determined by doubling your age and subtracting seven. This is not helpful, really, or even relevant, but we amuse ourselves with calculations for a while. For the rest of the afternoon.

Last names first

Every payday we go to Henry in HR and he asks who we are, last names first, though he should know us by now. We oblige him, as if bringing up the issue would risk stoppage of pay. He must have attended an HR meeting in which it was stressed that check disbursers must orally confirm the identity of each recipient. Still, Henry invariably confuses the two Asian workers, giving one the other's check before stopping himself, finding the right one. He also did this to the two black workers, before one of them was fired. He used to apologize for the confusion but even he realizes how ridiculous it's become.

Does anyone remember anything about Jason?

Jonah is still trying to figure out the mystery of the CD that Maxine broke into pieces and threw away, her plan for world domination lost forever. *Jason*, it said. He still has the shards in his desk drawer and every so often will stare at them moodily, his reflection evocatively fractured.

Surely the title was tongue in cheek. But why did it say *Jason* underneath? He's been gone since the Firings, a late October victim. Jill was close to him but she says the last time she saw him was at the holiday party. He had crashed it, dressed like the Sprout.

Wait, he was at the holiday party? asks Lizzie.

We remember Jules had a love-hate relationship with Jason. One time they didn't speak to each other for a month, a dispute over a paper jam. Actually, there was rarely any love—it was more or less hate all the time. Both of them are long gone now. The rest of us liked Jason but now we can't remember a thing.

He punched the wall that one time, offers Jenny. *Way too intense.*

Laars coughs. *That was me.*

Pru wonders if Maxine has a disc for each of us. She imagines files full of closed-circuit footage from tiny cameras hidden in our monitors.

Jack II floats a theory: that Maxine and Jason were lovers, and the disc has highlights of their afternoon romps. Lizzie points out the obvious.

Wait, says Jack II. *Jason was gay?*

Crease puts up his hand for a high five.

Jonah points out that Maxine only started in the office earlier *this* year—February, maybe March. Meaning she wouldn't have been around at all while Jason was still here. It can take a while for new presences to make themselves felt, but Jonah's chronology seems sound. Maxine and Jason never overlapped. Jack II still thinks we should try to glue the pieces together and see if the thing will play.

< **8** >

Major tool

Jenny has stopped coming out with us for drinks, either on the advice of her life coach or because she has a serious boyfriend. We've met him, though his name escapes us. He has a baby face and incipient dreadlocks and favors the loose-fitting, heavily braided clothes associated with the better class of sherpa. He tutors inner-city kids in math. *That's so great*, Pru says. They have the most difficulty with division, though this is of course true for everyone.

He splits a huge loft with a roommate, an actress who is never around. Pru went to a New Year's bash there and can't imagine how he affords it.

Laars misses Jenny. He might even like her. He refers to her boyfriend as a *tool* or occasionally a *major tool*.

All we do is stare

Most of us are in therapy. Occasionally one of us will quit for a while, laughably convinced we are better, before realizing there's no such thing as *better*. Haven't we learned that by now? Nothing will ever get better, nothing will ever be fixed. Fixing is not even the point. *What is the point?*

Jules used to see a sketchy Lacanian but we hear that he's now seeing a very good Brentian. It's a slow process because a Brentian session is conducted entirely in French. Jules's French is actually *pas mal* but his therapist's isn't so great.

Jenny scoffs at the method, even as she confesses to Pru that her relationship with her life coach is deteriorating. *All we do is stare at each other,* she says.

The situation in the workplace is stressful enough without worrying about her life coach. She doesn't need this. She almost wants to see a therapist about it. Maybe the answer to her problems is to quit her job and become a life coach herself.

Jules in disguise

About a month after Jules was laid off, he happened to see the Sprout and Sheila at a diner. The Sprout had coffee. Sheila drank water. They sat on the same side of the table but said nothing, just stared straight out at the traffic going downtown. It was the *American Gothic* of breakfasts.

They left after ten wordless minutes. Jules paid his bill and walked out. He had nowhere to go and so followed them up to Seventy-second. They walked west. Jules slipped on his sunglasses and mussed his hair for a disguise, using saliva as a stiffener. Then he started moving his jaw in a gradually more spastic manner suggesting, to any witnesses, that though his clothes looked neat, he was most likely a mentally unstable drifter.

The Sprout and Sheila slipped into the vestibule of a brownstone halfway down the block. He counted to a hundred before going up for a closer look at the sign.

He e-mailed Jonah with the news that the Sprout and

Sheila were getting couples therapy. Now almost every week he finds himself lingering down the block, waiting for a glimpse of them, occasionally cackling before dashing around the corner, out of sight. Some of us are worried about Jules.

Fictional damage control

Don't tell Jonah about HABAW, Crease says to Jill as she's shaking crumbs out of her keyboard.

HA-wha?

Half Asian British Accent Woman.

Who?

Elevator lady!

He can't remember whom he's told and whom he hasn't. His need to control the information is puzzling, as he has yet to speak to the object of his obsession. It's been weeks since he's seen her. Talking about her to others, imagining that they are likewise obsessed and even competitive, gives him a thrill that's safer than actually talking *to* her. It also helps him believe that she still exists.

Middle of the pack

Our latest Maxine theory has nothing to do with the Californians. We believe she is a corporate spy, working for the competition. The *Jason* disc, then, was her evaluation of the work done by a former member of the team.

Her retroactive evaluation, Laars clarifies.

The theory wobbles upon examination. Spy? On *us*? Our company is hardly a trailblazer. Its MO is to follow the industry norm as closely as possible, sticking to the middle of the pack to ensure its survival.

Also, if Maxine *were* a spy, wouldn't she be making more of an attempt to get to know us—more specifically, hanging out/sleeping with us?

Jules implies that Maxine's the one who got him fired last November, but it's not clear that she even knew who he was. Jules had tardiness issues and walked around scowling all the time. He also had padded his expense account to include office supplies that were actually groceries. Once he not only stole a whole bunch of office supplies but FedExed them to his home so he wouldn't have to carry them on the subway.

Siberia

At noon on Monday the Sprout moves Jill to Siberia. It's a spacious cubicle on the sixth floor, miles from anyone else, next to the door leading to the fire exit.

It wasn't always like this. Before the Firings, a large team worked here, and traces of their residence can still be found. We knew some of them, though not well. We don't really recognize the scattering of remaining employees, who sit hunched with their backs toward us as if awaiting the death blow. Supposedly there are more survivors on the fifth floor, but not too many. These are people whose tasks never intersect with ours, people we never even need to e-mail.

The Sprout's reasons for relocating Jill are opaque, even more mysterious than his usual reasons for doing anything. At first he makes it sound like a promotion. Then he adds that the HR department will be taking over her former desk area. This seems dubious. The HR department now consists of one person, Henry. They fired everyone else.

No one wants to mention that, shortly before Jules was canned, the Sprout praised him and then moved him up to six and gave him a pay cut.

This is turning out to be the Mother of all Deprotions.

The days pass. *I'm dying here*, she e-mails, and we e-mail back, *We're coming—be right there!!* or *OK hold on . . . !* but we don't visit for hours, if we visit at all.

Space shapes psychology, psychology shapes behavior, according to Pru. We imagine Jill roasting pigeons over a space heater, carving pictograms into the side of her monitor and then coloring them with blood from her perpetual hangnails.

Jill boldly e-mails Jack II, *Shoulders are killing me, I could use a backrub!* But he doesn't write back.

Going to Siberia is an event. We gird ourselves for the climb, make sure our schedules are clear, pack provisions. Then we get distracted by a phone call and fail to swing by. Maybe once a week, at the end of a slow afternoon, one of us will make the journey. From Jill's desk you can hear the yawning of ancient door hinges coursing through the stairwell. People from other offices head to the stairs for an illicit cigarette or silent sob session. In Jill's mind they grope each other under twitchy fluorescent lighting, mouths slack with pleasure, all this lust right outside her door.

I don't dare open it, Jill e-mails us, sounding like a child in a book to whom something very bad or very fun is going to happen.

I'm fantasizing about the Sprout, she e-mails us a few hours later, when the phantom groans get too much. *He's in the stairwell with Maxine.*

And Sheila, reply-alls Pru, who is obsessed, intellectually, with threesomes.

And Laars, reply-alls Laars, who is obsessed, despite the vow of chastity, with foursomes.

K.

We shouldn't discuss Sprout-Maxine relations on e-mail, Jenny writes to Jill. Except she mistypes a *K* in the to-field, which causes Kristen's name to automatically appear. Jenny sees this—*Kristen?*—but the error doesn't register until a split second after she clicks send. *KRISTEN!* Now she's a nervous wreck.

Kristen is the Sprout's supervisor.

We know her, if at all, by her initial, K., which periodically appears at the bottom of certain petrifying memos that the Sprout photocopies for us.

Jenny has always lived in fear that the company could monitor our e-correspondence, but it's only when trying to alert others that she puts herself in jeopardy.

Moral: Don't try to help people.

The feminine mystique

Only a few of us have ever even *seen* K. before. She must have access to a private elevator or else get teleported in. One time, about a year ago, Pru said she was shocked to see her at the Good Starbucks. We all said, *Who?*

She's never at meetings, though sometimes we suspect she's listening in remotely.

K. sits in an enclosed office on the fifth floor, one above us, one below Jill. Her door is always shut, the venetian blind impenetrable. No one knows what goes on in there. We can imagine her scolding the Sprout and Maxine via speakerphone, sipping Diet Cokes and throwing the empties out the window.

We are so removed from her realm that when we say her

name, sometimes we say Karen or Kiersten, and no one's a hundred percent sure if a correction is in order. Lizzie thinks that *any* name would sound too feminine, masking her power. Better just to think of her as K.

Police blotter

The top magenta Post-it of the stack on Crease's southern desk bears a message: *Please stop stealing me.* Nobody has been stealing them, but now some of us start, just to confirm his fears. We keep removing the top Post-it, taking a few of the ones beneath, and replacing the one with Crease's request.

He can always tell. The edges are never perfectly aligned.

Eight blank pages

Maxine e-mails the Sprout a PDF titled PLANS2. The Sprout somehow can't deal with PDFs. He's reasonably tech-savvy otherwise, so this amounts to a superstition or weird phobia. Maybe the initials *PDF* remind him of a lost love or buried trauma. He always asks Jenny to download the files and print them out.

The Sprout has a fax-printer in his office, but it doesn't connect to Jenny's computer. She has to use the asthmatic printer in the mail room, practically a time zone away.

She opens the PDF. She hits print and goes on her journey, only to find eight blank pages. She spends the next hour fiddling with the document until the Sprout phones her and asks how it's going. She thinks he thinks she forgot. She brings the pages in and tries to explain, but the Sprout doesn't seem to be listening.

Eight blank pages. He turns white when he sees them, as if a horse head has been deposited on his bed. He leaves early and the next morning there's a message on Jenny's voice mail saying he's taking a personal day.

The worst time in the world

Jenny is essentially the Sprout's assistant now, on top of her other duties. The position was formerly filled by the Original Jack, who was fired on 9/11. Not *the* 9/11, but the fourth anniversary. A Sunday. The Sprout called him at home. We consider this the unofficial start of the Firings.

We don't even like when we look at the clocks on our computers and they say 9:11.

The Sprout told her that Henry in HR was doing a search for a Jack replacement. Three months passed. Then he started asking Jenny to print out schedules and drafts and PDFs, keep the supply closet filled with highlighters, and call the IT department whenever the Internet went down, which it did— which it does—every other week.

A year went by, Jenny subbing for the Original Jack. Then everything was set in stone.

Things grow in Siberia

We all visit Jill bearing iced coffee, cookies, and about a dozen packs of sugar, as if she lives in a land where sugar is used as currency. We want her to stockpile the sugar and use it sparingly because we don't want to visit her again. There is something forcefully sad about her elaborately decorated cubicle. She has pinned up pictures of all of us from our short-lived softball days. We look slightly deranged, wide-eyed, and well-fed and for some reason not depressed. It's weird to see Laars holding a bat and pointing proudly to the Finnish clip-art logo on his jersey.

Who's that? asks Jenny.

Otto, says Laars. *I should give that guy a call.*

Things grow here: a spider plant, a scary cactus thingy, a healthy aloe. We joke about her green thumb. But all the personal effects that we remember from when she was closer to us now look sad and infected. It hurts too much to look at pictures of her family, her dog, an alarmingly good-looking guy who is probably her brother but maybe is her boyfriend. There is a strong citrus scent in the air, a swarm of chemical lemon fighting against all the dust that begins to surround her encampment at a radius of ten feet or so.

All I've done today is check e-mail, she says.

Later Crease asks if we noticed that there was ink all over her hands.

Pru hadn't, but did notice the odd new haircut and the flashy new scarf. The scarf looked awkward, like an eel from the future, or something worn by a vampire victim. *Like if you unraveled it, her head would fall off and roll away.*

Help wanted

Every few minutes Pru e-mails us her keyboard woes: *I can't make an exclamation point or question mark anymore. Help. HELP.* We can all sympathize. The decay of punctuational capability is a common theme here. The Sprout promised us new computers. But that was two years ago.

Elevator revelations

We sense something new in the elevator today. We smell it before we see it: a stone gray, footstep-muffling carpet.

By late afternoon we have forgotten what the floor looked like before. We're transfixed by the bits of color hiding in the dull gray weave, visible only upon prolonged inspection. We stare at it as if hoping to induce an optical illusion, something we can believe in, a secret porthole into another world.

I could live here, jokes Jonah.

We like that it looks so clean, but by the end of the day it has a coffee stain, a gum wrapper, and a few stray ribbons of shredded lime green paper.

Let go

Jill is one of those rare people who are more timid on e-mail than in real life. Sometimes she waits till Friday to send her nonurgent business e-mails, because then she can add *Have a nice weekend!* as a tagline. *You need to pepper your messages with a little small talk,* Jill says in an android voice. There's nothing as universal as the weekend and one's modest hopes for it.

Before leaving the office one Friday, she stops on our floor, but we've already fled, away to our own lives, away to our good weekends. Walking by Jenny's desk, she sees an index card on the floor. It reads:

  3. Let go of anger! Be more efficient. Exercise more!

< **9** >

The Unnamable

This man has been here forever but has only recently coalesced into an identifiable being. We don't know his name, though Jack II claims this person's name is *also* Jack. This is too unsettling—the mind cannot contain three Jacks, fired Jack I a.k.a. the Original Jack and current Jack II and this supposed Jack III—and so we think of him as *The Unnamable*.

The Unnamable is fiftyish, tall, with a healthy fringe of white hair and gleaming, inquisitive eyes. His ponderous gait gives the impression that he is rooted in the land: a spirit, a proud protector, an aristocrat of the corridors and cubicles. But the fact is—he's *different*. Slow. Language eludes him. When he tries to talk, it sounds like he's gasping. It's hard to isolate the words in his vast loud whisper and so we just nod and smile. This seems sufficient for him, and he replies in kind. The response makes you feel good, though it's unclear why it should.

His job, as far as we can tell, is intra-office messenger. We mark envelopes with initials and he matches these symbols to the ones on the bins by each desk. He does it so silently, moves so secretly, that often you don't realize something's waiting for you. His shoes must be made of feathers. Mostly you see the Unnamable only by accident. We wish he would make more noise.

We e-mail everything and there's rarely a need to send actual pieces of paper to people, but Maxine uses him with regularity and we have gradually fallen in line.

Jill wants to use him to keep us connected. *I got some pictures developed*, she'll e-mail one of us. *I'm putting them in my out-box.*

But the Unnamable has an aversion to Siberia. He does not go to her desk, her bin, unless one of us addresses something to her, which is somehow never on the list of priorities. When Jill's pictures finally arrive it is hard to attach meaning to them. We think they're from that time we got drinks and ran into Jason—fired, unhappy Jason—wearing a dress, but it's hard to say.

Pru once asked the Unnamable what his name was, but he only mumbled. Maybe he didn't understand. Sometimes she calls him *Pops* or *Gramps*. That's the only time he smiles.

The Mexican distress frog

Jonah goes to Mexico for a week. He sends us pictures from his cell phone. We can't tell what it was he meant to capture. The ocean? Birds in the town square? Clouds? We have clouds here, too. One picture looks like a giant chocolate bar.

He later explains that it was the entrance to the tomb of a chieftain who ruled by confusion. He would tell his subjects that a tribe was attacking from the north, then later in the day tell them the tribe had been spotted coming from the south. The militia would be spread thin. It was a matter of debate how such puzzling tactics could benefit anyone, but this obscure pocket of civilization managed to thrive for centuries. The court artisans sculpted very tall, thin figures wearing what appear to be bell-bottoms. The tribe was wiped out not by marauding forces but by three women who stumbled into town and enchanted the men with their beauty. The chieftain claimed all three as his wives. There was a blood sacrifice involved, for the first time in the people's history, though Jonah can't remember who was sacrificed—the new women, the old women, the men, the chief, the children.

Jonah says he bought souvenirs for all of us but left them in his hotel room. We are not sure if he went to Mexico alone or with someone. He doesn't offer this information. Come to that, we also don't know whether he's straight or gay. On one occasion he spoke out, with strange and exciting stridency, against bisexuality. He said his therapist, actually now his ex-therapist, said it was a bogus position. *Just choose one or the other and stop being so dramatic.* This outburst made us all conclude that he's bisexual.

On his desk now is a Mexican distress frog, a wooden icon about half a foot long with a ridged back, which you stroke using a wooden rod to create a soothing, some would say irritating, noise.

It sounds like this when you stroke from tail to head: *Takata takata tak.*

When you move the rod in the opposite direction, the rhythm is more *Tak-tak, kataka-ta.*

He plays it practically nonstop these days.

Toastmaster

Jules, mad Jules, does many things now that he's no longer with us. *Getting fired is the best thing that's ever happened to me,* he says. But they all say that.

Most of his hours are spent at his much-photographed restaurant in which everything is cooked in a toaster oven. How did he scare up the money? As things went sour for him at the office, he began moonlighting as a valet at an exclusive strip club on Eleventh Avenue. The tips must have been fantastic and Pru jokes that maybe *he* was the one taking it all off.

The toaster-oven place has one of those trisyllabic names that are all the rage now. Terrapin, Parapet, Happenstance? We can never remember. We regret not making it to the grand opening. Maybe it's just Restaurant.

Business was so brisk the first month that he bought two more toaster ovens and hired a part-time toastmaster to help out during the busy lunch hour.

Circumflex, Herringbone, Anagram?

Some of us finally visit him for lunch, a field trip. We're happy he's doing so well. The goodwill lasts about five minutes before we become completely jealous.

He keeps making weird remarks about the office, not to make us feel bad but because he's still obsessed with it. He wants up-to-the-minute details on Maxine, whom he's never even met.

You don't know what it's like working alone, Jules says. *There's no one to talk to.*

Is he bored already? Now we're disappointed. Our interest was in seeing someone thrive, post-firing. And not just doing another office gig but pursuing the creative life, if putting things in a toaster can be called creative.

We all have our little side projects that we don't like talking about. Jack II takes blurry Polaroids of urban detritus and unusual pavement cracks. Lizzie goes to Central Park or the Met most Saturdays and sketches. Laars has lead-guitar ambitions. Sometimes when he doesn't know you're there you can see his left hand squeezing out imaginary notes as his head nods to a secret beat. Pru knits more than she cares to admit, sweaters and scarves and baby socks for distant nieces. When Crease took over Jason's desk, he found a hundred poems sealed in an envelope. And surely the aloof Jonah has an alternate life—weekend woodworking, novel in drawer, libretto in its fifteenth draft.

Celery, Colophon, Venison?

All present agree that Jules looks better than before. At his low points, back in the office, he resembled someone you might find in a film for a college psychology course: sleep-deprived, robotic, convinced that it was OK to apply electric shocks to small plasticine dolls labeled MOM and DAD. Now a photo crew from a Japanese magazine arranges his collar and smoothes his hair and dabs his brow.

Cataract, Polyglot, Rolodex?

We help ourselves to more lemonade and order the eggs Benedict. *Is this how you get salmonella?* Lizzie wonders.

The photographer says, *Big smile!*

The deletionists

Pru reads novels on the subway for her book club, stern-looking paperbacks with matte covers and enigmatic titles. She gets a record-breaking *four* personal days a year, which she negotiated when she was hired, and traditionally she's used them to finish a novel she couldn't put down. She likes curling up on the couch but she says she actually gets the most reading done while on the subway. We imagine her getting on the train with a tote bag full of books and reading as she loops around the city, from Herald Square up to Inwood, from Astoria to Coney Island.

She's read several that have *-ist* in the title: *The Pragmatist. The Vertiginist. The Deletionist.* Then there's a crop of books with the possessive form of a famous person's last name, followed by a noun. *Napoleon's Pencil. Freud's Knickers. Shakespeare's Quandary.*

Lizzie says she hates books, which is somehow adorable. She uses her personal days for manicures and things like that. In May, Laars called in sick and went to the movies instead. It was three in the afternoon and as he put his Coke in the cup holder he saw Lizzie walk in, wearing sweatpants and a baggy sweater. It was so startling he slumped in his seat till the previews began.

Shooting the moon

Every other month a film or TV crew shoots outside the office for a couple of days. Trailers hog the curb. Preening lackeys with headsets move purposefully along the sidewalk, coffee in hand, trained to address any trespass. Laars has taken to insulting them. Pru says she once flashed them, and the thought of it makes Jonah quiver like a jelly. One summer Jules would pitch water balloons from the sixth-floor window.

Our building's rugged façade, with its lone quizzical gargoyle, appears in advertisements for a luminous sports drink, three different cell phone plans, a financial management firm, a protein bar, and a pain reliever.

Best of all is for a website that contained thousands of easy-to-use job listings for cities across the country. It's called Job-milla. The camera dives through an open window into a cavernous room, very Industrial Revolution, with the sinister sound of chains clanking and liquids dripping from bare rafters. A conveyor belt transports depressed-looking, obviously jobless people along a figure-eight route. At the end they get crammed into a computer monitor—representing the Jobmilla site—and are subjected to a brisk off-camera churning. Then they pop out of the building, onto the sparkling sidewalk, holding briefcases and looking thrilled to have a job and use of a comb.

The motto is *What goes around comes around.*™

The pit

There was a parking lot that many of us used as a shortcut on our way in from the subway. On rainy days it was like one big puddle with tiny islands here and there, so far apart that disparate life-forms no doubt grew and developed independently.

This spring, or was it last year, they put up boards around it and we learned to walk the long way round, using the sidewalk like good citizens. Now we can see, through holes in the boards, that a giant pit has totally erased our former route.

The pit marks the future basement of an enormous glass-skinned building shaped like the symbol for infinity. Lizzie thinks it's going to be turned into lofts for millionaires. Jack II hopes it's a vertical mall, or at least that it has a few benches where he can sit down and de-stress with a coffee and a fresh cinnamon roll. He says there are surprisingly few spots in the city where you can find a proper cinnamon roll. A mom-and-pop operation in Yorkville is the only one that comes to mind.

Something tells us he's misremembering a Talk of the Town piece from an old *New Yorker*.

The Red Alcove

In the office Lizzie, Pru, and Jenny sometimes eat together in the alcove by the window. They order clear plastic boxes of sprouts, sip at tinted water. *Alcove* is a nice real estate term for a disused storage closet with one of the walls knocked down. Even when Jill was on the fourth floor, she was usually too shy to join them. The alcove is directly under where Jill's desk is on the sixth floor, so it's sort of like she's with them in spirit now.

They look at fashion magazines, make fun of the ads, or maybe they're not making fun.

Do you like these velour hoodies?

They never say anything but it's clear that this refuge is for girls only.

I hate the ones with the arrow thing on the back.

Laars has started calling it the Red Alcove. Since his vow of chastity, he has joined a book club. His ex-roommate introduced him to it, then quit, making Laars the only man left. The club just read a book called *The Red Tent*, about a special tent in which women used to hang out whenever they were getting their periods.

It was pretty interesting, he says diplomatically.

Four attempts

Laars is about to go on vacation. He's using two vacation days and two personal days. He asks everyone to remind him to change his outgoing message before he leaves, but how are we supposed to remember that?

He has to head out to the airport by 5:30. At 5:20 we can hear him trying to leave a suitable outgoing message. Ten minutes seems like a lot of time, but everyone thinks he's cutting it close.

Hi, this is Laars. I'm out of the office. Until the twenty-first. So. Please leave a message, or actually don't *leave a message—I'll— CRAP.*

This is Laars I'll be on vacation from the seventeenth till the twenty-first and so I'll be out of the office on vacation aaarggg.

It's a Tourette's convention in there. Laars buries his head in his arms. Slivers of sweat darken his going-on-vacation shirt, the blue country-and-western-style shirt with the white piping.

I'm out of, I'm on— No, no.

This is—Laa— Fuck me, fuck.

The backlog

It doesn't matter what you say on your outgoing message. Having listened to you, people feel the need to comment. When Laars gets back from vacation, his voice mail is clogged anyway.

Hope you had a great time, everyone says, even people he's never spoken to before. *Welcome back.*

He knows from the display screen whether the message was from someone important or not. For long stretches he plows through the backlog, pressing 1 to hear a new message, then 9 to erase the call without even letting the robot-phone voice tell him who it was.

Message received from 2-1-2— Message deleted.

There are long stretches in which he hits 1 and then 9 so

fast, 1-9-1-9-1-9, that all the robot voice can say is *Mess—Mess— Mess— Mess— Mess— Mess.*

Later, he worries that he erased something important, like a message from a random low-maintenance billionaire asking if he'd like to spearhead a new project, a combination art gallery–Web empire–environmental magazine–snowboarding camp–counterculture festival.

< *10* >

The confession

I can't help it, Jack II is saying to Lizzie as he microwaves something with a high cheese content. *I'm in love with Half Asian British Accent Woman.*

He tries to get her to swear she won't tell Crease. *He'll kick the crap out of me*, he says, always ready to add unnecessary drama to his life. Instead she tells Pru, who tells Crease.

One if by land

Lizzie has this whole mini-rant about how British sitcoms and movies and books are overrated. In fact the whole country and all the people in it are given a free ride in the U.S. It was sort of zany-charming at first, but she needs to find a way to freshen her delivery. For starters, she could stop invoking the Boston Tea Party.

She goes on this tear again, set off by an ad for a film involving the Isle of Wight and the whimsical codgers who start a nudist colony. But we suspect it has something to do with Crease's new obsession with HABAW, Jack II's even newer infatuation, and the possibility that all the men in the office will follow suit.

Can't undo

Pru's résumé has taken on a life of its own. She thinks she's finally solved the double-line-space problem by turning everything into a font called Lemuria, then copy-pasting it into another document. It looks like hieroglyphics, but you can see that the double line space has miraculously resolved into a single line space.

Let's party, she e-mails us.

Then she selects all the text to change the font to Bookman Old Style. She releases the mouse too quickly and it becomes Braggadocio, which is appropriate only for menus at restaurants that have an old-timey, organ grinder theme to the decor.

Now I can get a job with a barbershop quartet.

I hear the telegraph company is hiring, says Crease.

She's stuck. The dialogue box gives her a *Can't undo.*

It's a double negative, says Jenny helpfully.

When Pru selects the text and tries to change the font to something normal, the double line space reappears.

What goes around comes around, says Pru, quoting Jobmilla.

Two words

Pru walks by the Sprout's office. He's just dialed a number and is waiting for a beep to leave a message. He says two words: *Veal stew.* Then he hangs up.

He notices her.

I'm calling myself to remind myself to go out later and buy ingredients for veal stew!

Just some old crap

Jonah listens to music while he works. He uses the CD player in his computer. He wears blue plastic headphones that are either really cheap or really expensive. We can hear sounds leak through, tiny voices squawking impotently. This isn't so bad. It makes us think we're working in a relaxed, groovy environment instead of a disaster area.

What we don't like is when Jonah starts tapping a pencil to the music, or pumping his legs so hard his desk shakes. You can hear it from outside his office. Crease makes a loud show of migrating to his other desk whenever Jonah gets into his musical phase.

If you ask Jonah what he's listening to, he'll say, *Just some old crap*. We figure it's country music or show tunes. But Pru corners him and learns that the CD in Jonah's heavy rotation is a recording of a Czech opera about a woman who is three hundred years old and from a different planet or something.

Is *Jonah* from a different planet? This might account for the weirdly glowing slate-colored eyes, the sleek briefcase made of futuristic water-repellent material, the tendency to predict the future with better than average accuracy. The trips to Mexico are to deliver complex information and late-capitalist artifacts to the mothership.

Also, once Laars saw him in the office early in the morning, the lights still off, typing with his eyes closed.

Recently, Jonah explained that his name is properly pronounced *Yawner*, a Czech pronunciation perhaps, but no one's going to make the switch. It could also be that Jonah wants the Sprout and Maxine to think he spells his name with a *Y*, since all the *J*s are getting fired these days.

FYA

Maxine e-mails some of us a link to an article she thought was funny, from a blog we've never heard of. *FYA*, she writes in the subject field, followed by a smiley face.

Opening the link crashes everyone's computer, except Pru's. We reboot. She copy-pastes us some of the photos and text. The site is devoted to images of dogs and cats nuzzling each other.

We expect more from Maxine, somehow.

After Pru hits Send, her computer crashes. Then our computers all crash again.

An hour later, Crease says, *I think it means For Your Amusement?*

$$< \quad \textbf{\textit{11}} \quad >$$

Laser Henry

Magic realism in the HR department: Henry gets the LASIK surgery and is out for a week. When he comes back, the blues of his irises have intensified fivefold.

Today he tells Jonah that he can see through things—clothes, metal, wood, brick. Not all the time, and the image goes in and out of focus. He has no control over the clarity or power. Sometimes he can see people's inner organs. It is as much a curse as a gift.

Since when has he been totally insane? asks Jonah.

Still, we make ourselves scarce when Henry walks by, scatter from his line of sight as fast as possible.

Background check

Periodically, Jill suffers repetitive stress disorder, though Jonah calls *his* pains carpal tunnel syndrome. They are not the same thing, though neither victim can quite delineate the difference.

She used to wonder if it was all in her mind. She gives us a synopsis of a book she's been reading about back pain. The writer asserts that nearly all such agonies are manifestations of pent-up stress. The psychosomatic explanation is attractive but leads to problems. We all develop back pain within a week of hearing this viewpoint.

Make it stop

Another of Maxine's FYA e-mails leads to a website showing cats curled up in bathroom sinks, gazing up with oppressive cuteness. What is wrong with her? Unless maybe it's some sort of virus that's hijacked her address book. We've heard of things like that before.

Laars read about a virus called YourPhyred that lurked around certain job websites. When you try to upload your résumé for potential employers, the virus turns it to gibberish or worse. Except *you* never know it. Your CV just hangs out there, in cyberspace, until an employer downloads it. Then it turns into a document filled with yards of random characters, or pictures of rainbows, or reviews of hard-core porn.

The humming

The Unnamable has taken to humming as he makes his rounds, picking up and dropping off paper. In another person this would annoy us, but his pitch is perfect and the songs are unfamiliar and instantly calming. Melodies from Jonah's Czech alien opera, perhaps. Sometimes we put paper in our out-bins as bait, drawing him near in the hope that he'll trot out a tune.

Today Jill hears someone in the stairwell for what seems like hours, humming the Cole Porter songbook with gusto.

But when she opens the door the song stops. She strains to hear any human sound: a footfall, a cough, the rustle of clothes.

I'm going crazy up here, she e-mails Pru, who doesn't write back, because you can go crazy on any floor.

The Republic of Smokistan

Those of us who smoke have to do it outside, creating a slovenly knot on the sidewalk about thirty times a day. Workers from other offices in the building also congregate here to light up, of course, and though at first some of us tried to make small talk, now barely a nod passes between the various factions. They are not like us.

Crease doesn't smoke but has taken up the habit to increase his chances of seeing HABAW. Is this what stalkers do? Laars says that Jenny met her boyfriend out here. The *major tool* worked at a graphic design studio on the top floor but was laid off and started his own studio out of his apartment.

People who can barely draw a straight line are becoming graphic designers, says Laars. His tone suggests that he's content to wait for a time when graphic design becomes an obsolete trade and things are allowed to emerge unmediated, pure human symbols, hand-scrawled sandwich boards, everything a sort of instinctive folk art.

People knock their ashes into the tiny opening at the top of a buoy-shaped receptacle. Sometimes even when no one's outside you can see a ghostly finger of smoke emerging from the hole as you approach the office, a signal of recent stress and despair.

Random poignancy circa 2:30

Is Excel crashing everyone's computer?

Keep the deli on the left

Pru gets invited to parties. She always goes and always complains about them. It's her most appealing quality. We picture her stepping out in boas and shawls. We also like that she never invites any of us to go with her. How is it that she has a whole life outside the office? Everyone must, but most days this seems like too much to ask.

More and more the parties are in strange parts of Brooklyn. *Everybody lives in Brooklyn now,* says Pru, who doesn't realize most of *us* live in Brooklyn now. We like that she complains about Brooklyn—the distances, the erratic subways, having to take a forty-dollar car service back home. She lives uptown in a place her stepfather's first wife snapped up as a pied-à-terre for like five dollars and some bottle caps back in the '70s.

But she has to go to the parties, and the parties are now in Brooklyn. She has no conception of how the neighborhoods fit together, which trains go where. The directions are elaborate, vaguely ritualistic. She writes them down and fears losing them. She tries to memorize them but can't. She keeps them in her coat pocket and refers to them repeatedly on the subway, shading the scrap of paper with her hand. Broadcasting your outsider status could be fatal. *Stay in the last car. When you exit the station, take the staircase on the right. Walk three blocks north toward the big clock, staying on the west side of the street. The deli should be on your left. If you see the laundromat, you're going the wrong way.*

Pru says, *It should be Walk three blocks and say your prayers.*

She has the sense that if she doesn't follow the directions to the letter, she will die and her body will never be found. All of us crave this sort of excitement.

Budapest

At one party Pru sees none other than the Original Jack. He looks a little rounder, but since he was rail-thin before, this means he's basically perfect. His skin glows. He's not exactly handsome but Pru says there's a certain newfound allure. The baldness is a recent development but somehow it works.

We're working on a theory that everyone looks better once they leave the office forever.

The party was thrown by someone Pru went to school with. The way she says this makes it sound like they dated briefly freshman year until he slept with her roommate. At first the party was the height of awkwardness, people sitting in a circle and pushing potato chips around their plates, but then at 11 more people showed up and things got slightly more fun. There was disco music and people who came dressed up as scientists.

The main lesson we take away is that the Original Jack is somehow a consultant and makes more money than all of us combined. When she saw him, he had just returned from a business trip to Budapest, which he pronounced in an authentically unfamiliar way.

Also, I think he was hitting on me.

Lizzie makes a how-disgusting face but Pru just shrugs.

More time with the cats

Maxine calls a meeting in the fourth-floor conference room, then cancels it. Instead she wants to meet each of us individually, one person every twenty minutes, beginning at noon. This can't be good.

We drift toward the coffee machine. Nobody feels like making any. In truth nobody has made coffee in weeks. The pots hold bluish water, a nontoxic chemical cleanser that theoretically leaves no cleanser taste. We're not convinced. We've been buying our coffee at the Bad Starbucks or at the new tasty hippie coffee van that has replaced the mobile taco stand around the corner. Laars thinks the hippie coffee van is maybe run by Scientologists.

Scientologists can't drink coffee, says Crease.

You're thinking of Mormons, says Laars.

Jonah jokes that he's going to get fired. He *wants* to get fired, he tells us, provided he gets severance. If he does, he'll go to Mexico again for a few months. Then he'll come back and collect unemployment and spend more time with his cats. He blushes as he says this, which makes *cats* sound like a euphemism for something else.

He says he's nearly done with night school. This is news to us. While we've been sitting around and complaining, he's been complaining and improving himself. We feel he should have told us. Maybe we would have enrolled in night school as well.

< *12* >

That sinking feeling

Work picks up. There's hardly time to talk. Pru doesn't think Maxine wants to fire us. She says there's no way the company can function if they cut anyone else.

We agree. *They must know that*, says Laars. *They can't be that stupid.*

But actually they can. And then time will pass, and the company will still be afloat, and we'll wonder who's next.

Maxine should fire herself, says Jonah. When did he grow a mustache? It's light, much lighter than his hair.

I'm getting that sinking feeling, says Laars. He fiddles with the coffeemaking elements, but decides against the actual making of coffee.

I need a smoke, says Pru, heading for the elevator. Crease is about to go with her, then remembers he's quit smoking. He wants to hang out and see if HABAW will pass, but the other day his former student came hurtling down the sidewalk, excited shouts of *Crease!* filling the air.

We stand around nervously for another minute. Maxine

struts by with a weird vicious but kind of hot smile and we all watch her as she passes.

She's really amazing, says Laars. *Like, different-life-form amazing.*

Later we hear Jonah running the wooden rod across the back of his Mexican distress frog. The verdict is still out on his mustache.

Some percentage

There's a meeting. It's pretty bad. Some of us wonder if it's a dream.

I want each of you to think about what it is you're bringing to the table, the Sprout says.

After work, we compare notes over drinks. It might as well have been over potato chips, though. We're too frazzled to drink.

According to Laars, Maxine said that the company was deducting 15 percent from everyone's gross salary to cover an unexpected rise in costs, a one-time-only thing. Jonah understood that, in order to comply with new city and state taxes, a 15 percent cut was necessary, over two pay periods, meaning 15 percent *each* paycheck, or 7.5 each for a total of 15? We are trying to remember how percentages work. On a napkin Lizzie has drawn the little hut you make when you're about to divide a number, but she hasn't written any numbers down.

Pru came away with the sense that the Sprout insisted on trimming 20 percent from half of the paychecks and 10 percent from the other half, but that she, Maxine, had approached him with a flat 15 percent across the board. And Laars is under the impression she had told him 1.5 percent, but for the rest of the year.

It's like our own little *Rashomon*. We are either the victims of deliberate obfuscation or we are all complete morons. *The Californians are going to have a field day with us*, Jack II says.

Vow of chastity

Laars's self-Googling has reached another level. He keeps turning up more stuff: more people with his name, more women he's been involved with. Both his doppelgängers and his exes are having more fun, leading more interesting lives, than he is.

His arms hurt. He's in a rut and needs to lift the curse. He restates his vow of chastity to Jenny, which makes everyone think that he must have recently broken it, that he's hitting on Jenny, or preferably both.

I've been thinking about going to church, he says.

In the meantime, Laars plans to stop all gallivanting and carousing, all pointless crushes and ludicrous Maxine obsessing, all shadowy self-abuse. The Googling will end. He is going to become a serious worker and a spiritual being.

The Sprout overhears this last part and laughs: *Hoo-hoo!*

Valid actions

Lizzie drags an icon out of a cluttered corner of her screen but lets go too soon. It falls into the document she's working on, which happens to be her résumé. The icon bounces back to its starting place with a *boinggg* noise she's never heard before. She learns that *Word cannot insert a file into itself.*

Word can seriously go fuck itself, she mutters. She's been talking to herself a lot lately but maybe we all have.

Later she's trying to put a chart into a different document but gets scolded: *That is not a valid action for footnotes.*

This is funny—the quick response, the finger-wagging

strictness—but it also creeps her out. She calls up Pru except she accidentally dials her own extension and the little screen says, *You cannot call yourself.*

Our machines know more than we do, Pru thinks. Even their deficiencies and failures are instructive. They are trying to tell us about the limits of the human, the nature of the possible. *Or something like that,* says Pru, who has been reading a novel about cyborgs set in the year 2012.

The message that kills us is the one that pops up on the rare occasions when we remember to shut everything down for the weekend, just before we turn the computer off.

Are you sure you want to quit?

The misrecognitions

Jonah sees Jules in a coffee shop on Twenty-second, wearing a baseball cap and glasses with enormous frames, just one millimeter away from being joke glasses. Jules says his toaster-oven restaurant is closed for renovations. Something exploded last week.

Now I have time to polish off my screenplay, he says, thwacking a grubby stack of paper perched unsteadily on the chair beside him.

Despite a lack of interest in all but three or four films ever projected in the history of cinema, Jules was apparently hard at work on a script before he was let go. The title is *Personal Daze*—Daze *with a* z, he says, which confuses Jonah until he sees the cover page.

Jules has a younger brother whose friend is friends with one of the people who wrote the movie about the stolen horse. *You need a foot in the door,* he explains.

It all came together shortly *before* he got fired, during his brief exile on the sixth floor. Otto in IT wanted to try out Glottis, a fancy new voice-recognition program, so he hooked it up to Jules's computer and asked him to say anything. This pretty much became his job for that last strange month. He would read newspaper stories aloud, bits of whatever book was at hand. Otto would study the results. Jules began to freestyle, yapping about the weather, lunch, things he overheard on the way to the office, childhood. He did different voices. Before long he was making up a story in which certain characters reappeared. The screenplay was born.

Jules would experiment with how low he could speak and still produce legible results on the screen. At first Glottis gave him a lot of errors, thirty misrecognitions for every hundred words. Over time it adapted to his voice, learned to negotiate the peculiar Julesian cadences and frequent slurring, and the error rate went down significantly.

Still, there was something wild about the words that would occasionally appear—surreal juxtapositions, such as when a cop character tells a perp to *Keep wool* instead of *Keep cool* or the periodic greeting *Jello!*

Sometimes when Jules wanted to open a file via Glottis, words would appear on the screen: *Open fire!*

The title, *Personal Daze*, also came about this way. *Let's just say it's the name of someone I met, a customer at the club*, says Jules. *I don't want to talk about it.*

A bad egg, says Jonah.

Worse than that—this guy was like the bad chicken!

How can *Personal Daze* be someone's name? Jules won't elaborate, as if he still fears retribution.

Jules dictated reams of material during work hours. Every

night he'd boil down his ramblings to half a page. By the time he was fired he'd compiled nearly 150 pages of fast-moving, wisecracking, bittersweet dialogue.

Now he estimates he only has twenty-five pages left to go before he can stop composing and begin revising. But somehow it's harder to write now that he doesn't work in the office.

You need something to push against, he says. He compares the creative process to an oyster requiring sand for a pearl. *Also, I need an ending.*

He attributes his current writer's block to the fact that he no longer has the voice-recognition system. Glottis costs a bundle, as does the brand of microphone headset with just the right sensitivity. He misses the surreptitious muttering, the magical appearance of words on the glowing monitor like a parade of ants materializing out of a pool of milk. More than anything else, he longs for the faulty wording, the slips between thought and expression. The misrecognitions had been his inspiration.

Jules is cagey at first, but then lets Jonah read certain scenes. Mostly it's a ghost story set in a haunted gentleman's club on Eleventh Avenue. The main character, Jude, appears to be modeled on Jules, down to the precision-cut sideburns. The rest is a little hard to follow but seems to take place in our office, except that everybody likes the boss and plays basketball with him.

I must have been reading a dream sequence, Jonah tells us afterward.

Playing the frog
Jonah keeps his door shut lately. Is he working on his own screenplay? Listening to opera nonstop?

Sometimes we forget about him for days at a stretch, until we hear the Mexican distress frog's plaintive call: *Takata takata takata, kat-kat ka-tak.*

A mouse in the hand

Three of us meet with the Sprout. He hums tunelessly as he toggles between files on his computer desktop, smiling unhappily as he eyes various charts. Like some of us, he has a second, older computer on his desk, which he also glances at now and again. *It's a period of transition,* he likes to say: The new system hasn't been successfully phased in yet and no one wants to get rid of the old data, just in case. No one ever wants to get rid of anything, though once something is gone there's a mild sensation of improved health and wide-open desktop vistas.

The IT people always look harried, barking into two-way radios, and so you don't feel right bugging them. Old-timers like Jonah know that it's *always* a period of transition.

At one point the Sprout has a different mouse in each hand, clicking in counterpoint. When he double-clicks on the top of a document, it flies to the bottom of his screen like a little bat. He talks while he moves from one set of data to the other.

Every time he saves something, the computer makes a sound, a coin dropped into a box of xylophone parts.

He e-mails himself an enormous Excel file from the old computer to the new one. But the new one can't open it. He downloads some sort of Excel upgrade onto the old computer, crashing it.

I'm not sure why I did that, he says, rebooting.

We gaze at the bookshelf. There's now a gauzy photo of Sheila in a black wooden frame dotted with seashells. We trade glances, trying to read each other's eyes. One of us seems to be saying, *She's hot*, another, *Weird frame*, another, *Wait, did she die?*

Some of the old books are gone. The new titles include a massive bird-watcher's guide and a coffee-table book in which people across America take pictures of their shoes at different hours of the day.

The Sprout is still saying *hmmm*. We detect a vein throbbing on his forehead. We always forget about the vein until we see it again.

Then he relaxes. He arches an eyebrow comically as the fax machine in the far corner of the office begins receiving. It's actually a fax from *himself*.

Hoo-hoo!

He plucks the printouts from the machine.

Read 'em and weep, he says. Like most of his statements these days, it's either totally meaningless or somehow evil.

Random poignancy, continued

The next day, Friday, the Sprout asks Laars for a file from last year. Laars's system of folders is so byzantine, his naming conventions so idiosyncratic, and his memory so poor, that he often has to do a global search of all the contents on his computer if he's looking for a file more than a few weeks old. He tries to guess what word might spring up in the document title, then hits Search.

I don't understand, the computer says.

The air of mystery

For some reason Jonah uses a mug that says *Joan*. He's had it for a while, but Pru just noticed the spelling recently.

Hey Joan, Pru says.

Jonah just smiles and cultivates his air of mystery.

The letters are in a painfully dated '80s font, a red not quite cursive, like something used on the newsletter for a dodgy Myrtle Beach time-share. The mug is white with thin multi-colored horizontal stripes above and below the name.

What's shaking, Joan?

He looks like he's going to reach for the Mexican distress frog.

Crease says *Joan* is the name of Jonah's robust common-law wife, now ex, who lives in Texas with their ornery love child. He claims he heard this from Jules.

Pru keeps calling Jonah *Joan.*

The long good-bye

The Sprout is leaving the office for the weekend. There's a spring in his step, a thin jacket draped over his arm, and a bag from the Italian bakery dangling from a finger.

Have a good one, he says to Jenny, closing his door and locking it smoothly.

Later, man, he barks at Jonah while turning the corner by the mail room, the very picture of managerial friendliness.

Any fun weekend plans? he asks Pru, not quite pausing as he heads to the elevator. She says she'll probably see a movie and go to a party in Brooklyn. He nods and says, *Excellent plan— don't do anything I wouldn't do.*

He gives Lizzie a little wink and Laars a big salute and hits the Down button. The elevator takes its time arriving. He taps one tennis-sneakered foot in time to the jaunty tune in his head.

Crap, says the Sprout just as the doors open. He's forgotten something. He trots back the way he came, not saying anything to the people he's just passed. He unlocks his door and grabs his briefcase and sprints back to the elevator, which has long since gone.

The layoff narrative

We have assorted dietary restrictions and particular aversions, which makes group meals untenable, generally speaking, and so the decision to lunch together is sort of impulsive.

Jill is in Siberia and no one feels like going up to get her. She sits too far from the elevator. We could e-mail her, but no one does. Pru says she thinks Jill might be out, taking a personal day to help a friend move into an apartment. This relieves us of guilt.

Our high hopes for the new Chinese restaurant are dashed by the time the soup arrives. Everything tastes a little like soap. *At least we know it's clean,* Jonah says.

Whatever you say, Joan, says Pru.

Oh, stop it, says Lizzie. *Seriously.*

We talk about how getting fired might not be the worst thing. We calculate severance, add it to how much we'd get in unemployment. The sum would be distressingly close to how much some of us are making as it is. *It's inhumane,* someone says.

I'd be OK for three months, says Laars. *Unless I got in an accident.*

Define OK, says Lizzie.

They always try to wriggle out of paying severance, says Jonah. There's a disobedience clause that they like to use. Jules made out decently, but Jason didn't get a penny. The Original Jack signed a nondisclosure agreement and made out so-so. You can't get him to tell you what happened, why he was fired, even if you say *I promise I won't tell anyone.*

Pru says what we're doing is constructing a layoff narrative. The idea is that you look back on your period of employment, highlight all the abuses suffered, tally the lessons gained, and use these negatives and positives to mentally withstand what you anticipate will be a series of events culminating in expulsion. You look to termination as rebirth, liberation, an expansion of horizons.

Once you start constructing the layoff narrative, it's only a matter of time. It starts to feel like a fait accompli.

Nobody knows what to say. Suddenly we wish we'd invited Jill, a collective guilt twinge. We talk about Jules and his screenplay, *Personal Daze.* We speculate, a lot, about Maxine's sex life. Laars describes a TV show he saw last night, some stalker drama or cancer drama, possibly stalker cancer drama, with that guy from the *X-Files* spin-off and the woman from a French movie none of us have seen. *I should write a pilot,* he says. It's his new thing to say.

Jack II says he's started a blog. He tells us the address, but nobody writes it down.

Pru's fortune is a good one: *You are the master of every situation.*

On the back it gives the Chinese word for *ninety.* We aren't sure of the pronunciation, though there are accent marks galore. It seems like a singularly useless piece of information. Imagine going to China knowing how to say a single number. Someone in the fortune cookie factory was clearly slacking, perhaps just translating all the numbers from one to a hundred.

Pru puts the slip of paper carefully in her wallet. She says she's been reading her horoscope every day this week.

We remember that Jules used to eat fortunes if he wanted them to come true. Once he got one that said *What goes around comes around*. We can't remember whether he ate it or not. A month later we saw that it had become the motto for Jobmilla.

The punctuationist

When we return to the office, Jill's gone. We wouldn't have known—it could have been like one of those situations where a dead body isn't found for weeks, and then suddenly there's a smell—except she's left a very brief note on Jenny's desk. It's on Hello Kitty stationery. She writes that she wanted to message all of us individually but her e-mail account's already been eliminated and she's being escorted out of the building.

I'm sad to go. Please water my plants

Who does the escorting? None of us has ever witnessed the actual exits of any of our former co-workers, as if the removals were precisely timed to minimize visibility. Does the Sprout press a button to summon men in dark uniforms, wielding biceps and Tasers? Maybe the Sprout himself grabs you by the arm, doesn't say a word as he pushes you out the door.

Already we're thinking of Jill in the past tense.

Please water my plants

There's no period. Somehow this is the worst thing—Jill was always the most meticulous punctuationist. We imagine her getting yanked out of her seat, a firm hand at her back. The terminal *s* seems to be swooping upward in an unnatural way.

The mail cart stands unattended in the hallway.

It's because she didn't complete the self-evaluation, says Crease. We remember Jill's blank essay. Why hadn't she written anything down?

Jenny feels a chill. She has a sudden premonition that she'll be moved to Jill's freshly vacated Siberian desk. In five minutes Jenny looks like she's lost ten pounds. She's not wearing any makeup and her hair stands up in places.

Please water my

Jenny says she saw something yesterday, a Post-it on the Sprout's desk. All it said was, *Jill?* The name was underlined. The handwriting was not the Sprout's. Was it *K.'s* decree?

Please water

Jenny says she also put together a conference call between K., the Sprout, and a number in California. It only lasted ten minutes. The door was closed and she couldn't hear a word. She didn't think anything of it at the time.

The Sprout walks by, whistling. He halts the tune when he sees us, his eyes doubling psychotically. Then he bolts down the corridor and tries to disguise that he's bolting by doing weird circular motions with his head. This is supposed to represent the natural, spontaneous movement of a carefree individual, someone out for a nonthreatening, non-guilt-filled turn about the office. We hear him crash into the abandoned mail cart and let out a *fuck*.

Please

Pru mumbles her Chinese word, *ninety,* an impotent mantra. Jonah goes to his desk. Laars is looking at the walls, hands tightening into fists.

Jenny stares at the Sprout's door, listening to the ventilation system's roar. She feels like she's waiting for the last straw. But every straw these days is the last straw.

We hear: *Takata-takata-tak.*

< **II** >

REPLACE
ALL

II (A) Asylum

<u>II (A) i:</u> *That's crazy!—It was an* insane *idea.—I'm so* crazed *right now I can't even think.—It was like total* insanity.— *Hysterical.*

   <u>II (A) ii (a):</u> They often talked like that in the office, everything nudged to the rhetoric of the breaking point.

   <u>II (A) ii (b):</u> But nothing was ever *that* crazy. It was a badge they hadn't earned. If someone ate two bagels—watch out. *That's some freaky shit.*

   <u>II (A) ii (c):</u> Any minor eccentricity could be deemed *wild* or *out of control.* Such language convinced them they were more interesting than they suspected they really were. It was crucial that they never contemplated the possibility of their inherent, overwhelming dullness.

II (A) iii: Grime

<u>II (A) iii (a):</u> This analysis held true, mostly. Except that after Grime came onboard, they started monitoring his behavior, and it turned out he *was* crazy, crazy in what was actually a bad way.

<u>II (A) iii (b):</u> It wasn't so obvious at first.

   <u>II (A) iii (c) 1:</u> He was Grime because after a few weeks working there, during which they had only a distant notion that someone new was on the floor, he rang Pru with an ur-

gent PowerPoint question. Her phone extension and that of the IT department differed by one digit.

<u>II (A) iii (c) 2:</u> He said, *It's Grime, from down the hall, the one with glasses.* Pru went searching for the punch line.

<u>II (A) iii (c) 3:</u> He was saying *Graham* but his thick British accent got in the way. She'd never actually used PowerPoint before, but she went to help him anyway.

II (B) i: A New Kind of Sleeping

<u>II (B) i (a) 1:</u> That whole area where Grime had his cubicle was an obstacle course, a treacherous maze. There were monitors coated with dust, upturned scraps of radiator shielding. Abandoned poster tubes littered the floor in a manner anticipating vaudeville pratfalls. There was half a bike chained to a pipe with the insulation falling off. Everything was a shade darker there, and grainy to the touch. A wine bottle with no label held a plastic flower. It was like the prop room for a theater company based in Pompeii.

There used to be more people in that area but three of them fell in a wave of firings two years before, back when the Sprout thought he was a sea captain. He'd say things like *We'll have to run a tighter ship* and *I don't like the cut of her jib,* and often invoked the *Titanic.* Even his clothes had a nautical bent, lots of navy, lots of stripes. Jules offered odds on when the Sprout would adopt an eye patch.

He also started using words like *fungible* and *egregious,* which he got from his word-a-day e-mail. More recently, expressions like *As the crow flies* and *We'll just have to eat crow* had worked their way into Sproutian rotation.

They couldn't remember the names of those ex-workers of

yore. There had maybe been a David, a Dawn or a Donna, and a Marlboro Man type whose name was something like *Dirk*.

You are running out of memory, Jonah's computer warns him every few weeks.

II (B) i (a) 2: The weirdest thing: *an ax*. It looked about twenty years old. Laars once picked it up, thinking it would be made of Halloween plastic. He dropped it and the heavy handle crushed his toe purple. Everyone thought someone else would get rid of it but no one ever did.

II (B) i (b): At last Pru found Grime, slumped at his desk, his glasses on top of his monitor. He had a screen saver of the city going up in flames.

Grime had one eye open. He explained that he was trying to sleep like a duck. A duck can shut down half its brain at a time. It's harder for humans, he said, because our eyes are on the same plane. He said bullfrogs never close their eyes.

II (B) i (c): That thing about the sleeping and ducks and bullfrogs—that monologue alone was doing things to Pru that she didn't understand.

II (B) i (d) 1: Plus he was dressed in a pin-striped shirt that looked like it had been stepped on, with a loosened tie that also looked like it had been stepped on. Two cute little impromptu horns rose from his mop of hair. His appearance could best be described as *rumpled*.

II (B) i (d) 2: This comported with Pru's idea of how British people should look. The next day she said she was in love. The one drawback was that Grime thought she was with the IT department. He kept calling her with minor queries. She wasn't sure how to break the news.

Later in the day Grime stopped Lizzie in the hall and asked where the watercooler was, except he called it something else—whatever was British for *watercooler. Aquifer? Thirst-station? Liquids dispens'ry?*

Lizzie told Pru that she was charmed as well, despite her abiding hatred of all things British. They were joking but they weren't joking. It was clear Lizzie thought Pru should refixate on Crease, but of course Crease was intoxicated with Half Asian British Accent Woman.

Aren't we still supposed to be in mourning? asked Laars.

Pru and Lizzie stared, bullfrog style.

For Jill, he said.

Jill?

II (B) i (e): That Friday, Grime called Pru but she was away from her desk. He left a message, thanking her again for her PowerPoint assistance and asking for her help with a different program. His voice was at once chipper and lazy, and soon he got tangled up in the words. The message was an amusing shambles. He concluded with: *Well . . . what I mean to sigh is . . . Oil just toke to ya afta lunch!*

II (B) i (f): Pru kept that message on her machine for over a week. It was so adorable. She hadn't mastered the voice-mail system after nearly three years on the job and didn't know how to skip over a message, or how to archive it. This meant that when she got other, newer messages, she had to listen to the first Grime message in full. She didn't mind and in fact she sometimes listened to it just to listen to it. She played it once for Jonah, who said, *That's pathetic.*

II (B) i (g): Lizzie and Pru had a friendly, imaginary, passive-aggressive bet about which one of them Grime would ask out first.

What if it's Jenny? asked Lizzie.

Who?

<u>II (B) i (h):</u> It might be noted that, several years ago, Lizzie and Pru had been roommates for about five minutes. They didn't like to talk about it. Lizzie had been working at the office for six months when Pru started staying with her. Pru's half sister and Lizzie's brother's best friend had been friends in forestry school.

Pru had come from Boston to New York for grad school. She eventually moved out of Lizzie's place because she wanted to be closer to campus. Or so she said. The rumor was that Pru's then-boyfriend, a gravel-voiced graffiti artist, had taken a shine to Lizzie, and Pru wanted to squash any flowering side romance. It wound up not mattering, because shortly after Pru moved out, he joined the Peace Corps or said he joined the Peace Corps.

<u>II (B) i (i):</u> So there was that history between them. They were very different people, or so they wanted Grime to believe. Lizzie was very down-to-earth, though that might have been largely by reputation. Someone would say to a new hire, *She's so down-to-earth*, cementing her personality in the newcomer's mind.

Lizzie gave the impression of being very organized. At meetings she was constantly creating one-week to-do lists in a little notepad, six boxes marked M, T, W, Th, F, S/S, which she filled with tasks in minuscule handwriting. Actually what it meant was that the meeting was putting her to sleep and that she had to keep the pen moving in order not to collapse.

She had a toothbrush in a crazy little '60s glass by her desk, which said to the world that the office was her home.

<u>II (B) i (j):</u> Pru on the other hand kept a spartan cubicle, all the easier to abandon at a moment's notice. She always radiated a faint but definite socialite vibe, like she was slumming in that

dead-end environment by day and moving around in glamorous circles by night. This might explain her belated discovery of Brooklyn. Jules claimed he saw her in the society pages, posing at a medical gala with two oldsters and a stethoscope carved out of ice. Maybe one of them was a baron.

<u>II (B) i (k):</u> Pru had a different surname than her second stepfather, who they thought was the guy whose name was preceded by *real estate developer and philanthropist* when it was in the newspapers. He was about five times her age and in articles was regularly described as boarding his private jet, relaxing on it, or disembarking from it.

It was the departed Jules, of course, who'd kept the mental file on Pru, so some of the facts were shaky. Jason had also been fixated on her pedigree, back when he was still at the office, and claimed she paid five hundred dollars for a haircut.

It was believed that Pru went to college in the Boston area. They were all pretty sure it was Harvard, but she never said one way or the other. Laars, the Aorta College grad, had an anti-Harvard chip on his shoulder, for no real reason except maybe that his father and brother went there and he hated them.

II (B) ii: Not-flinching

<u>II (B) ii (a) 1:</u> Grime never called Russell by his recognized nickname, The Sprout. He would just laugh and say *Ahhh, HA-ha* when one of the others used it. New employees were typically uneasy about participating in all the name-calling and the grievous, pointed sighing. Even Laars had been that way at first. Same with Crease. Same with Jill. They all had to be broken in.

You could understand a newcomer's position. On the surface, the Sprout didn't seem totally evil. His evilness was subtle, deep-seated, inconsistently revealed, to the extent that on occasion they wondered if they'd had him pegged all wrong. A Jekyll and Hyde element was proposed. *It's his job that's made him evil*, Lizzie sometimes said.

<u>II (B) ii (a) 2:</u> For a while they were all fascinated by Grime. He was like a new toy. He ate constantly yet remained enviably trim. He always had a tweed or corduroy blazer in the vicinity, slung across a shoulder or molded to his chairback. His glasses were never on his face but tucked in his shirt pocket like a giant sleeping insect or dangling from his mouth. Sometimes when he talked he cleaned the lenses using a soft gray cloth.

His hair was full and dark save for a shock of white at the very back, about an inch square. Pru pegged Grime as in his mid-thirties. Possibly he was as old as his mid-forties, but a *young* mid-forties.

He might have been partly deaf. He always asked you to repeat things, and in any conversation would invariably cock his head a few degrees to the right, like a dog discovering a new form of food. When compelled to walk, he moved like he'd just come out of a disco, the music still swirling in his good ear.

Grime's first words to Laars, to Jonah, to Jack II were not *Hello* or *Nice to meet you* but *What's today?* He never knew the date. It wasn't clear that he knew the *year*. And he seemed to find the men more or less interchangeable.

He told anecdotes that usually hinged on names none of them knew—British stage actresses from the '40s and football greats, Fleet Street legends and MPs.

Laars had to Google *Fleet Street*. He could have sworn it was where Sherlock Holmes lived and even bet Pru five bucks, but he was so wrong.

II (B) ii (a) 3: A couple weeks in, Grime made a big production of going to each person and grilling them playfully about what it was they did. *So basically you're a useless piece of crap*, he joked, at the end of each encounter. His delivery was excellent and it was very funny at the time but a little unnerving about two minutes later. There should be a French term for that, along the lines of *esprit d'escalier.*

II (B) ii (a) 4: They could listen to Grime talk forever, but it was hard to read anything he'd written. His e-mails were amazing. Sometimes nearly every word would be misspelled or find itself adjacent to incorrect punctuation.

> Thnaks, for the heads-op! Aprecite it.
> I can't priny this docment.
> I;m gong out for coffee will be bacj in 10.

Sometimes the meaning was completely obscure. They would either call him or ignore the message. *Its not clar how I shold stile sit.*

The most memorable line, the one some of them repeated when he wasn't in earshot or even when he was, was *Keep me in the lopp.* He'd written this to Crease regarding some project that none of them would start thinking about till the spring.

II (B) ii (a) 5: Crease joked that Grime must put his outgoing correspondence through a turbo-powered spell-check, some program developed by the military that cost four hundred dollars an hour to operate and needed to be supplemented twice a year.

Whenever the fluorescent lights flickered, someone would say, *Grime's spell-checking again.*

<u>II (B) ii (a) 6:</u> Grime found something better than an industrial-grade spell-check. He asked Lizzie if she could help him proofread his stuff. He said he wasn't used to the keyboards in their office. Maybe he was trained on those non-QWERTY ones or the kind that looked broken, fingers meeting at a ninety-degree angle. Maybe his hands were too big or too small.

He said he was going to ask Pru but she seemed a little uptight.

Uptight and whatnot was the actual phrase.

An hour later Lizzie was sorry she'd said yes. Grime's write-ups and summaries—documents that he had to send out on actual paper, with an actual signature—reminded her of the second half of *Flowers for Algernon.* He kept looking at her while she proofread, and she could feel sweat break out across her brow. Looking up, she saw him licking the corners of his lips, and later she wondered whether she liked that or not. It was getting hard to be *down-to-earth.*

<u>II (B) ii (a) 7:</u> Lizzie soon reverted to the style of dress she wore when she first started there. Pru described the look as Eccentric Librarian. A pencil could always be found tucked behind Lizzie's ear, or impaling her scrappy chignon.

<u>II (B) ii (b) 1.1:</u> Jonah and Laars were the first to be disenchanted by Grime.

Laars thought it was obscene that the Sprout hired someone so soon after getting rid of Jill. Admittedly Jill wasn't the most dazzling human being, but she was solid, a hard worker who got the job done. Grime's role was unclear, and Laars imagined he was getting paid more than Jill ever did.

The thing is he won't shut up, Jonah complained to Crease. *Also I have no idea what he's saying half the time.*

Jonah was also probably upset because he used to say *Cheers* when getting off the phone. With the appearance of an actual British person on the premises he couldn't say it without feeling fraudulent.

<u>II (B) ii (b) 1.1.1:</u> Actually, when Grime said it, it sounded more like *Chairs.*

<u>II (B) ii (b) 1.2:</u> Most of them were used to Jonah's mustache by that point. That did not mean they liked it. Jonah wasn't sure *he* liked it, but shaving it off would be admitting defeat.

<u>II (B) ii (b) 2.1:</u> Laars was suspicious of Grime's connection to the Sprout. Were they friends? It seemed like they'd worked together somewhere before. Also he'd seen them both toting athletic bags on the same day—did they face off every week on the racquetball court?

<u>II (B) ii (b) 2.2:</u> They heard the Sprout say *How's the Cracker?* to Grime. It took a second to figure out: *Graham.* The Sprout never bestowed nicknames on any of them, a fact that left them curiously dejected.

Jenny said she overheard the Sprout saying to Grime, *Operation JASON—working like a charm!*

Operation JASON? Naturally they assumed it had to do with the broken CD of files that Maxine threw in the trash.

Jonah asked Jules to get in touch with Jason, but he didn't know how to anymore. He thought Jason might have moved to Madrid.

They began to doubt that Jenny heard what she heard. *She* began to doubt it. She said her boyfriend was renting all these spy movies.

<u>II (B) ii (b) 2.3:</u> One day Pru received a mysterious message from Grime:

floor?ds\\\\\\\\\\\\\\\J\A\S\\\

It went on like that for a while, winding up with

]\\\\\\\\\\\\\\\\\0\
???????//////

It was like typographical Rorschach. Later Grime explained that he thought he'd already sent the message and then saw that his slash key was absolutely filthy, so he started scrubbing it with a wad of paper.

That still didn't explain *floor?ds.*

Or *J\A\S.*

<u>II (B) ii (b) 3:</u> Grime and Lizzie went out to lunch together once, alone, accidentally. She bumped into him at the post office and they decided to stop by the new fish and chips stand, sample his native fare. The chips were presented in fresh copies of the *Telegraph* and *The Guardian,* adding to the overall cost. The lunch went fine, a few laughs, maybe not as many sparks as she'd hoped. Lizzie was so cute when she said *sparks.* The food was pretty bleh but at least her Diet Coke was properly carbonated.

What killed her was that on the way back, about half a block from the office, Grime picked up speed. She asked where he was going as she raced to keep up. He said it was probably a good idea for the two of them to enter the building separately. He didn't want people to get the wrong idea about them.

Was Grime playing hard to get? There was nothing to do

but laugh nervously. In truth she wanted to cry or kick him in the shins, but his sudden skittishness also made him that much more attractive. She tried to imagine the kind of woman he went for and in her mind she conjured up Pru in a leopard-skin teddy.

Lizzie favored pencil skirts and pencils in her hair and those shirts with cuffs that buttoned up halfway down the forearm.

<u>II (B) ii (b) 4.1:</u> The next day Grime swung by the Red Alcove after lunch. Pru and Lizzie were studying the Victoria's Secret catalog in a non-ironic manner. Jenny was sipping a green tea latte and looking through last month's *Allure*, stopping on an article about green tea lattes.

Grime did a fake-embarrassed cough and said, *Ladies.* He said he had an important question, maybe the most important question ever.

They all straightened up, chins thrust fetchingly forward, eyes widening.

I don't know how to describe it . . .

Yes . . . ?

<u>II (B) ii (b) 4.2:</u> He wanted to know what it meant when there was a red toolbox pulsating on the menu bar of a Word document.

Lizzie wished Pru wasn't around at the moment, and vice versa. They both offered to take a look. Jenny stayed behind because she had to go back to her desk in a second. She was becoming a little wary of Grime.

Grime led them to his lair, loping. His head was at an unnatural angle, as if he had a crick in his neck from pubbing till the wee hours. His gait was mellow, a beach-comber's stride. Unseen waves lapped his toes. His harem converted to his dreamtime pace as he detailed additional problems he was having with his document.

II (B) ii (b) 4.3: En route they nearly collided with Maxine, who emitted a perfectly calibrated squeal of delight.

She was wearing something that none of them could really describe. She'd been in full plumage of late, inspiring daily fashion rundowns by the rest of the office. Jack II even started devoting part of his blog to the study of Maxine, craftily changing her name to *Minnie*. Someone was leaving lewd comments on the site. He suspected Jules.

Maxine's new outfit was completely inappropriate for winter, in fact for any season or situation, with the possible exception of world domination. It had two kinds of pink going on, and ornate beaded strappy things, and a fairly explicit bondage motif. There were parallelograms of exposed flesh that were illegal in most states, a bow in the back that looked like a winding key. One area involved *fur*. Her hair had a fresh-from-salon bounce that clashed with the rest of the getup, but this being Maxine, everything kind of went together in the end.

II (B) ii (b) 4.4: Pru and Lizzie instinctively flinched. They might as well have been rolling on the ground like bowling pins, with *x*s for eyes.

With the female competition out of the way, Maxine leveled her extremely hot gaze right at Grime, who stood his ground. He swayed in place, gently rocking on one heel. Maxine was saying something about Wednesday, but it wasn't clear whether she meant tomorrow or last Wednesday.

Grime's not-flinching was making *Maxine* flinch. It looked like a nod but it was actually a flinch. Lizzie and

Pru saw it all unfold. They're filing away the subtleties for Jack II and his blog. Maxine lost the thread of what she was saying, eyes gleaming in panic. She could have been talking about the general concept of Wednesday, its status as hump day, its complicated spelling. No one had seen her quiver like this before. It was like she'd been set in italics.

There was a historical vibe to the scene. Lizzie got so nervous just from watching that she stuck another pen into her hair.

Time was upended. *Wednesday* derived from Wotan or Odin, god of the victorious, god of the dead.

The air grew thick with non-flinches. Then the flinches burst forth. Lizzie looked away from Maxine. Maxine looked at Pru and then at Lizzie and then, finding no moral support, back at Grime.

From down the hall came a loud tinkle of coins. A can of soda fell from its perch in the sad old vending machine, the one with half its red sold-out lights always on.

The can's tumble sounded loud as thunder.

<u>II (B) ii (b) 4.5:</u> Maxine reflexively clasped Grime's shoulder and murmured something unintelligible. It was a good reminder that she could be quite *touchy*, though she hadn't been in a while, not to her regular admirers. When this *did* happen, traditionally, most of them were unable to stop at mere flinching. They would gasp and stagger away, extremities shaking. They would take a long slow drink at the watercooler and generally need to lie down on Jonah's sofa for a couple of minutes, staring at the ceiling as strains of his Czech opera laced the air. On these occasions, Jonah would lend his Mexican distress frog.

But Grime barely responded to the surprise caress. A corner of his mouth rose a micrometer. The encounter had already bored him and he wanted to get back to his Word document and the mystery of the pulsating toolbox. The shoulder touching was just a neutral thing that happened. Maxine's arsenal had failed to make a dent. Maxine's arsenal had imploded.

She mentioned a mandatory seminar in two weeks, hoped he would help lead it. Another sexual-harassment seminar! The words caused no change in affect. His face betrayed no sign that he would attend, let alone lead it. With increasing discomfort Lizzie and Pru watched Maxine try to make an impression. An attempt to gaily link arms with him came to grief. He just stood there without any sort of accommodating elbow movement. Nothing in her experience had prepared Maxine for such pure indifference. She reversed course and disappeared.

II (B) ii (b) 5: Appendix I: Potential Problems

A semi-important development: Just when it seemed like Grime was the walking embodiment of cool, so unaffected by maximum Maxining that Lizzie and Pru wondered for the first time if maybe he was gay, he stopped and did this brisk John Travolta dance-floor maneuver, one index finger pointing up, the other pointing down.

Lizzie's and Pru's irritating maybe-he's-gay thoughts were quickly replaced by *So that's sort of weird, sort of something you don't see every day.*

Grime pumped away in his disco stance for two seconds, flexing a little. A barely discernible melody played on his lips.

Maybe this is what they do in England, Lizzie thought. *Maybe this is how they walk.*

Pru believed she was simply witnessing the age-old English tradition of fierce eccentricity.

They took a step back and observed him as he froze, smiled, and let out a deep baritone fart.

<u>II (B) ii (b) 6:</u> It was totally deliberate. It wasn't an embarrassing slip. It wasn't the chance rubbing of a shoe against the linoleum or anything like that.

It was like the loudest thing imaginable, louder than the falling can of soda. Geiger counters in Japan went haywire. Satellites got shaken out of orbit, crashed into the sun.

Pru and Lizzie weren't sure how to react. They needed a seminar for this, special counseling. They kept walking, blushing, feeling like nuns. Grime's computer mouse was dangling off the desk edge, its infrared eye beaming out at them as though passing judgment. They helped him fix his Word document—he had opened a document header and didn't know how to get out—and then the two of them walked back in silence, still in their mental wimples.

Later they said, *He's insane.* Pru said it so that the last syllable trilled out as two notes, a full octave higher. Jack II offered to start a new blog devoted to the subject. Pru finally deleted the two-week-old Grime message from her phone, not without sadness.

II (B) ii (c): Appendix II: Pronouns and Abbreviations (a.k.a. P & A)

<u>II (B) ii (c) 1:</u> Somehow Crease thought that Grime, being British, *must* know Half Asian British Accent Woman, but

how to bring it up? Crease liked to refer to her in e-mails as HABAW or .5ABW or even just AB. They always had to pause and untangle the abbreviations.

In conversation he would just say *she* and *her* and expect them to know who he was talking about.

II (B) ii (c) 2: Three weeks and two days have passed since he last saw *her.* He noted that patience had always been his strong suit. It was how he had managed to stay at his job for seven years, weathering storms, rising slowly through the ranks. Crease said he'd been there so long he remembered when people got excited by Minesweeper. Now it was just e-mail, surfing the Web, and good old-fashioned erotic reverie.

II (B) ii (c) 3: Crease admitted he would be devastated if he were fired, not because he loved the job, obviously, or even because of the stop in cash flow, but because it would mean losing all hope of seeing HABAW again.

Pru said he needed to work a little harder on his layoff narrative.

At this point I'd give it a C/C-, she said.

II (B) ii (c) 4: Crease nearly flipped out two days ago because as he was waiting to take the elevator up, the door opened and the Sprout and HABAW got out, chatting comfortably about the weather. Their paths diverged, but he still sensed some connection between the two.

Crease's small-talk skills needed a polish. He would carry out a HABAW conversation in his mind and get stumped after the first short sentence. He needed to be prepared. He bookmarked a weather report website and checked it every two minutes.

So if she says, It's so nice out, *what do I say?*

You agree, and then you compliment her on an article of clothing, said Jonah.

Then you ask for her number, said Pru. A wave of fear and excitement passed over Crease. *No, actually, you definitely don't.*

Later he confessed to Pru, *I'm not used to beautiful women.*

She gave him a what-am-I-chopped-liver look, but he was oblivious.

II (B) ii (c) 5.1: Jack II confided to Laars and Pru about his own mini-crush on HABAW and said not to tell the rest of them, who already knew about it from Lizzie. He forgot that he'd been writing about her on his blog, in the style of a blind-item gossip column.

Confiding something to Laars and Pru pretty much ensured that everyone would know about it. Most of them had yet to see HABAW, but they imagined she was out of his league, if she looked anything like the way Crease described her.

II (B) ii (c) 5.2: Was Jack II's parallel obsession in jest? He was living with his girlfriend, an office manager in midtown. Pru described her as a *real character,* meaning she had a thick Queens accent.

At last year's holiday party she did shots with the Sprout, commenting every few minutes, *So* you're *the SPROUT!* It was very strange. Of course none of them had ever called him *the Sprout* to his face. But clearly he knew. He kept bellowing *Hoo-hoo!* and the shots kept coming.

They wondered if she now knew about HABAW.

II (B) iii (a): Initials had a way of getting out of control. Pru kept saying TMI, even if all you said was that you'd meet her at the elevator in a minute because you wanted to wash your hands first.

Jason used to say DGT, or *Don't Go There.* That one never caught on.

Crease was fond of scrawling ASAP on everything, most recently on a Post-it addressed to the janitorial staff: *Please fix soap dispenser in bathroom ASAP. This is a good way to spread germs, flu, etc.*

FYI was what Lizzie said for something as simple as the sun coming out. *FYI, I think it's not going to rain today.*

Jonah put HFS into e-mails, usually trailed by a long string of ellipses. Nobody wanted to ask him what it meant. Crease thought it stood for *Holy fucking shit.* It tended to appear after some account of the Sprout's particular brand of spineless evil.

II (B) iii (b): Maxine's thing was still FYA—For Your Amusement. She sent another message with that subject line. It had a link to a website full of Polish jokes.

Weird, said Lizzie.

Polish jokes are so Elks club 1978, said Pru. She theorized that it was the rise of Solidarity and the ascension of Pope John Paul II that killed the Polish joke.

It seemed like Maxine meant to send this only to Grime, because she prefaced it with a jaunty reference to England. There was also a line about bed linens that was totally DGT and TMI and, if you thought about it, OMFG.

The website froze everyone's screens. IT sent a faintly amused message via voice mail: *Please don't send, open, or even think about Polish jokes.*

II (B) iv (a): In the office, new alliances were forged from time to time. One Wednesday some of them were talking to Big Sal from IT and Henry from HR in the elevator, and all of a sudden Lizzie said, *Come grab drinks with us.*

It was strangely not that awkward. They learned that Big Sal had just started a few months ago. He'd overlapped with

Bernhard, whom he then replaced. He liked the office but thought he was due to get canned soon. *The problem is, you guys have like three different systems and they're not really talking to each other,* he explained. He began half his sentences with *The problem is.* His job was to make all lines of communication interact smoothly, a pretty much impossible task. *Your office is like the Bermuda Triangle of IT jobs,* he said.

Pru was expecting a whole big layoff narrative, but Big Sal said that was just how IT was. He didn't seem too worried about his imminent canning, prospects for reemployment, or life in general.

<u>II (B) iv (b)</u>: They learned that Henry from HR was married, had three kids, one of whom had just graduated from college, and conceivably could have been part of their little office gang. Henry was older than they thought.

His son had an internship with the Parks Department but what he really wanted to do was dance. *The kind where you wear rolls of toilet paper and walk backwards.*

They all nodded and tried to look like they respected that sort of dancing, or even knew what he was talking about.

<u>II (B) iv (c)</u>: Henry had a daughter in high school and a daughter who was only five. He was obsessed with the LASIK surgery he'd gotten. Most people had forgotten that he used to wear enormous glasses in which you could see your whole head and torso, glasses with frames the color of ice-diluted cola.

He said he loved not having to wear them but sometimes his eyes took in too much information. First was the X-ray vision. Now he received random glimpses into the future. Whole lives played out in his gaze. He looked at his son and saw an old man in a plastic loincloth, doing somersaults on a stage meant to evoke a windswept plain. His older daughter, twenty years hence, was wearing a welding mask—she'll become a mechanic, or maybe a sculptor.

The strangest vision was of his younger daughter. He saw her as having the same job he did, heading an HR department at a medium-size office. *And I'm fine with that,* he said.

No one felt confident enough to ask Henry what the future held for them.

II (B) iv (d): Grime, quiet up to that point, said good night and headed out of the bar. Big Sal studied their faces and finally asked, *What's with that guy?*

When they asked what he meant, he said, *There's a skull on his desk.*

No there isn't, said Lizzie, who was one to know.

I mean, there was. *On his old desk.*

Jonah, whose class had been canceled, came in and had a seat right as Big Sal said that Grime used to be on the *fifth* floor until recently, working out of an undecorated cubicle near the broken refrigerator.

Since when? asked Jonah.

Big Sal didn't know. They forgot that he hadn't actually been with the company that long. He remembered that the first time he saw Grime was in July. *The problem is, the guy refuses to stay put.*

II (B) iv (e): Henry from HR said he liked being his own boss. He didn't consider himself accountable to the Sprout or Maxine or anyone—if anything, they had to answer to *him.* He knew everything about you: vacation days, personal days, sick days, address and social security, taxes. It was a radical, HR-centric view of the universe.

He said that having a boss was infantilizing. You felt the

need to please, to explain constantly, to request permission for every little thing. And even if you thought you got along fine with your boss—even if you thought you *liked* your boss—the possibility of punishment always hovered.

All children are a little paranoid, he said, speaking as someone with actual children.

Just then Big Sal's beeper purred. He was needed back in the office. The e-mail server had to come down so he could root out a virus. The Polish joke website had sent spyware into their consoles. Every time the system crashed, he said, he was that much closer to losing his job, even though crashes happen all the time, everywhere. Dozens of small crashes happened in the office every day, he explained, crashes the rest of them knew nothing about.

IT people are like the doctors of the twenty-first century, said Henry admiringly, as Big Sal headed back to work.

II (B) iv (f): Pru recapped the story of Henry's psychic powers for Jonah, who wanted to know about his own future. Henry said he saw big things, big changes.

Good or bad?

Answer cloudy, try again, he said, wiggling his fingers in front of his face like a carnival mystic.

The response satisfied Jonah, who had been at loose ends lately, ever since his Mexican distress frog went AWOL.

II (B) iv (g): The night was fun, but none of them would ever drink and talk like that with either Henry or Big Sal again. It was a onetime workplace bonding event. Spontaneous bursts of boundary-crossing fellowship had happened before. But it was rare, like that one Christmas during World War I when the British and German soldiers climbed out of their trenches and played soccer with each other. Usually Big Sal and Henry were the distant targets of their anger—they'd stamp their feet at how slow IT was to fix things, how HR managed to bungle a date on a vacation form. Later, in the clear light of the work-day, everything was awkward and they wound up wishing it had never happened.

II (C): Return to Siberia

<u>II (C) i (a):</u> One morning not long after, Laars realized he'd run out of paper clips. It wasn't that he had a lot to clip to-gether, but a packet had been taunting him since Friday in all its loose-leaf glory. He wanted to be a man of action. He had recently stopped saying *What is the point?* and had undertaken a vow of chastity and now he was going to get some paper clips.

He additionally needed staples and, for that matter, a func-tioning stapler. The one he had was an ancient gray model that he'd inherited from Jules. It worked approximately every third time. It was more objet d'art than true stapler. Long ago someone had added layers of masking tape over the hood for a bit of hand cushion. The tape was sepia now and bore the ominous name KRASH. The letters had been carved deep into the tape with ballpoint—mostly red, with notes of black and blue, as though they had been traced over every day, in mind-less desperation, for years on end.

<u>II (C) i (b):</u> Jenny remembered that Jill used to hoard paper clips, staples, every sort of fastener and fixative. *She had a huge thing of rubber cement*, Jenny said.

<u>II (C) i (c):</u> Pru, Grime, Jack II, and Crease joined the party as it continued its travels, heading up to Siberia, footsteps echo-ing in the stairwell. Grime started in with a sea shanty—droll

at first, with mermaid imagery and calls for rum. Then they just wished he would stop. Lizzie and Pru kept their distance, alert to any sudden disco maneuvers. All of them were kind of holding their breath till they got upstairs.

Turning the corner, they stepped into a flood of light, a change in atmosphere. Siberia had its own weather. A soft sound: The Unnamable was emptying the contents of Jill's desk into a huge wheeled plastic trash bin, a thousand kinds of paper. Her chair was in there, the throne of Siberia turned upside down, silver wheels catching the early afternoon sun. It was a better chair than most of them had, but none of them wanted to be the one who lunged for it.

Jill's desk, said Jenny, like she was the phantom Jill's receptionist, answering a call.

It felt like years since Jill had been fired. They'd never even had farewell drinks for her. Everyone thought someone else was supposed to get in touch, organize. It was way too late now.

Jill, said Crease. *I can barely remember her. I can barely remember what she looks like.*

The weird thing was, everyone thought Crease had a minor crush on Jill. Even Pru could see them as a couple. It made sense. *They have the same body type,* Jack II said. But the advent of HABAW had completely obliterated those feelings in Crease, incinerated them and sealed the ashes off forever. She was like the Chinese emperor who built the Great Wall and burned all the books.

II (C) i (d): The Unnamable came by wearing an air-filtration mask. *Sky blue is definitely your color,* Pru said, and his smile was apparent even under the rubberized cloth. He squirted a double loop of cleanser on the desktop and removed one of the clean rags from his belt. He swiped with military precision, in rectangles of decreasing size. With each pass the surface whitened dramatically. It was amazing to see something actually work the way it was supposed to work. Jonah stared at the center of the swipe area, as if a long-buried message was about to be revealed.

The Unnamable heaved an armload of stuffed manila folders into the dumpster. Then he manned a broom too big for him, pushing a minor dirt formation down the hall a ways, where it merged with a larger cluster. If you kept going, if you turned and passed the vending machine and entered the most remote region of Siberia, you ran the risk of ambush by a creature made entirely of punched-paper holes and old hair and notebook frills.

Up to that point the Unnamable had only been seen as a bearer of interoffice mail, a patient trudger. By contrast, his upper body now moved with freedom, even a kind of wordless, elastic joy. His concentration was tremendous. Who else in the office worked that hard, that efficiently, at anything? You could imagine strains of Vivaldi as some faded television star narrated the story of artisanal desk cleaners who have been cleaning desks for five generations.

Jonah picked up something that had fallen off a pile of papers—a birthday card from Jason, dated March the fifth, but what was the year?

<u>II (C) i (e):</u> Two other men came by to make alarming dismantling noises. They wore flannel shirts and lime green hard hats that said KOHUT BROTHERS, though they were probably not *the* brothers, or even brothers, themselves. One was thin, the other barrel-chested. They ripped out a patch of linoleum for some reason, so now it looked like a UFO had blasted Jill from

above, capturing her in a teleportation beam. The plants, the thriving wildlife, were nowhere to be seen. A few insect skeletons lay scattered on the narrow sill, shiny and precise and sad as broken jewelry.

II (C) ii (a): Everyone marveled at the ample real estate in Siberia, the generous sunlight, all the while keeping an eye out for dust monsters. Jonah had a dim memory of coming up here once, long before Jill's exile, and seeing wood-paneled walls, plush sofas, elegant standing lamps. There had been chatty women with fun haircuts and crisp clothing, slim dudes in natty suits talking in an office argot he didn't understand. They called each other *Slick*, said things like *Smell ya later.* A little radio played NPR while typewriters rang out thrillingly. It was weird but kind of great, a civilized oasis. He didn't know anyone's name, or what exactly they did. He was too shy to speak back then—four, five years ago. He remembered dropping off a file, picking up a floppy disk from a beautiful girl in a rhomboid-print dress, a girl with a wonderful, untraceable accent and the most enchanting golden hair. The next time he was up there, less than a year later, everyone was gone except a severe-looking gnome in the corner, bald and with white hair in his ears like feathered nests, a figure nearly invisible behind towering stacks of paper. Jonah wondered if it had all been a dream.

Returning to Jill's desk, they peered into the dumpster, as if all her trash might have summoned her into being.

We should really call her sometime, said Jenny in a total robot voice.

They sifted through the detritus, no longer self-conscious now that the Unnamable and the Kohut Brothers had gone. At first they turned up nothing good: a battered dictionary, chipped mugs holding pencil ends, assorted small broken women's-hair-related items. A scattering of gray tic tacs and yards of mysterious dark green string were a running motif. Laars found a CD he'd lent her a year ago, but he didn't want it anymore.

<u>II (C) ii (b):</u> Lined up on Jill's old desk were three staplers, all in perfect working order. One bore the name KRASH, the letters deep as runes, carved into layers of Scotch tape.

It's following me! said Laars, making a crucifix with his fingers.

Laars imagined KRASH as a more desperate version of himself, toiling in Siberia, living out his days in office drudgery without even the Internet for distraction. KRASH's main activity was adopting, naming, and losing staplers.

<u>II (C) ii (c):</u> A paper clip, centered in the dark circle where a cactus pot used to be, drove a sliver of sun straight into Laars's eyes.

It obliterated my short-term memory, he said later, after realizing he'd forgotten to bring one of the staplers back downstairs.

II (D) The Worst Soup in the World

<u>II (D) i:</u> The cold weather was approaching. The Red Alcove didn't get good heat, so its denizens ventured outside the office for lunch. Some of the others came along, and as the group grew, the possibilities for a mutually agreeable venue diminished. Laars had gone through an intensive burrito phase. Jonah had completed a sub phase and never wanted to see another one again. Crease voted against anything Asian, including Indian food. Already that week he'd eaten Thai, Japanese, and Burmese.

Let's decide on a place before we step outside, Pru said, as they puttered in the lobby.

In the past, when they tried to order delivery together, the logistics would drive the designated order placer crazy, not to mention the order taker at the other end of the line. Jack II was a vegetarian who always wanted extra hot sauce. Lizzie eschewed carbs. Crease avoided vegetables at all costs. Someone—Jill?—didn't like mayo. Jenny once said she was going to make a chart of who couldn't eat what.

Pru said she ate everything except cheese and butter.

Oh, and eggs, she added.

Everyone longed for either converting the sixth floor into a cafeteria or hooking up an IV drip, or boarding a random bus for a spur-of-the-moment excursion to some outer-borough culinary Xanadu that would take them all day to reach and get them fired.

They agreed at last on soup.

II (D) ii: Grime wasn't with them. He was at home, taking a personal day. Before last week, he was hazy with the whole concept of personal days. Lizzie had filled him in and then he said he wanted to use them all up at once.

Lizzie also said that she was no longer speaking with Grime.

He told me the most disgusting thing the other day, totally out of the blue. We were walking to the subway and I was explaining the personal day thing to him. We stopped for a drink and for some reason he was talking about India and then all of a sudden he was talking about something else. So awful. I'm sorry. I really, really can't tell you what it was.

Is it something bad? asked Pru.

Lizzie nodded.

Something about who's getting fired?

Now everyone was listening.

Lizzie shook her head. *No, nothing like that. It's worse, maybe. I think it's worse. I don't even know why he told me. It's the filthiest thing.*

What—what? Tell us, tell us.

I can't. Not now. Forget it.

II (D) iii: Laars observed how he never packed a lunch anymore. *I'm a good cook, too,* he claimed. Anything homemade always ended up making you a little sad. The look, the taste, the lack of colorful packaging. Occasionally someone would bring leftovers from a big dinner, but then the smell became kind of a downer, evoking decay and the passage of time. Another problem was the microwave in the pantry. Even on its lowest setting it would blacken things, smelling up the office, or otherwise cause a mess so extensive that the guilty party wouldn't even begin to clean up.

This soup is like water, said Jack II, unloading half a salt-shaker into the bowl.

Lizzie said Grime's thing recently has been popcorn. He couldn't stop raving about it. Apparently British popcorn was the absolute worst. It was a New World food. They analyzed this information for clues.

II (D) iv: Pru wanted to change the subject. She didn't care to hear more about what she understood to be Lizzie and Grime's burgeoning relationship, even if it appeared the two were no longer on speaking terms.

Remember those oat bars? asked Pru.

For a while Jonah was bringing in about ten of these weird little snack bars every day, offering them to anyone who asked and even those who didn't. Pru would take two and give one to the Unnamable.

The bars tasted like they'd been dipped in V8 and left to dry atop an old radiator. The story went that Jonah's aunt had gotten involved in a pyramid scheme with these oat bars, and he'd bought two institutional-size boxes' worth to help her out. He still had half a box of oat bars. They were two years old now but probably tasted the same.

II (D) v: Pru said she was at a party in Brooklyn and the Original Jack was there again. He'd been to Jules's restaurant—Mannequin? Gallivant?—and reported that it served a deluxe toasted version of Jonah's staple: two oat bars sandwiching a thick slice of cheddar, with a light tofu-based frosting. The chalkboard listing the house specials described it as *decadent*. The Original Jack also mentioned that Jules was thinking of changing his name, something about tax irregularities. Jules had asked if he could use the Original Jack's mailing address, a request that was denied.

II (D) vi: They talked about physical ailments, recurring nightmares, psychosomatic afflictions, all of it blamed on the job. It was pure TMI of the most compelling variety. Jonah's carpal tunnel syndrome had been so bad he'd asked Robb, Otto's successor in IT, to set him up with Glottis, the voice-recognition program that Jules used for *Personal Daze*. But then the symptoms suddenly vanished—a miracle.

Unfortunately, he now had a form of vertigo, which he said was even worse than searing limb pain. The discomfort was more abstract and thus more worrying. He had some tests done and the doctors couldn't figure out what was wrong. Whenever he went out of the city, even just to New Jersey to visit his aunt, the oat-bar aunt, his dizziness subsided completely. Did that mean it was purely psychological? Whenever he traveled to Mexico it evaporated almost as soon as he boarded the plane, faded even from memory as he clambered over steep Mayan ruins. It returned, like clockwork, the moment he touched down at JFK.

II (D) vii: Crease said his left eyelid fluttered of its own accord. At first he thought it was from too much coffee, but he weaned himself off caffeine and the lid was still moving.

Can you see it? Oh wait, it's stopped. Oh there it goes.

They stared at his eyes, but it was hard to catch such small movements under the soupery's dim lighting. Crease said he was going bald as well, but that might just be age. He maintained that the construction from the infinity-shaped building next door was making his ears ring. *Don't you guys hear it?* Most days he wore earplugs, which helped but made him think he was underwater.

The really heavy machinery kicked in at one o'clock, he explained. Crease basically had to have his work finished by then, or at least anything that required problem-solving skills. Even with the earplugs in, he could feel the vibrations, and it became impossible to arrange his thoughts toward any productive end. He had two desks but claimed he could feel the vibrations at either one. He could even feel them at home, he said, lying in bed, staring at a shadow on the ceiling.

The construction was not just ruining his hearing and depleting his brainpower but also shaking the hair out of his head.

Pru said she had no sex drive and that she recently had a dream in which Grime killed the Sprout using a plastic shovel. The stuff about the sex drive was definitely TMI, but a good sort of TMI.

II (D) viii: *I'm getting fat,* offered Jack II, mixing a pack of oyster crackers into the dregs of his bisque. He had been saying that for years, indeed tended to say it shortly upon meeting someone for the first time. It used to be people would tell him he was crazy, a tallish, rail-thin narcissist, but now when they looked at him, the green sweater *did* seem to bulge significantly.

You look avuncular, said Lizzie. Jack II nodded grimly. He knew he was doomed. Biology had it in for him. His whole family was avuncular—not only his uncles but even his aunts.

Laars said he'd been going to the gym every other day, where he'd run three miles, do three hundred sit-ups and a hundred push-ups, and regard himself moodily in the floor-length mirrors.

Crease said that his eyelid didn't flutter when he was at the gym. It kicked in when he waited for the elevator in the morning, anxious and hopeful that HABAW would arrive.

II (D) ix: Lizzie said she'd been dreaming of sharks again, but that these were friendly sharks, with big happy eyes, or at least not the sorts of sharks that attacked her. This was an improvement over earlier in the year, right around when Jason and the Original Jack were fired, when it seemed that every night she was torn apart, by one shark or two or twenty. Back then, sleep had been like tuning in to a particularly gruesome radio serial.

This is the worst soup in the world, said Laars.

Speaking of food, said Lizzie, *there's a banana in the fridge that's seriously been there since Labor Day.*

II (E): The Jilliad

II (E) i: In flowing greatcoat and knit black skullcap, with a fat black notebook clamped under his arm, Laars presented a distinctly monklike aspect as he stepped outside on that crisp autumn afternoon.

He asked the smokers huddled on the pavement for a

piece of gum. He'd just gorged on a chicken curry lunch special, chased by some pungent unagi from the day before.

I have the most amazing breath.

Pru proffered an Orbit. *What's in the notebook?*

How much time do you have? Smoke escaped from the upright ash stand as he laid out a curious episode against the dying light.

II (E) ii: Laars explained to those gathered outside that he had just returned from a solo expedition to Siberia—having remembered, as it were, that he'd forgotten to take a stapler the other day. Several weeks had passed since that first journey, and now Siberia was starting to live up to its name. The heat was off, and you could see your breath against the wan light from the windows. The vending machines stood empty and dark. It was so quiet you could hear the clock tick.

Dust touched everything, as if it had traveled from every corner of the sixth floor to gather around Jill's desk, a silent pilgrimage. Laars shuddered as he noted the cobwebs now softening the edges. His nape hairs detected a spectral presence and at one point he actually said Jill's name aloud, half-shutting his eyes in fear of who knows what.

Alas, Jill's three staplers were nowhere to be found.

Most of the old junk had been carted away, and a new heap of things lay in the dumpsterette: five pairs of sunglasses, a disposable camera, and a small bookcase that must have been tucked under her desk.

The stout dark wood shelves held a dozen titles, books that promised to help you navigate the workplace, negotiate from a position of power, and otherwise claw your way to the top. In other words, titles that would have found their most timid reader in Jill, whose idea of asserting herself at work was answering the phone after the first ring. Each text appeared carefully read—dog-eared and heavily underlined in three different inks. Her microscopic notes clouded the margins, and the endpapers teemed with page numbers and keywords. Her elaborate outlines went beyond the standard markings—Roman numerals, capital letters—and into Greek symbols, decimal places. A flurry of red arrows tied the information together in a swirling, almost three-dimensional mass.

Laars concluded that Jill, exiled and scared, had been trying—*really* trying—to get back on track. Not only that: She was determined to advance *beyond* her previous station. If her fate was to be stuck in an office, she would arm herself with the cutthroat wisdom of sages from Moses to Bill Gates to the guy who invented that new vacuum cleaner. She would study the way of moguls. She would sell out former friends, volunteer for onerous tasks, anything to *get a leg up*. She would become a winner for maybe the first time in her life.

Had anyone noticed, toward the end, her confident new haircut, fortified with power highlights, set off by those hypnotic scarlet earrings?

II (E) iii: Maybe the Sprout had. Maybe he'd read the same books, memorized the same guru-sanctioned moves, and knew—as soon as he saw that overpowering pair of pendulous ear decorations—what was in store: a power play from below. Decisive action was called for, and he ruthlessly cut her loose before she could do any damage.

II (E) iv: *It's heartbreaking,* said Pru as a twister of receipts and Styrofoam take-out containers blew past.

Seriously, Lizzie agreed.

That's what I thought—at first, said Laars. *Listen.*

<u>II (E) v:</u> Jill's spidery handwriting, usually deployed for such pleasantries as thank-you notes and birthday cards, took on an altogether different cast in the margins of these mercenary books. Here it suggested ancient formulae—as if to utter what had been inscribed would unleash a plague of amphibians or a dark unsavory wind.

Listen.

He lit a cigarette and continued the account of his expedition.

On the bottom shelf, hidden under a sheaf of old newspapers, was a spiral notebook. The black cardboard, leathery with age, had gone white along the edges, but the pages were still tight around the spine. Laars opened it under the woozy overhead lighting, holding his breath against the unsettled dust.

What was this—Jill's diary?

There were two or three entries per page, undated, filling most of the book. The handwriting here was bigger, looser, with a slight calligraphic flair. The ink was hard to read at first, somewhere between red and orange but so light it floated, an extract of sunset. The supply cabinet never stocked colors like this.

<u>II (E) vi:</u> *Is this where she wrote down her true feelings about us?* asked Pru.

She seemed nice but she could be a bitch when she wanted to, said Lizzie preemptively.

I think she secretly hated me, said Crease.

Laars held up a hand. *It's not what you think it is.* He opened the notebook, cleared his throat, and read aloud from the first page:

This you must know: Your colleagues are your most irreplaceable assets. Treat them like you would the hammer, awl, and clamp in your tool kit.
—*Every Worker's War Chest,* by Fred Glass

What's an awl again exactly? asked Lizzie.

It's like that pokey thing, said Pru, miming awl usage, or else the shower scene from *Psycho*.

II (E) vii: Laars intoned the next entry:

Don't be the one who says, I told you so. Tell them so to begin with. Tell them often.
—*Office Politics 101,* by Randall Slurry

II (E) viii: And then the last one on the page:

Think of the office as an ocean liner. Are you the captain? A passenger? Or the person who plays xylophone for the lido deck band?
—*Climbing the Seven-Rung Ladder: The Business of Business,* by Chad Ravioli and Khâder Adipose

I think I'm the person barfing over the rail, said Pru.

It's all too sad if you think about it, said Jack II. *It's depressing to imagine her sitting up there and copying out all that junk.*

II (E) ix: Laars closed the notebook but kept a finger in it. All of the passages came from different books, he explained, but none were from the books Jill had under her desk. This suggested that she drew from an even larger library of ghostwritten CEO memoirs, Machiavellian road maps, and PowerPoint-friendly wealth manuals. Her apartment must have been full to the ceiling with them.

An army of pigeons rolled across the sky, reversed itself, modified its course yet again, then soared out of sight to the west. What warmth there was to the day had drained completely but no one was quite ready to go inside yet. They began to pass the notebook around, and to absorb what wisdom was entered there.

<u>II (E) x:</u> Pru read:

> *My father used to say that impossible situations require intestinal fortitude. Think about that word: intestinal. Every morning before coming into the office, ask yourself this simple, five-word question: Do I have the guts?*
>
> *Much hinges on your answer.*
> —*The Business Warrior's 30-Day* Mental *Fitness Plan* (*Revised Edition*), by Cody Waxing, Founder of MTech Solutions

<u>II (E) xi:</u> Some eyes rolled.

Isn't he that guy who got arrested for embezzlement? said Crease.

I think it was prostitutes, said Lizzie.

It was strippers, said Laars.

Strippers aren't illegal, said Crease.

Pru continued:

> *Confusion is inevitable. Ride the wave.*
> —*The Manager's Bible: The New Memory System for Daily Insights,* by Wayne V. Hammer with Juliette Earp

<u>II (E) xii:</u> Pru took a deep breath.

> *Two words, and they might be the most important two words in this book: Document everything. Be terse in e-mails, but let your colleagues—who could turn into your opponents—spill their guts, tell their dirty jokes, whine about this, that, and the other.*

Again *with the guts,* said Lizzie.

> *Be the shoulder they want to cry on, the confidant, the best friend. And every month, make a hard copy of the entire contents of your in-box. Even if something seems insignificant, print it out.*
>
> *Maybe you'll never need to produce this huge stack of evidence. But trust me: You'll be kicking yourself seven ways to Sunday if it*

comes down to you and the fool down the hall—and he's got the
goods, and you've got squat.
—*How to Win in the Workplace Every Damn Time,* by Sue Locke
Villareal and Edmund Villareal

II (E) xiii: The notebook passed to Jack II.

Got a problem? Put a number to it. Break it down. Do the digits.
Give a percentage, a ratio, the odds. You don't have to be a math-
elete—you just have to be smart. If your boss asks you about the
weather, don't just say it's warm or it's cold—give the Celsius, the
Fahrenheit, the Kelvin if you know it. If you don't know it, give him
a guesstimate. Bottom line: Always use numbers.

Numbers will also help you think like a pro. Organize your
thoughts by numbering every paragraph. Do this for a quick memo
the same way you'd do it for an annual report. Outline, quantify,
digit-ize.

The way you number things tells a boss all he needs to know.
—*Three Easy Rules for Impressing the Powers That Be (and Maybe*
Becoming One Yourself) (A Simpleton's™ Guide), by Douglas
Salgado and Uri Boris

II (E) xiv: He wagged a finger.

Listen up because I'm only going to say this once. I'm in the market
for employees who are willing to give me 110 percent.

You heard me right.

Most people don't even have 50 percent to give. Very few can
drum up 75. One in a thousand can offer 100 percent, the typical
maximum amount. I'm looking for that one person in ten thousand
who will give me 110 percent.

And you know what? I've been a student of statistics all my life.
I'm going to find that one in ten thousand. And I'm going to hire
him. And then I'm going to kick me some ass.
—*Yes, I Drank the Kool-Aid—and I Went Back for Seconds,* by
M. Halsey Patterson

II (E) xv: *Can I kill myself now?* asked Pru.

Jack II read the next one in a homier but still nostalgia-
soaked voice:

*Hell's bells! We were like kids in a candy store, snapping up proper-
ties left and right, renaming them, and squeezing every blessed dol-
lar before throwing them aside. No guts, no glory is one of the oldest
clichés, but you have to know that it's also the only business philosophy I've ever found that—hold on to your hats—actually* works.
*—Mine for the Taking: or, Some (INCREDIBLY!) Irreverent Notes
on the Business of Wealth*, by Parker Edwards

II (E) xvi: It was Lizzie's turn.

*Waste not time on correspondence; no great wealth ever came of
words.
—Letters to a Young Tycoon*, by Percy Ampersand, edited by
Percy Ampersand IV

II (E) xvii:

*Drinking problem? Fuggedaboudit. Drugs? Take a long hike off a
short pier. I'm not saying you have to be a teetotaler. But understand that an effective company is all about* control, *and there's no
place on my ship for people who can't even control themselves.
—The Pegasus Plan: How to Get the Job You Want, the Respect You
Deserve, and the Employees You Need in Order to Succeed for Life*,
by D. M. S. Shrapnel, with an introduction by Whittles Langley,
CEO of Ptarmigan Group

II (E) xviii: The streetlamp hummed to life, dousing them in pearlescent light.

*Imagine you've just stepped into the elevator with the CEO of your
company. Door closes. It's just the two of you.
    What are you going to say?
    You need to put across your present responsibilities, recent tri-
umphs, and personal goals. And you need to do it in a way that
makes it clear how your objectives mesh with the company's.
    Think of the Elevator Speech as a 30-second sound bite. An
advertisement—for yourself.*

The Sprout is totally into Elevator Speeches, said Lizzie. *Have
you noticed?*

Except I think he's misinterpreting the concept, said Pru. *He'll draw all these bogus analogies between the upward movement of the elevator and the upward movement of the company.*

Crease continued:

> *Every employee—never mind how high or how low—should have his or her Elevator Speech ready. Why not practice it in front of a mirror? Don't throw away an opportunity to shine.*
> *—Are You Going Up or Going Down? Learn How to Sell Yourself Every Time,* by Dobbs Redondo

II (E) xix:

> *I don't care about the bottom line. Let me repeat that:* I don't care about the bottom line. *No CEO with a brain in his head and (excuse me, ladies) a set of bona fide cojones gives a rat's ass (pardon my French) about the bottom line. Once you start thinking about it, you're finished.*
> *Done.*
> *Toast.*
> *Your enemies will eat you alive—and not even bother finishing the meal.*
> *—Give Me a Break Already: An Inside Man Thinks Outside the Box,* by Thomas Feeley with Moss Jervins

Toast! said Lizzie. *We should show this to Jules!*

II (E) xx: Crease read the last entry for the day, a puzzling one indeed:

> *If your boss is in the way, get a new boss. This obviously doesn't mean you have to jump ship and send that CV out into the big bad world. No. Getting a new boss can be as simple as making your* current *boss change—to conform to* your *needs. Show him who's in charge. Answer every question—and each time, make sure you ask one of your own. If you can co-opt the information flow, channel it to do your bidding, you can put him in a position where he can't help but depend on you. Hey presto: Your job has become more secure than his.*
> *—Real Advice You Can Take to the Bank,* by Rhona Chen, with an introduction by Gordon G. Knott

Cheers, said Grime, who had just stepped out for a smoke. *What's all this then?*

<u>II (E) xxi:</u> Something changed over the course of the public reading. Though the gems of hard-won wisdom made them laugh, at a certain point they weren't really laughing at Jill anymore.

Something *clicked.* She wasn't a gullible follower of those mandates and routines, some rube from West Virginia or was it regular Virginia trying to turn herself into a soulless, win-at-any-cost shark. She was taking a buzz saw to the rules, pointing out the absurd contradictions, the glib b.s. of corporate culture.

That no one suspected Jill had this side to her made the whole thing a sort of modern cautionary tale, or myth, or something. Pru was still working on the wording.

Laars took back the notebook. He'd removed his gloves to light another cigarette, and with his bare fingers he could feel something on the blank black cover, something he hadn't noticed before: deep grooves done with dead ballpoint, marks in the shapes of letters. As he tilted the notebook toward the light from the streetlamp, the title was revealed:

THE JILLIAD

<u>II (E) xxii:</u> Soon they were all in love with *The Jilliad.* It became an obsession: the encyclopedia of their despair, a catalog of futility written by someone they thought they knew well but in fact did not know at all. Jill had been the artist in exile, the anonymous, merciless genius of the sixth floor.

She's my hero, said Jenny.

It's working for me on all these different levels, said Pru. She and Lizzie had a feminist take on it, and Grime claimed he did, too.

In one afternoon Jill went from grade-A milquetoast to ironic literary master. In an e-mail that read like a press release, Pru called her *a deadpan poet of devastating wit who revives the lost art of quotation.*

II (E) xxiii: Lizzie tried to reach Jill but nothing worked. Her cell phone number was out of service. No home phone could be found. Lizzie even tried calling directory assistance in Jill's hometown, hoping to locate her parents, to no avail.

The author was a ghost.

II (E) xxiv: The manuscript was unstable. There were exactly 322 excerpts in *The Jilliad*, most just a few lines long, a handful of them overrunning a page. For a stretch in the middle, Jill switched to a delicate pencil, as if tracing the letters straight from her source books. Sometimes she skipped pages, or started an entry close to the bottom of a blank one. Was that significant? The organization had its own logic, its own rhythm. She adorned later entries with amusing caricatures of salarymen in severe suits, exuding tadpoles of sweat as they waved calculators in the air and pointed at pie charts. The bosses in these sketches resembled the Sprout of the future, with a potbelly and nose hair. In the corner one could generally find a fretful female employee drawn at a quarter of the scale, dutifully taking notes while having a nervous breakdown. This was likely a Jill figure.

Crease was in charge of making photocopies of *The Jilliad* for everyone, but the machine was having trouble reading the unusual ink. So Lizzie kept the notebook in her desk for safekeeping, and the rest of them took turns borrowing it from her, transcribing a page or two each time. The idea was to merge all the finished pieces into one master file, which they could then annotate, print, e-mail, and otherwise control.

Laars said he was uneasy about sharing it outside their little circle.

Lizzie thought *The Jilliad* could be a hit on the Internet, a piece of homegrown cubicle art. Maybe Jack II could design a website. Pru agreed that it deserved to exist outside of the office, but wanted to think about what form it should take.

There was talk of detaching individual pages in order to expedite transcription, a motion voted down by the circle, but just barely.

Laars was getting the sense he wasn't even part of the circle anymore.

<u>II (E) xxv:</u> Without Laars, *The Jilliad* would surely have disappeared forever, tossed out with the rest of the rubbish. Now he wished he hadn't saved it. He wanted to show it to everyone because they all knew Jill, but it was quickly becoming something greater. Their real memories of her didn't stand a chance. It was like killing her off a second time.

And what was Grime's deal? He didn't even know her but now he was talking as if he did.

Laars searched his computer for any photos of Jill—from nights out, from last year's holiday party—but he couldn't find her face. She was probably the person taking the pictures. In one, the flash was caught in the window behind a laughing Pru and a tipsy Lizzie, and you could see a pale arm and a ghost of a smile floating in the glass, the photographer capturing a sliver of herself.

But when Laars tried to reconstruct her from these hints, he only came up with Jill as he never knew her: in her last,

too-sleek haircut, her chin held high, the would-be office war-
rior with a master plan in her refurnished head.

II (E) xxvi: Everyone devoted spare time to the transcription
of *The Jilliad*, all except Jonah, who was missing out on the
whole adventure—studying for his night school exams, using
up the last of his personal days.

Grime had been asked *not* to assist in the typing, but he
was definitely still in the loop, as it were, offering his interpre-
tations free of charge.

It looked like Lizzie was talking to Grime again. She still
hadn't told anyone what he'd said to her that was so disturbing.
She always had a minimum of two pens sticking out of her hair.

Pru borrowed *The Jilliad* and kept it for a long time, for so
long that she usurped the librarian position from Lizzie. She
buzzed with theories. She said that Jill fit into a great American tradition of outsider artists, who created purely in private.
They lived superficially humdrum lives until their breathtaking work was discovered.

Laars wasn't sure what she meant, so she gave some
examples: The deaf-mute farmhand who made haunting
charcoal-and-saliva sketches. The savant dishwasher with the
photographic memory who drew every bird he ever saw. The
prisoner who stitched tableaux of ballparks and football
fields using the colored threads plucked from his socks.

The life becomes part of the art, said Pru. In such cases the
dead-end existence led not to despair but to wild acts of cre-
ation. Most of these were lost forever. One had a moral duty
to rescue and preserve such works whenever possible.

She alluded to friends she had, or friends of friends, people
in the gallery world with names like Nico and Eduardo.

Laars didn't think they should be exploiting Jill without

her knowledge. He got catty and brought up Pru's unfinished graduate thesis. *What was it called? The Aesthetics of Boredom?*

Lizzie finally removed the decayed banana from the fridge in the pantry. She held it with a paper towel, as far away from her body as possible. The shape was very unbananalike, as though the matter had liquefied and reconsolidated several times.

She refocused her eyes just long enough to see a name written in green marker on the Dole sticker.

This had been Jill's banana, pre-Siberia. Nobody wanted to do the math.

II (F) To Recap

II (F) i: Laars came into work looking like someone had punched him in the mouth with a sock full of salt and then insulted his grandmother. He wasn't talking much and his lips drooped so maybe it really happened. Everyone steered clear. He had a temper and once exchanged blows with a cabbie at the foot of the Brooklyn Bridge.

Before lunch he e-mailed Lizzie and told her he went to the dentist for the first time in six years and was now thoroughly depressed. All his old fillings, the fillings of his childhood, were in danger of coming loose. He could choke on them and *die*. They needed to be replaced. He'd hated them for years but now he was getting sentimental, lost in memories of the matronly dental technician who smelled like flowers and held his hand during the procedure.

II (F) ii: The dentist called it *bruxism*, the unconscious grinding of teeth. The wear was great. Certain molars needed recapping.

The dentist said that it happened at night. Laars begged to differ, but how would he know? The dentist was trying delicately to ask him whether there was someone he was sleeping with, someone who could monitor him during the night. This depressed him even more. Also the dentist didn't explicitly say *girlfriend*, which suggested that Laars was giving off gay vibes again, an occasional problem he had.

I need new teeth and I need a woman, he wrote. He formally renounced the vow of chastity, probably a good move regardless. He wasn't trying to pick Lizzie up but on the other hand he wouldn't mind. It might do the trick. The office romance aspect didn't bother him. His teeth were more important than Maxine's sexual harassment guidelines.

The worst part was that he needed to wear a mouth guard every night. A lab in Michigan was making one for him, working off the plaster mold. Even with insurance, it would set him back around nine million dollars.

Most of this was in an e-mail to Lizzie, in response to a simple *What's shakin'?*

II (F) iii: Lizzie multitasked as she read Laars's lament. She was finessing a report that Jonah had written, looking for run-on sentences, and changing all the active constructions to passive ones. Jonah was a very fluid writer, maybe too fluid. If you diagrammed one of his sentences, the result would look like a subway map mating with the remains of a fish dinner. Lizzie might have been the best writer of them all, but she got none of the glory. This was because she was very *down-to-earth*.

Another part of Lizzie's brain was involved in a long instant-messaging exchange with Pru about what she suspected was her blossoming Ambien addiction. Pru was the person to talk to for something like this. She was a total Ambien addict in good standing and had the lingo down cold.

<u>II (F) iv:</u> Stress caused the grinding, according to the dentist. Laars wrote to Lizzie that he hadn't felt stressed before, but now he did. He felt stressed out of his mind. The high cost of the dental procedures gnawed at him. So did the idea that his body was doing stuff to itself late at night, beyond conscious control.

Maybe discovering *The Jilliad* had pushed him over the edge.

Bruxism's bad enough, Laars wrote. *What if I start to sleep-walk? What if I throw myself off a bridge?*

Lizzie told him not to sweat it. He lived too far from significant water. There was an outside chance he'd sleepwalk downstairs and into the street and take a cab to the river. But unless he brought his wallet, he probably wouldn't make it.

<u>II (F) v:</u> Later Pru walked by Laars's desk. In the trash was a pamphlet from the dentist's office entitled *Tooth—and Consequences.* It was all marked up and perhaps tearstained.

Crease tried to tempt Laars with a cigarette. Laars went outside and lit up but then remembered he was under dentist's orders not to smoke. Crease made some crack about Grime's teeth, the old British stereotype, to make Laars feel better. Grime flashed a set of bright, neatly aligned choppers. This made Laars feel even worse.

Grime said, *Cheers, mate.*

II (G) The Outside World

<u>II (G) i:</u> Big Sal from IT joked that he was losing weight from having to run from desk to desk. The e-mail program had been

updated a week ago and now all of them were having problems. Unfortunately for Big Sal, everyone's problem was different.

Whenever Laars or Lizzie wrote to Jonah, Pru, or Crease, all the dashes turned into this mystical cluster:

â€□

It was like some supercondensed commentary on the history of Europe.

All of Pru's apostrophes turned into ™s, a chilling foretaste of the future of intellectual property law.

With Crease's e-mails, all the dashes became question marks, so he had to remember to go through his correspondence before clicking Send and change every dash to a period, colon, or ellipses. Otherwise he wound up sounding like a Valley Girl.

Jonah complained that his period key wasn't working. He sent his wafty prose to Lizzie, who inserted full stops wherever they felt right. Jonah called his laptop a *craptop*. He'd been after them for months to get him a replacement. The Sprout said he could buy one himself and expense it, but Jonah knew that if he did he would never see that money again.

II (G) ii: Worse, Jonah's Mexican distress frog was still missing. He turned his office upside down. Who would want to steal it? Maybe it had absorbed so much grimness that it had no choice but to hop away. Even totems had their limits. The loss of the Mexican distress frog was itself distressing. Added to everything else, it was too much, and Jonah took a day off—a bonus personal day he squeezed out of the Sprout in recognition of putting in so much overtime.

II (G) iii: These days the Sprout was barely in his office. Was he upstairs, hashing out the numbers with K. and Maxine?

Out west, negotiating with the Californians? Or simply at home, staring at his hands and drinking gin?

II (G) iv: Pru made what would universally be regarded as the most significant discovery in *The Jilliad*, in the middle of page 27:

> *Are you an Ernie—or a Bert? You remember this comical duo from your youth. Ernie is a carefree sort, always up for a gag or a razz, ready to bust out into gales of laughter—usually at Bert's expense. He's a classic hysteric. Bert, on the other hand, is his exact opposite: an organized, goal-driven, no-nonsense dude. He's an obsessive, the sort of person who probably spends a lot of time organizing his sock drawer. He's a nebbish, and maybe a bit of a dud.*
>
> *Most people like to think of themselves as Ernies—the life of the party, having a good time. That's fine, as far as it goes. But guess what? Your boss doesn't want an office full of free spirits. Such a workforce would get nothing done, and spend the hours from 9 to 5 blowing dandelion seeds and skipping stones. Your boss is most likely a Bert—and he's going to want more Berts on his team. Wouldn't you?*
>
> *—Ernie and Bert in the Boardroom,* by Dr. Tal Champers, Ph.D.

They spent a lot of time trying to figure out who was an Ernie, who was a Bert. It was true: Everyone wanted to be an Ernie. Tempers flared. It was decided that Lizzie, Jenny, and Jonah were Berts, and the rest were Ernies or Ernie-Bert blends. Lizzie protested, but she couldn't sway public opinion.

Jenny was the exception. She accepted the judgment of her peers gracefully. *I always liked Bert,* she said. The next day she wore a shirt with vertical stripes in clashing colors. Jonah wasn't around to weigh in but probably wouldn't care. He'd become a total Bert.

Strangely, no one thought the Sprout was a Bert. They imagined he might be a better supervisor if he *were* a Bert.

K. was definitely a Bert.

Jack II used to be a hard-core Bert, but recently he'd turned into more of an Ernie, an impression supported by his progressive roundness, especially in the cheek area.

Grime, being British, wasn't quite sure what they were talking about—he thought that Ernie and Bert were cartoon characters, or toys of some sort—and thus his colleagues spent much time reenacting various segments from yesteryear. Laars did a passable Ernie imitation, and Lizzie, though she still denied being a Bert, did a very good Bert.

There's this thing they do where they get too close to the camera and their noses fall off, Pru explained, to Grime's utter incomprehension.

Grime is a total Ernie, Lizzie later concluded, *but he has Bert's eyebrows.*

II (G) v: Jack II never left his desk anymore. He sat like a pasha on his swivel chair, with his cuffs rolled high and each bare foot tucked underneath the opposite thigh. Any spare time got funneled into the upkeep of his blog—an Ernie activity on the surface, though blogs also encouraged a Bert-like obsessiveness. He'd been posting photos of bare-limbed trees, manhole covers, his sister's dog, the infinity-shaped building going up next door.

The others started to avoid him. If you entered his field of vision, he'd ask, *Are you going anywhere near coffee?* He was acting like everyone was his servant.

Pru expressly denied him permission to post *Jilliad* excerpts on his blog until the entire thing was transcribed. Was this *her* layoff narrative—riding the discovery of *The Jilliad* to a curatorial position somewhere? Book deal, movie deal. She'd been hogging the notebook for weeks now. She said she was finding great new stuff every day and didn't want to break the momentum. Laars was at the end of his rope.

Does anyone want anything from the outside world? asked Lizzie.

II (H): The New Layoff Narrative

<u>II (H) i:</u> How did Jack II go from meticulous Bert to free-wheeling Ernie? Observers agreed that at a certain point last year, not long after Jules was let go, something shifted in his mind. He began to see the cloud of failure everywhere he turned.

All of them knew there was no way he'd get fired, but in his mind it was as if the deed were done. Hence the erratic hours, the blatant blogging, the two or three personal calls that stretched across any given afternoon. He still did his job with Bert-like precision and swiftness, but these qualities themselves galled him. They suggested that he might as well construct a Jack II robot and send it to the office every day. He could stay home in his pajamas and update his blog.

The nickname Jack II started to bug him. What was so special about the Original Jack? Why hadn't he, Jack II, been able to supplant him as *the* Jack?

It took a while for them to notice, but he'd stopped giving his spontaneous massages. *I kind of miss the Jackrubs,* said Lizzie.

<u>II (H) ii:</u> He had a document, right on his work computer desktop, entitled WhatToDo.doc, a list of people to contact, possible escape routes. The most intriguing of these contacts was his uncle, a genuine oil tycoon. Jack II said his family and the uncle had been estranged for fifteen years but it might be

worth a shot. For graduation the uncle gave him a pen set and a business-card holder, still in their boxes. Jack II couldn't remember if he'd written him a thank-you note.

Now he talked about work projects in some dour variant of the conditional tense, saying that he'd do such and such a task *provided I'm still around*. Even his most casual e-mails came laden with doom. *I'm never going to forget this place.* All of them in that office felt this way to an extent, but Jack II was really bumming them out.

<u>II (H) iii:</u> Jack II and Lizzie got called into the Sprout's office at just after nine one morning. Maxine was there but she was staring at the carpet. The room was already involved in what felt like the unending middle of a very long conference call with the new owners.

The Californians? Jack II scribbled on a pad to Lizzie.

They exist! she wrote back.

So they were now the property of the Californians. Exactly *when* the handoff happened wasn't clear. How had they missed it? It had stretched out for months, flickering in and out of reality. Up till now none of them knew whether it would turn out to be a good thing or a bad thing, but now it seemed like it was definitely a bad thing.

Unlike the former people at the top, every word the new owners said could be heard with horrible clarity, from all the way across the country. Continuing to think of them as *the Californians* was probably not the best idea, conjuring as it did an image of sunglassed, zinc-nosed layabouts toting Boogie boards. From the first syllable, it was obvious these were not poolside-lounging Californians. They wanted new IDs made for every employee, a new receptionist trained at their facilities, personalized long-distance and Xerox codes, pay phones installed in the lobby for all nonbusiness calls, endless other complications. Every employee would soon be required to create a new log-on password consisting of a mix of nonsequential capital letters and a three-digit prime number and a punctuation mark, and then change it once a month by sending an Excel form to a secure website in Oakland. This was just *standard operating procedure.*

Each demand felt like the securing of a strap on a straitjacket.

What's in Oakland? Lizzie wrote.

The Californians were saying things like *effective immediately* and *compliance is mandatory.* Lizzie imagined there was a dartboard in that West Coast boardroom with a stern phrase printed on each wedge. The Californians were picking phrases at random. It was a new world of all sticks and no carrots.

The carrot is you don't get fired, Lizzie whispered.

Are you sure that's the carrot? Jack II whispered back.

What?

Nothing.

What?

Nothing.

The Sprout kept forming a fist and almost pounding the table. It looked like an exercise you would do at mime camp. His sleeves were rolled up and his tie was loose.

Didn't you get the PDF? asked one of the Californians. *Didn't you read the file?*

Maxine's outfit could be described as *psychic Catholic schoolgirl.* It was like she knew something bad was going to happen before she left home today.

Lizzie decided that Maxine was a Bert about clothing, but probably an Ernie about everything else.

II (H) iv: The collective blood pressure in the room spiked when Henry from HR entered. For a second they thought maybe he'd come by on other matters, but the Sprout motioned for him to have a seat. Henry from HR stared out the window with his superhero eyes, reading omens in the clouds or looking through someone's shirt two avenues away.

At first Lizzie and Jack II thought that the Californians were doing a good cop, bad cop scenario. But there were actually three of them on the phone, and they were doing something along the lines of bad cop, bad cop, *really* bad cop. They were Berts gone over completely to the dark side.

The worst cop said she wanted Maxine out. She said her name as *Maxie*, without the *n*. The Sprout shook his head while saying, *Of course*, his right hand clutching the edge of the desk.

Effective immediately, snapped one of the new people. *Is Maxie still in the room?*

Maxine was looking like she'd just lost a fairly important limb in addition to a consonant. The Sprout told the Californians that she wasn't in the room anymore. *She's meeting with a client*. The spur-of-the-moment, completely pointless lie was touching in its own way. He said that he'd tell Maxine about the change in her employment status right after the call. Lizzie strained to hear if he pronounced the *n*.

The Californians started insulting Maxie's work, describing her as subpar, *sub*-subpar, *the pits*. Maxine didn't say a word. Her plans for world domination had come to an end, at least in that office.

Henry from HR, his face an undertaker's mix of sympathy and purpose, opened a folder and wordlessly handed a piece of paper to Maxine. The Sprout was scrolling through some file on his computer, tilting the screen for the exact right angle, as if that could make any difference to anyone now. Lizzie heard a *thwack* sound: a tear had rolled off Maxine's cheek and hit the form she was just given. Without lifting her head, Maxine asked in the smallest voice possible if she could borrow a pen. Lizzie handed over her prized Japanese Gel-Magik 8000, a gift from Jason, knowing she'd never see it again.

More tears hit the paper, hit the paper like rain.

It went on. Nobody was ready for this sort of crying, not from Maxine. She finished filling out the form and Henry led her out the door. She looked devastated but also amazing.

II (H) v: One of the Californians, the middle bad cop, started talking about Phoenix, apparently one of their cities. He asked the Sprout if he knew what Phoenix was. Not *where*, but *what*.

It was all prelude to a tagline they'd probably been using for years.

Phoenix is not just a city, said the middle bad cop. He asked if everyone on the New York end was familiar with the story of how the phoenix rose from the ashes. *That's exactly what we're going to do with this place.*

They're going to burn it down first! Lizzie whispered, but Jack II didn't respond. She noticed that he'd gone dangerously pale, his head weaving a bit. A cold sore had formed on the corner of his mouth, and he kept licking his lips, lingering on the tiny painful vesicles.

II (H) vi: The other Californians pointed out, in extreme but vague terms, the way the office had mishandled New York, as if the city had been dropped, kicked to the curb, dented beyond repair. New York—all of New York?—had become *dysfunctional*.

It's snowing, Lizzie mouthed at Jack II. She could see the edges of him tremble and wondered if she should be trembling, too.

On the phone came K.'s voice, a touch louder than the voices of the Californians. She was upstairs, in her own glass-enclosed office, no doubt looking at a dry-erase board with numbers written in different colors. She spoke without hesitation, in complete sentences, her phrasing seamless. The Sprout inched away from the phone as she talked until he was part of the wall.

At first it sounded like she was defending the Sprout and his team. She'd conceded Maxine, but maybe she was going to draw the line at any further firings. It was a skeleton crew, and at this rate all that would be left were a couple of ribs, a portion of kneecap. But then she directed a question at the already pale Sprout, who went a few shades whiter before sputtering *I don't know.* She asked him something else, and something else, and something else, and he said, *I really don't know. I'll check. I just don't know right now.*

K. didn't say anything.

The Californians didn't say anything.

Lizzie was in a pink sweater and looking at the snow.

Then K. said: *Well,* know *already!*

The Sprout agreed that he *should* know, swore that he *would* know, that everything would be known very shortly. He became a spokesperson for knowledge and its virtues. Ignorance was not part of his makeup. The rest of the call went by like the last writhings of a bad dream, the falling snow inappropriately beautiful, the Sprout blanching, K. aligning firmly with the Californians, or so she thought.

II (H) vii: When it was over, the Sprout told Jack II that he had to suspend him for two weeks. He said that this was his decision, not based on anything the California crew wanted, but this sounded instantly like a lie.

Lizzie gasped. Jack II looked at his hands so long they took on the appearance of moist vinyl. By this point the cold sore had colonized much of his upper lip. He couldn't say a word, as if the wound had welded his mouth shut.

The Sprout told Lizzie to leave and to ask Jenny to come in. Instantly it occurred to Lizzie that the Sprout had meant for *Jenny* to be at the meeting from the beginning, rather than herself, but had mixed up their names somehow. He always got them confused, despite the fact that Jenny did roughly half his work for him.

Jenny came in and Lizzie lingered by the door, just out of sight, listening. The Sprout told Jenny to have a seat. There was silence for ten seconds. Then he told her to go see Henry in HR. Why had he told her to sit down first? Maybe protocol required the expendable party to be seated, to prevent lawsuits based on fainting-related injuries.

Does this mean I'm fired? Jenny asked, hands on armrests, ready to rise.

It means you should go see Henry in HR.

I'm not going to cry if you fire me, she said, rising and banging her knee on the edge of the desk and sitting back down.

II (H) viii: When Jenny finally left, she was breathing in a scary, untrackable rhythm, like she'd just rolled down a flight of stairs. The speakerphone blipped and K.'s voice returned. Lizzie could hear it all. At first she thought K. was saying something to Jenny, condolences of some sort, but in fact she had moved on to a completely different subject. Jenny apparently realized this, too, and stumbled out to see Henry in HR.

K. was scolding the Sprout for mishandling the conference call. She said it was a crucial test and he'd failed it.

How was that a test? the Sprout asked.

I don't know what I expected from you, but I didn't expect that, said K.

I said, How was that even a test?

K. laughed. *Do you know that you're an embarrassment? This has been the most embarrassing day.* She stayed on the phone with him for another ten minutes, using *embarrassment* twenty-seven times. Crease kept count.

II (I): American Worker's Habitat, Early Twenty-first Century

<u>II (I) i:</u> Weaving her way out of HR, Jenny knocked over a wastebasket, stopped to set it aright, then didn't. It was like the biggest transgression of her adult life, and she took a moment to acknowledge the enormity. It suggested a sudden rupture in her moral universe, a heady escape into a life of crime. Next thing you knew she'd tossed her stringy, tear-soaked Kleenex to the floor and let it stay there. It could stay there forever, for all she cared, fossilize for centuries, perplex future archaeologists with its high salt content.

Her small hands were in tight red fists and her face had gone a vivid pink, cheeks nearly the shade of Lizzie's sweater.

I should smile, said Jenny, choking back tears. *Right?*

Futile lines from *The Jilliad* came to mind. She stared at her stuff.

> *If your boss is in the way, get a new boss.*
> *Think of the office as an ocean liner.*

Lizzie put a hand on Jenny's shoulder and steered her like that for a while. It became a procession, as more people joined them en route to the elevator.

Jack II was long gone. His cubicle already looked like a museum display, *American Worker's Habitat, Early Twenty-first Century.* His screen saver had kicked in, a platoon of Smurf-like creatures digging luminous tunnels that crisscrossed the black of the screen.

<u>II (I) ii:</u> They all rode down in silence. It was barely 3 but a drink was in order. Outside Pru was smoking and Jenny told her in a tiny voice what everyone else already knew, the full list of casualties. Pru wrapped an elbow around her in a complicated way, a hug that didn't require abandoning her cigarette.

Where's Maxine? someone said.

Jenny wasn't crying yet but it sounded like someone was. It was the crane at the construction site down the street, squeaking as it lowered a voluptuous payload. The infinity building was shaping up, with much of the curved blue glass already in place for the lower floors.

They found their faces in it as they walked by. When they looked up they saw that the snow was really coming down, so swiftly it unmoored them. It felt like the world was rushing up to meet the sky.

Over drinks Jenny was fine for five minutes and then started to break down. Chunks of her seemed to fall off and die and for the rest of the night she was crying or just about to start. *You guys are, never going to, see me again,* she said, gasping. They knew this was true but told her it wasn't.

We see Jules all the time, they said. *We go to his toaster-oven restaurant.*

The verb tense was dubious. They went only once as a group and would never go again if they could help it.

But Jules is different, said Jenny. *Jules is fun. I'm so boring. You'll forget about me. It's OK. It's OK.*

Jules is a nutcase, said Laars.

We'll keep in touch, said Pru. *We'll e-mail.* Pru was always realistic about those sorts of things.

Grime wandered in late. He made a loud offer to buy drinks for the evening and said he'd set up a tab at the bar but never got around to it.

Despite all the crying, Jenny looked pretty good, indeed noticeably better than she usually did.

Her eyes shimmered and her mouth had an appealing pout. Several of them remarked on this the next day at work. <u>II (I) iii:</u> Jenny said it sounded crazy but she thought she got fired for accidentally sending that e-mail to Kristen.

Who's Kristen? said Laars.

Do you mean Karen? said Crease.

What e-mail? said Pru.

She means K., said Laars. *I thought her name was Kierstin.*

Grime didn't know what was going on. Jenny explained how she had meant to forward something to Jill, but hit *K* instead of *J*. K.'s name had then appeared in the To field.

This was going to be a key component of Jenny's layoff narrative.

She knew it was the wrong name, that *Jill didn't even work here anymore*, but she clicked Send before her conscious mind kicked in.

Didn't that happen months ago? Lizzie asked. Jenny said yes but that it happened *again* a week ago.

Crease brought over another drink for Jenny. He was trying to call Jack II's cell but no one was answering.

Please call us back if you get this, Crease said.

II (I) iv: Lizzie asked Jenny what it was that she'd forwarded to K.

That's the other thing that sucks, Jenny said. She was sending Jill the Polish joke website, to show her how crazy Maxine was. Maybe sending it had gotten *Maxine* fired.

Oh, and one other thing, said Jenny.

She'd also attached a link for Jack II's blog, with the note: *Check it out he's losing his mind!*

II (I) v: Jack II's two-week suspension ended with his termination. He never came back to the office. It was unsettling to see someone so frequently and then to lose touch altogether. Oddly, his cell phone stopped accepting messages a few days into his suspension, as if the phone company disapproved of him as well, and when one of them tried to get in touch a week later, the number no longer worked at all. *It's like he never existed,* said Jonah.

The empty cubicles echoed. Toward evening, with the outside light failing, the office looked like the carcass of a beached whale, split open, immense and exposed and way too intimate.

Crease used to whistle as he walked from the subway to the office, but he didn't anymore. It used to be that several times a week he'd run into Jack II approaching the building from the opposite direction. Jack II was like Crease's uptown shadow, his mirror self.

All of Jack II's stuff was still in his cubicle, including his bicycle. No one knew what to do. They assumed he'd return for it, but later the Kohut Brothers were back, putting everything into boxes. Even the bike went into a big box that the brothers, or whatever they were, stuffed with bubble wrap and shrouded with packing tape. Laars looked around for a CD he'd lent him but couldn't find it.

Later they had the idea to go to Maxine's desk, with the secret hope that they'd find smashed discs in the trash, more abandoned files for world domination, fragments that had something to do with Operation JASON or else held Maxine's secret fantasies about them. But her space was even emptier than Jack II's.

Laars finally received his mouth guard from Michigan. He started to wear it at his desk.

I think I'm grinding my teeth when I'm awake, too, he said.

<u>II (I) vi:</u> Now that there was no Jenny, they couldn't get anything to work. Everything existed at a level of raging confusion. Things they all assumed they knew by heart were now forgotten. *Does anyone remember how to add up a column in Excel?*

There were clusters of boxes everywhere, and file cabinets nudged out of true, giving the office the look of an apiary, hives waiting to explode. Lizzie pierced her hair with no fewer than three pens. *It's a way to gauge her anxiety*, Pru pointed out helpfully.

<u>II (I) vii:</u> After days of buildup Laars finally demanded to talk to the Sprout about the dismissal of Jenny and Jack II. Not enough people—that is, nobody—had stood up when Jill was let go. Laars didn't want that to happen again.

The trouble was that while Laars could be articulate among equals or over a pint, he tended to either rant Tourettishly or clam up altogether when talking to the Sprout. Today he was doing the former, or else simply speaking in tongues. The crazy factor was upped by the fact that for the first half of the meeting Laars was holding his mouth guard, occasionally waving it in a threatening manner.

The Sprout laughed: *Hoo-hoo.* He held his palms up to the ceiling, at nearly shoulder level, elbows at his sides, a gesture of innocence under duress.

Think of the office as a work in progress, said the Sprout at last.

I'm not one to point fingers, said the Sprout.

I'm as upset as you are, said the Sprout.

He then made the astonishing claim that, based on his best information, Jenny and Jack II were far and away the least productive people on the team.

I need everyone to bring their A game, said the Sprout, shuffling two pieces of paper with a practiced frown. *The whole thing is really out of my hands at this point.*

He didn't *quite* show the papers to Laars, but he made it clear that they were efficiency reports of some sort, full of damning information. But it didn't make sense. Who was writing up the reports? Jenny and Jack II were the *most* efficient workers—it was obvious to everyone. Both of them always had their work schedules mapped out weeks, even months, in advance. In truth they made the others look bad.

The Sprout kept talking, not just about A games but about a *plan B.* He wasn't making much sense. Bogus reports aside, he was probably still stunned by the loss of Jenny, though maybe less so about Jack II, whose name he periodically forgot.

Laars was unsure how to proceed. He had grown to suspect that Maxine had been devising ways to get rid of them. But now that *she* was gone, the mystery deepened. Could it be

that Maxine *had* written the efficiency reports—but so ineffi-
ciently that she herself was shown the door?

<u>II (I) viii:</u> Lost in questions he couldn't quite phrase, Laars
spotted a curious memo on a Post-it, stuck on a tape dispenser:

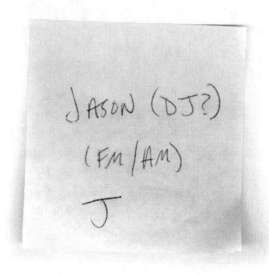

He grew more baffled than ever. First there was Maxine's broken world-domination disc, which had Jason's name on it—
now this.

What did *Jason* have to do with anything? Did he have a
higher-level job than any of them suspected? Was *he* a double
agent?

The evidence suggested, nonsensically, that he'd become a
disc jockey, on both the AM and FM dials.

Even so, why should the Sprout care?

Of course, maybe the name referred to someone else entirely: a different Jason, a powerful, hidden Jason, who lived in

a shed on the roof, eating instant noodles and Lorna Doones, tapping out directives in Morse code.

Allowances need to be made, the Sprout was saying.

The message was a stumper. Not to mention the signature, the *J:* Had the memo come from Jonah? From Jenny or Jack II, RIP? Laars felt his sanity seeping away, but he managed to surreptitiously copy each mysterious letter onto his pad, pretending to take notes, nodding while the Sprout said, *The idea is to make the operation as lean as possible.*

Mmm-hmming while the Sprout said, *We have to take it apart.*

Smiling while the Sprout said, *Then we want to rebuild gradually.*

II (I) ix: The meeting left Laars so depressed that later, after some time at his desk, checking the hour-by-hour performance of the one stock he owned, he felt the undeniable urge to get a doughnut.

The Sprout was at the elevator. The silence doubled as they waited. What more was there to say? In the Sprout's eyes, Laars saw his own exhaustion reflected. At last they stepped in, but the carriage was going up. Laars thought of *The Jilliad,* that passage about always having an Elevator Speech ready. He was about to say something, but then the Sprout started talking, as if picking up from their earlier conversation.

In this new environment, in this claustrophobic pen, the Sprout explained that costs needed to be cut by a certain fixed amount every month. The Californians wanted results. The quickest remedy, in the short term, was to let go of extraneous workers. Everyone was going to be scrutinized.

We've all got to step up to the plate, the Sprout said. *We've all got to work outside our comfort zone.*

Laars kept thinking about Jason, but couldn't recall what he looked like. They had barely overlapped. Small head, pleasant features. How horrible, he thought, if someone were to remember him that way. He thought harder. He could visualize the one deep furrow on Jason's otherwise blank brow. During moments of concentration or intense malaise it resembled a second mouth.

The Sprout said that the cost cutting was a long-range goal, which they had a year to meet—as if this information would inspire Laars. Maybe he was trying to inspire him to quit. The Sprout didn't say anything about how the workers who were left now had to do all the abandoned work, in the same amount of time and for the same amount of pay.

Laars wondered why the Sprout was revealing so much— surely *The Jilliad* would have sharp words for a boss who opened up to his employees. Then he started thinking about the Post-it again: *DJ.* Did Jason have a talk-radio personality, or was he more of a smooth-rock navigator? Laars couldn't remember the voice *or* the face.

The elevator doors opened at seven. No one was there. Then the secret love of Crease's life stepped aboard. Laars wanted to send Crease a text message: HABAW ELEV ASAP! But the Sprout was still talking. He said that the layoffs would be on a rolling basis for at least the remainder of the year. Then hopefully there'd be a *break in the clouds.*

HABAW stared at the descending lighted numbers, tapping her toe gently.

These things tend to be cyclical, the Sprout droned on. He was making a motion with his finger, but it wasn't a twirling, rounded motion. It was more like a square that becomes an asterisk.

The elevator finally reached the lobby. HABAW stepped out and in four long and fairly breathtaking strides evaporated into the sun.

At the same moment Grime walked in the front door, bound for the office. He made a gun gesture at the security guard, who put down his Bible and mimed falling backward, bleeding, only to be resurrected with laughter.

Join me, Russell? Grime said to the Sprout, who nodded and went back up with him, no doubt readying another Elevator Speech.

II (I) x: No one could make head or tail of the *Jason DJ* memo.

So I don't get it, he's on the radio now? asked Jonah. One thing he remembered was that Jason had the worst taste in music, though this statement was regarded skeptically, coming as it did from a devotee of Czech opera.

Laars spent an hour, two hours, the rest of the afternoon doing a slow purge of his e-mail correspondence with Jenny. After a while it was too painful to read the messages, so he just stared at the subject lines.

Hey
Oh and
Hey Laars
questions
idea
Re: Hey Laars
Re: Re: Jenny
Hi!
Re: questions
report

    Re: report
    Potential problem(s)(??!)
    Scratch that
    Re: Scratch that
    Re: idea
    sorry
    Hey
    Re: Hey
    NEIN!
    hi
    One thing
    sproutage
    whassup
    Re: Scratch that
    Don't forget . . .
    Re: Hi!
    Re: Re: report
    drinxx
    Re: sproutage
    Sproutaggio
    Re: NEIN!
    Re: Re: Re: Hey Jenny
    Re: Re: idea
    Re: Re: Re: report
    Re: Re: Re: Re: Re: Re

He wondered how many e-mails he wrote a week, a month, a
year. One day he was going to sit down and count. He realized
he'd only written to Jenny twice since she was fired. He started
typing a message to her, but couldn't think of anything to say.
II (I) xi: Was Lizzie the new Jenny? She said she wasn't. The
Sprout kept calling her in, though, and soon had her switch to
Jenny's old desk so that she was closer to his office. This also
meant that she had to get in before he did, a situation that

might have been acceptable had she been able to leave a little earlier than before. But she always wound up staying late—it was otherwise impossible to finish even a fraction of the necessary tasks. He talked to her in a voice that was barely audible. She kept saying *Sorry?* She hated it when people said *Sorry?* instead of *Excuse me?*—she thought it was some sort of Britishism. But somehow it was her first response.

Was it *good* to be the new Jenny? Yes and no but mostly no. Lizzie now had a slightly more comfortable chair and a much better computer that didn't sound like it was on the verge of exploding every time she opened an application. But she wasn't getting paid extra and she was definitely doing more work. Some of it involved what she called manual labor, such as sharpening the Sprout's pencils and printing out mailing labels. She felt herself slipping down some job-description sinkhole.

This wasn't quite a *deprotion.* It might have simply been a demotion.

The Sprout also e-mailed Lizzie from home, at midnight, at three in the morning, asking her to print out various files and leave them on his desk so that they would be the first things he saw when he got into the office. Often he had her print out his to-do lists, cryptic commands that read like he was shouting:

ASK LS abt next wk!
CHECK w/K abt conf call
NO MORE TTM?!
CANCEL CC, M, VX ASAP
SHEILA CAR FIX CALL!

He would sometimes send identical to-do lists two or three days in a row, suggesting either that the items were not actually high priorities or that he wasn't doing any work at all, just letting his mind drift into space.

She also got sent this one:

JASON DJ FM AM J

The sequence was exactly the same as it was on the Post-it Laars had seen. Nobody could figure it out.

Jason's such a mystery man, said Pru. *Who would have guessed?*

II (I) xii: Sometimes when Lizzie put printouts on the Sprout's desk, she couldn't help but notice things.

The bag with all his racquetball gear was perpetually in the corner. She had never seen him take it out of the room.

There was a pad full of doodles by his phone. Usually the Sprout drew butterflies, treble clefs, igloos attacked by flying saucers. Sometimes he drew a dense forest with birds pouring out of it, obscuring the imperfect circle of sun.

Every so often, like a form of bureaucratic weather, Post-its appeared like scales on a corner of the Sprout's monitor. The handwriting wasn't his. The messages were in red pencil, written in a way that maximized the number of sharp corners in any given letter. Even O looked needlessly harsh. The Sprout's face always fell upon seeing them.

Where did they come from? How did they get there?

Lizzie thought they originated with K., though she gathered that K. was in California every other week, presumably undergoing a metamorphosis into yet another bad cop.

II (I) xiii: Lizzie was interested in the fact that Grime came by to see the Sprout so often, sometimes twice a day. Though the door was usually ajar, she could hear only murmurs, the occasional curse, the rare *Hoo-hoo!*

In extra early one morning, Lizzie saw Grime leaving the Sprout's office before the Sprout arrived.

A few minutes later, delivering a printout to his desk, she was startled by a coating of Post-its that definitely wasn't there before. The memos covered the monitor, the keyboard, parts of the desk itself. There were phone numbers and initials, dates and times, one-word questions underlined and repeated.

One read: OPERATION JASON UPDATE—ASAP.

Lizzie wondered: Was it *Grime* who was leaving the notes, the Post-its of Doom?

When the Sprout arrived, he took a legal pad out of his briefcase and carefully transferred all the Post-its to the cardboard backing one by one, their edges a centimeter apart. Then he told Lizzie he was taking a personal day.

Right before Lizzie went out for lunch, the Sprout returned to check something on his computer. Lizzie saw Grime approach. The Sprout shut down his computer, slammed the door, and hurried past Grime, saying, *I'm here but I'm not here.*

<u>II (I) xiv:</u> It appeared that Jonah had nothing to do. While the rest of them were busy, stretching their schedules to accommodate the work that used to be done by their ex-colleagues, he listened to his Czech arias, thumbed through fat textbooks, waited for the other shoe to drop. His screen saver was a flock of black birds and an opposite-facing flock of white birds, which eventually interlocked Escher style.

Whenever someone popped in to see him, he would quickly set his book flat, half-concealed under papers, and tap his keyboard to summon his darkened craptop screen back to life.

He was growing a beard to go along with his mustache. While the others tried not to call attention to themselves,

Jonah was pretty much waving a flag, jumping up and down, and playing a tuba for good measure.

Lately Jonah had been wearing the ratty blue work shirt that he'd kept draped over his chair for years. He wasn't talking as much as he used to, and Pru thought he was trying to get fired, consciously or unconsciously. Perversely, they came to appreciate what he was doing—it would give them that much more time if he attracted the Sprout's attention and got the boot. Lizzie kept saying, *I mean at this point I kind of want it to be me.* Everyone wanted to leave but no one wanted to be next.

<u>II (I) xv:</u> Jonah's beard grew quickly, arriving in a slightly different color than his mustache. There was less protest this time around, as the mustache was a complete failure to begin with and things could only get better for him in the facial hair department. In the Red Alcove, Pru pointed out to Lizzie that the Paul Bunyan look was in. Glassy-eyed models in Milan were going around looking like oatmeal-eating Gold Rush casualties.

<u>II (I) xvi:</u> One week later, Jonah's burgeoning resemblance to the Unabomber made them rethink their position.

II (J): Blastoff

<u>II (J) i:</u> Taped inside the elevator one morning was a notice from the Department of Environmental Protection. It looked like it had been sat on and re-Xeroxed with the wrinkles in place and then sat on again for good measure, this time by a horse.

In order to maintain service to area water mains, and to ensure a continued high-quality water supply, the city would be conducting its regularly scheduled underground blasting this week, not exceeding two times a day. Though the actual detonations would not endanger any buildings in the area, the note informed them, noise levels might be uncomfortably high for some people, and earplugs were recommended as a protective measure.

A system of whistles would precede each blast:

One whistle = Blasting begins in ten minutes
Two whistles = Blasting begins in five minutes
Three whistles = Blasting begins in one minute or less

II (J) ii: This startling document became an instant source of elevator banter. Someone would whistle three times and everyone would laugh. Laars told Crease he'd bumped into HABAW that morning and she'd done the whistling joke.

What a goddess! said Crease. *Admit it.*

Laars agreed and said she was a terrific whistler. Also, she called the elevator a *lift*. Crease was overwhelmed once again by the cuteness of that Britishism and made unironic pitter-pat motions over his heart.

Crease asked if Laars thought HABAW was an Ernie or a Bert and he said, *A little of both.*

I'm so jealous I could kill you, said Crease cheerfully.

II (J) iii: Even without a fresh firing, the week had its built-in drama. Everyone waited for the blasts, or rather for the whistles to sound. Was the blasting related to the infinity building? It was unclear where the alarm system was based. Jonah imagined that a van would circulate through the neighborhood when the time came.

Regularly scheduled made it sound like this had happened before, but no one could remember any blasting.

Crease showed everyone his earplugs, which he'd been using to block out noise from the construction site, and also as part of a general program of self-isolation. They were made of yellow foam and looked like little dollhouse sponge cakes. When he stuck them in his ears, they resembled those Frankenstein neck bolts. He did a little monster lurch, arms outstretched, and wished that HABAW could witness his lively sense of humor.

II (J) iv: Crease fantasized about a blast so loud that some of the floors collapse. Nobody's injured, thankfully, but while everyone else escapes, he and HABAW find themselves cut off from civilization. The computers are down, there's no e-mail, cell phones don't function. The company is in ruins, never to restart.

There's a water fountain that works. For the first week no one even knows that the two are missing. They eat vending machine food and she confesses that she noticed him the very first time they rode the elevator together.

In one variation, HABAW has lost her hearing from the blast and they must communicate using an improvised sign language, or by writing things on the wall with charred sticks. Crease's hearing of course is preserved, thanks to the earplugs.

II (J) v: Lizzie said maybe the whistles were the kind only dogs could hear. Whistles were going off all the time and nobody could detect them, and every day big things were happening just below the surface.

II (K): The Destiny of K.

II (K) i: *I hate this,* said Laars, on the morning of the last day of the non-blasting. *Did anyone else get this?*

It was a companywide e-mail, sent out at 9:11 a.m. Some of them were beginning to suspect that a virus was shifting e-mails so that they registered that ominous time stamp.

I don't want to open it, said Lizzie. *It's bad luck.*

As if everything else so far had been good luck.

<u>II (K) ii:</u> The e-mail was from K.

After fifteen fantastic years, she wrote, it was time to move on. Apparently she *hadn't* been absorbed by the Californians, despite all her efforts. Instead she'd been tossed out of the company altogether, an event which in her version became an opportunity to *pursue other projects.* This made Lizzie think of shoe-box dioramas, finger painting, the construction of piñatas.

K. included the standard line about being proud of the staff, singling out the Sprout as a skilled manager and her temporary successor.

That *temporary* was going to give the Sprout an ulcer. It was going to give his current ulcer an ulcer.

Then there was a little paragraph in which the tone shifted, a fascinating autobiography that breezed by in three quick sentences. K. had started out, fifteen years ago, in the sixth-floor mail room—a place that no longer existed, she wryly noted—and worked her way up the ladder, serving a stint in nearly every department, and briefly overseeing the successful restructuring of the Boston branch.

Didn't they close the Boston branch? asked Crease.

She had also participated in the national corporate training seminars for the past five years, including the one over the summer, held in California. She didn't say what her future plans included beyond *spending more time with my partner.*

She wrapped things up by saying how much she'd learned from dozens of generous people over the years. Most of them were no longer with the company, their names not ringing even the faintest bells.

She signed it K. R. Ash.

As they each reached the end of the e-mail at their separate work stations, Lizzie, Pru, and Crease could hear Laars saying: *Oh. My. God.*

<u>II (K) iii:</u> In a flash Laars figured out the provenance of his ancient, temperamental stapler, the bandaged beast that still sat on his desk and every so often could be coaxed to fasten papers together. It had been handed down for generations within the company, migrating over the years from floor to floor, desk to desk. It couldn't just be coincidence that the instrument had fallen to *him*.

That means there's hope, said Laars, popping out his mouth guard. He wiped a string of drool. *I could be the next K.*

Jonah, leaving his cave for a rare appearance, stroked his beard but didn't say anything. This gave the impression of a judgment, without him actually having to speak.

Nothing could puncture Laars's buoyant mood. *It's destiny. What else can it mean?*

Pru made a megaphone of her hands and said, *Ernie alert.*

<u>II (K) iv:</u> At quarter to five Grime sent a mass e-mail: *Ftinkd?* It was like the name of some forgotten Norse god. Nobody knew how to respond. Lizzie forwarded it to Pru, adding, *I'm scared.*

A few hours later Grime bumped into Crease in the hall and asked why no one wanted to get drinks to celebrate or at least contemplate the big K. news. Crease discovered that Grime had meant to type *Drinks?* but his left hand had been misaligned on the keyboard.

<u>II (K) v:</u> *Where does the time go?* Lizzie asked, in her poignant way. *Where does the life go?*

No one could answer this.

I can't believe it's already October, she said, sharpening a pencil for the Sprout.

Pru waited as long as humanly possible. *It's November.*

Sorry? said Lizzie. December was a week away.

II (K) vi: Lizzie was complaining to Jonah, to Big Sal, to anyone who'd listen, about Grime's misspellings. She understood that it was part of the Grime mystique, that for a man so rumpled it stood to reason that language would not emerge with the smoothness most of the species enjoyed.

But seriously? It's like a medical condition. He spells sincerely *with two* a*'s.*

There's no a *in* sincerely, said Big Sal.

Exactly.

Another hilarious thing was that he always rendered *definitely* as *defiantly.*

II (K) vii: Big Sal said that he'd see what he could do, and a week later he installed Glottis 3.0 on Grime's computer. It was a more advanced version of the software that Jules had used to compose his screenplay right before he got fired.

Big Sal replaced Grime's computer with the one Jules used to have. It made upgrading easier.

I just have to click on this thing, said Big Sal. One advantage of 3.0 was that it was specially designed to discern British, Australian, and Indian accents.

II (L): Swiping

II (L) i: Laars said that so far, this winter wasn't as bad as the last. It took a few seconds for them to realize he was talking about the temperature.

They all agreed, but it was based on the haziest of communal memories and a degree of tacit peer pressure. How many people really remembered what last winter was like? Winter was winter. Some days were colder than others. Some days were sunny. Some weeks were wet. Every winter had at least one blast of traffic-stopping snow, followed by a miserable stretch of slush and countless afternoons when you said *I can't believe this wind.*

Inside the office it didn't make too much difference, except that Lizzie's desk and both of Crease's were near drafts. The cold air poured in mysteriously from above. They kept calling Ray in maintenance, only to discover that the Sprout had fired Ray back in the summer. Lizzie's lips were a corpsey blue. She was wearing two sweaters and sometimes put her winter coat over her shoulders. The Sprout told her that he'd handle it.

They had a vision of him in the basement, rolling up his sleeves and manhandling the boiler, his trusty wrenches and tongs arrayed on a makeshift workbench. But all he did was tell Lizzie to go to Kmart and buy herself a portable heater and expense it.

Now everyone who didn't have a heater wanted one. Even people who were warm wanted a heater.

II (L) ii: Winter really kicked in a few days later, snow up to *here*, thuggish winds. Laars said, *This is like two winters ago.*

Winter, two winters, two years. *Where does the time go? Where does the* life *go?*

Laars said to Crease, *I have the worst hat head and I wasn't even wearing a hat today.*

II (L) iii (a): On Thursday some of them were at the Good Starbucks talking about Jules. No one had seen him in a while but Pru heard through the Original Jack, whom she seemed to be encountering with remarkable frequency, that he'd closed the toaster-oven place and had just opened a club done up '70s ski-lodge style. The name escaped her. Gondola? Snowmobile? Bunnyhill?

Laars wondered if Jules had ever finished his screenplay, *Personal Daze.*

Jonah might know, he said. Jonah wasn't with them—holed up studying as usual, getting smarter, growing hairier.

Crease was excited about *Personal Daze,* the movie, and hoped there were lots of office scenes. He fantasized that it was about him—the unrequited love of the Greek girl could make a good subplot. He thought Jules might have a better chance with producers if he changed the title to *Jobmilla.*

I can imagine what the poster would look like, he said.

<u>II (L) iii (b):</u> Lizzie explained to Grime that Jules had written most of the screenplay using an earlier version of Glottis.

Glottis is bloody brilliant, said Grime. *It's like magic.*

True, his spelling had improved. They were still scared of his e-mails, as Glottis tended to go all caps without warning, so that IT LOOKED LIKE HE WAS SHOUTING AT YOU. But the trade-off was worth it.

Grime's headset had an attachment that transmitted his voice up to fifty yards—it was overkill, but he liked the freedom to pace. It helped keep the ideas fresh. Pru said she'd seen him jawing away contentedly, musing over by the windows, and asked what project he was working on.

Oh, just writing me memoirs, he joked.

<u>II (L) iv:</u> The next morning they slung off satchels and handbags, settled at their desks, sorted through new e-mail, stared at their coffees. The Unnamable was making his shuffling rounds,

dropping an interoffice-mail envelope into everyone's in-box. The missive came courtesy of Henry from HR, and even before they started reading, they knew something bad was happening.

At around the same time, at each desk on the fourth floor, a piece of black plastic, about the size and shape of a credit card, slipped out of an envelope and clattered to rest.

It had no name or number, no markings at all. Its power was entirely invisible.

Henry's note said that, beginning tomorrow, everyone would be required to swipe in and out whenever they started or stopped working. Each floor was equipped with a box that would take a digital time stamp.

You can't even see the magnetic strip, said Crease, studying his card under the light.

Strip or stripe? said Lizzie.

A black box was affixed to the right of the elevator, a thin metal box as blank and unyielding as their new cards. A somewhat crudely cut slit extended vertically down the center of the box, the space their cards would pass through two or more times a day—five inches that seemed to stretch to the length of the entire wall. Jonah approached the box cautiously and after a moment rapped it with his knuckles. They listened for any sound of life: gears turning, a hidden clock ticking away.

Silence.

Then the congregation headed for the Sprout's office, a united front.

But the Sprout just shrugged. *You can all thank your friend Graham for that,* he said and pointedly turned his attention back to his screen.

Graham? *Grime?*

The Sprout typed a line with exaggerated clatter, intent on

ignoring them. Then he picked up the phone and left a message for Lizzie—who was standing in his office with everyone else—to look up various numbers and e-mail addresses. *Whenever you get a chance*, he said.

The Sprout swiveled his body to face the window and kept talking to Lizzie until his visitors eventually went away.

After looking up the information, Lizzie came into the office, where she saw the Sprout peering at his own swipe card. *I don't see where the magnetic stripe is, do you?*

II (L) v: Grime, conveniently, wasn't in the office. He'd phoned the Sprout that morning, off to England for a spell.

Everyone wound up staying later than normal that day, in thrall to the new swipe box, the heartless new regime. Minutes, seconds, were being counted by the Californians. Pru bore down on Lizzie, wagging her card. *Is this the thing that you didn't want to tell us before, the plan that Grime told you about?*

What?

The thing so awful you couldn't say what it was?

This is totally separate, she said. *I swear I had no idea.* But Pru didn't believe her. No one did.

I bet Grime's not even on vacation, said Crease. *I bet he's with the Californians somewhere.*

Pru demanded that Lizzie spill the beans.

II (L) vi: *If you want me to tell you, I'll tell you*, said Lizzie. *But you're going to wish I hadn't.*

Tell us, said Laars.

It doesn't even make sense. I don't even know why he told me. Just tell us already.

I can't even tell my therapist. It would mean I'd have to be in therapy another five years. It's just so awful and I don't want to think about it.

Don't be such a Bert, said Pru.

Lizzie insisted she needed three drinks before she could even *start* to tell it.

II (L) vii: The jukebox was loud. They humored Lizzie, playing a drinking game that they constructed on the fly—you had to knock one back any time you used a word with a *g* in it. It was a difficult thing to stay sober, hard to pick words as you grew tipsier.

Laars, attempting to drink with his mouth guard in, avoided talking altogether. Pru, too. Crease and Lizzie were three sheets to the wind. Before long Crease had taken his shiny new swipe card out and was making it do a little dance on the table to an old Van Halen song.

I feel dirty just thinking about it, said Lizzie. *You're going to hate me.*

We already *hate you.*

That's what I thought.

Everyone kept quiet until she began.

II (L) viii: *So this is what Grime said that night. Grime—his name! Grime! It makes total sense now in a cosmic linguistic, linguistico-cosmical way. It's karma or— right. So we were talking about vacations, my buddy Grime and I, I suppose this was right after I explained the whole crucial concept of* personal days *to him, the Lizzie definition of personal days, how they weren't vacation days—you were supposed to spend them at* home, *doing* personal *things like reading a book or watching an old movie, or I suppose theoretically at least having nonstop sex with someone off Craigslist, and anyway I mentioned that I wanted to take a big vacation someday, possibly next year, to India—which I realize is kind of what I say whenever I don't know what to say. Not that it's not true. I suppose this was all a clumsy way of seeing what his idea of a vacation was, more to the point, whether he was single or had a girlfriend or whatever. I asked him if he'd ever been to India. He said yes, actually, he lived there for a year, working in strategy for Goneril. I had no idea what Goneril was, or really what strategy was, so I just nodded. I Googled it later, it's this pharmaceutical company that I think is bankrupt now. Grime was telling me about all the places he's been. He was sort of flirty. It both was and wasn't sleazy. What he was saying wasn't particularly risqué but something about him got me hot and bothered. The truth is I didn't really mind.*

TMI, Pru said.

OK, well, Pru? If you think that's TMI, I should just stop right here. I mean, let's talk about something else. Let's talk about climate change or waterfront development or maybe the stick up your butt. Because this whole story? This whole story is premised on TMI. It's the most TMI exchange in the history of TMI.

Sorry.

Anyway I asked Grime if he liked it and he said he didn't get to do much sightseeing, the work was relentless, but one time he took a trip out to a temple somewhere in, I don't know the name, I don't even think the temple was famous at all. Oh wait, it was famous for something, for its beveled something. It was a few hours from the city and he was on a bus and the bus was falling apart. He'd had some bad food the night before—tried to cook something and it turned out strange. Basically he's not feeling so great all of a sudden, trapped on this rickety bus. There's still almost an hour to go. He's sweating. He said that in India you're always sweating but this was sweating of a higher order. Higher odor? Something like that. It's hard to figure out everything he's saying.

<u>II (L) ix</u>: *He manages to fall asleep. When he gets off the bus, he isn't quite at the temple yet. He exited too early or too late. No vil-*

lage in sight. Cars go by, a few trucks. Across the road is a sign. He figures out using the bad map in his guidebook that he's a mile away. A mile! He's in agony and all of a sudden he feels like he's going to die—he knows he's going to die. He starts weeping. Who will find his body? He can imagine the vultures picking his bones. He thinks, How sad, how sad, to just disappear like that. The Goneril people don't care, they'll try to find him for a few days but after that they'll give up. Nobody even knows he's made this trip. So he's slumped and sweating by the side of the road and he just spontaneously sends up this prayer, sort of half-moaning, half-praying. He's not even sure if he's praying to the Christian God or whatever or some Indian god that happens to be hovering in the area. It doesn't matter. He just says, If you let me survive this, I'll always be grateful. Show me a sign and I'll worship you in my own way, is the gist. He's saying this out loud now, tears in his eyes, the words coming from who knows where: I'll worship you in my own way.

And just like that he has a moment of clarity. His stomach is in total revolt and he knows that he has to find the loo as he calls it ASAP.

But there's nothing around him. He bolts in what he guesses is the direction of the temple but it's just not going to happen. He's seeing double, his legs respond stiffly. And then he can't help it and he just—he—you know. He loses it and he just goes.

<u>II (L) x:</u> At this point everybody screamed.

<u>II (L) xi:</u> *That's not actually the bad part*, said Lizzie. *He's a mess but he's feeling a hundred times better. He's taken a few steps back from death's door. He keeps walking to the temple, where hopefully he can clean himself up. He's uncomfortable and soiled but at least he's not dead. In his mind the Judeo-Christian God or some random local deity has spared his life. He prayed and his prayer was answered. So now every year he has to keep*

his promise, to do it again, no matter where he is, as a sign of his devotion and thanks.

Do what? asked Pru.

Nobody said anything.

In his—pants? asked Pru.

Lizzie nodded, and everybody screamed again.

I so did not have to hear this, said Crease.

Grime says he's done this in all sorts of places since then. The time comes and he just knows. *He's done it in Berlin and Tokyo, Wichita Falls and Syracuse. One of the conditions is that he can't* plan *to be somewhere alone. He could be at home or he could be out in public. It has to be a natural thing. And he's had good luck ever since, he says, his career has taken off. He thinks the ritual keeps things real, hooks him up to the cycle of consumption and waste, matter and decay, Ernie and Bert, yin and yang. And I don't know, part of me was freaking out but part of me somehow wasn't. Until, OK, let me finish this drink. Until he said, You're a down-to-earth girl, I can tell—I knew that from the beginning. He said, You probably understand where I'm coming from. And I said, London? Because I was getting this weird feeling, I'm probably crazy, but I'm just remembering now that I was getting this really weird vibe.*

<u>II (L) xii:</u> *That he wanted me to do it with him. And I don't mean sleep with him.*

Everybody screamed.

<u>II (L) xiii:</u> Pru went to the bar and bought another round for the table. Grime! *Crazy!* Yes! *Of course!* They didn't know whether this made him the biggest Ernie or the biggest Bert. The Ernie-Bert paradigm was shattered. Drinks! Drinks! Lizzie looked both relieved and totally mortified that she had told the Grime story.

This all sounds like an urban legend, said Crease. *The corporate coprophile, or whatever you call them. People who, you know. Poopy people.*

It makes sense either way, said Pru. *On the one hand, Grime's eccentric. We knew that from the start. This behavior could be the tip of the iceberg. I mean I'm shocked but I'm not surprised. On the other hand, he could just be feeding Lizzie a line of—well. I don't think I trust him.*

He hasn't been an out-and-out liar, said Crease. *Has he?*

But he's kept us in the dark about what it is he's actually doing for the company, or doing to the company, said Laars. The alcohol made them talk in circles, forget the point. *And now, starting tomorrow and thanks to him, we have to swipe in like a bunch of assembly-line workers.*

My father had to swipe in for his job, every day for thirty years, said Lizzie morosely.

OK, sorry. But my point is that this sucks.

I can't believe you're still talking to him, Crease said to Lizzie.

Not after today, she said. *I agree. The swiping is the last straw.*

Every straw is the last straw, said Pru.

II (M): Who Moved My Mouse?

<u>II (M) i:</u> They swiped in the next day, groggy from drinks and uneasy Grime-tinged slumbers. They weren't sure they were doing it right. The black box by the elevator didn't beep or click or otherwise acknowledge that the card had successfully gone through. There was barely any friction. It was like waving your hand through the air.

No one could figure out whether up-down or down-up

was the preferred direction. Some of them swiped again, inadvertently swiping themselves *out*, perhaps creating the impression that they'd worked a forty-second shift.

Laars got in late because he had to go to the dentist. It was a bruxism emergency. He'd left his mouth guard at the bar last night, and apparently they threw it away. They must have thought it was a big horseshoe of hardened chewing gum.

I'm fucking so getting fired, he said, swiping in, out, in.

II (M) ii: Waiting in everyone's in-box was this message from IT, sent out at 9:11 a.m.:

> Dear Staff,
> Yo . . .
> I will be making administrative changes to your systems today. I'm going to be connecting to your desktops remotely, so don't be freaked out if/when your mouse starts behaving erratically and windows start popping up! I need to make sure everything is flowing and need to pinpoint problem areas. Hopefully in a few months we won't be having as many crashes etc.
>
> I will do my best to be as unobtrusive as possible and not interrupt your workflow! The changes should only take a minute or two, in most cases, though in some cases I might need a little more time. (I'm also trying to weed out this latest virus.)
> Any questions, please let me know ASAP—
> Later dudes/dudettes,
> Wynn in IT

II (M) iii: *What happened to Big Sal?* asked Laars. He disapproved of Wynn's casual greeting, the surfer sign-off. His inner Bert kicked in.

Laars had imagined that there was potential for further

bonding with Big Sal, but alas. It wasn't worth dwelling on. These IT people came and went, much like information itself.

II (M) iv: Lizzie said she got an e-mail from Jill, who was writing from an Internet café in Sebastopol. She was there with Ben for three months. None of them knew who Ben was, or to be honest where Sebastopol was.

At least she *thought* the message was from Jill. The e-mail address was cryptic and the message was signed *J.* Maybe it was from Jenny, or Jason for that matter. But the tone sounded more like Jill's.

Pru said it was the return of the repressed, but she said that about everything.

In her carefully constructed reply Lizzie mentioned the discovery of *The Jilliad*, relating their appreciation of that precious document. But the message bounced back.

Lizzie called up the original e-mail again and noticed that her name was actually misspelled *Lizzy* and that there was an attachment: a bizarre request for money involving a spendthrift uncle and a hospital in Burkina Faso. She wasn't able to read the whole thing because her computer crashed.

II (M) v: Grime left a message for the Sprout on Lizzie's voice mail. *I'm at the airport,* Grime said, speaking quickly between squawks of echoing terminal announcements. He was extending his vacation.

II (M) vi: The transcription of *The Jilliad* was nearly complete. Pru basically took over the last third. Now she was trying to track down the books that the quotations came from. But Google and Amazon searches failed to turn up any of the titles or authors cited. Lizzie asked a librarian friend to try more specialized lists for the texts in question, but without success.

<u>II (M) vii:</u> Crease was working on Excel when he suddenly lost control of the cursor. He flipped over his mouse for answers and the red light streamed into his eye. He wondered if he'd develop superpowers like Henry from HR, or at least 20/20 vision.

The cursor zipped about wildly for a while as if tied to a horsefly. Then it slowly floated to the upper left corner, cruised to the upper right, and twirled across the middle of the screen in a languorous figure eight.

When Crease tried to return to his spreadsheet, the arrow remained inert. Then he remembered Wynn's memo.

He waited to see what would happen. After about a minute, the arrow rose again, clicked through to the Web, and started calling up sites from his browser history. Each screen lasted for barely a second—assorted news sites, some blog about Indian food, Craigslist, Amazon. Then a succession of unfamiliar URLs filled the address field. Wynn was taking the browser places Crease had never seen. Most of these were horror movie sites. Some were porn sites. One was a fansite constructed around the heavy metal band Dio.

Finally it was over. The mouse was responding. He found the spreadsheet cell he had been working on. He positioned the cursor and double-clicked. Then his computer crashed.

<u>II (M) viii:</u> Her research exhausted, Pru was forced to come up with a new theory: Jill had simply made up all of the books quoted in *The Jilliad*. She hadn't planned to read up on the rules of the game, for her own future benefit. Nor had she really been critiquing the way these sorts of books were written. It was all a lark, pure invention. And the new haircut was just that: a new haircut. *A bad one, too,* added Pru.

They imagined Jill during her last days: bored to tears in Siberia, drowning in misery, aware that her career was grinding itself to dust. She'd messed up somewhere along the way. No one wanted her. No one even wanted to *look* at her. She was just trying to distract herself before the deathblow came.

Lizzie asked what this meant, in terms of their plans for *The Jilliad*. Pru sighed and said that now its value as a work of outsider art was virtually nil. Its main appeal—*its heterogeneous, magpie nature*, as Pru had once put it—had vanished completely. You *could* think of it as a piece of fiction, she explained, but no one would want to read it.

Lizzie didn't see why that should make any difference. But Laars was happy. *The Jilliad* wasn't supposed to be read in the first place, after all. *So anyway, I guess I'll take it back now,* he said.

That's the other thing I meant to tell you guys, said Pru. *It's not in my desk anymore.*

I don't understand.

I mean I think someone stole it.

II (N) Voice Recognition

<u>II (N) i</u>: Rumor flowed from one cubicle to the next, like water poured into one corner of an ice tray, spilling over to fill every mold.

It was said that the Californians were basically going to get rid of everyone, from top to bottom, and sell the machines for scrap.

It was said that they were doing it gradually for the sheer sadistic pleasure of it, and that they liked to tell companies that a third of the employees would remain. This encouraged amazing feats of self-promotion, all sorts of entertainingly vicious one-upmanship.

They'd done it before, in Boston, Cleveland, Nashville.

It was said that the Sprout had been interviewing for jobs as far away as Eugene, Oregon. It was said that Sheila was on the verge of leaving him.

It was said that K. was fired because she was a lesbian.

It was said that one of the Californians was also a lesbian, but the kind of lesbian who hated other lesbians.

It was said that because the company had lost so many people, this year's holiday party would include guests from the other offices in the building, which had also shed personnel. Maybe the whole building was cursed. This had the makings of the most depressing holiday party ever, held at a new club downtown with a retro-chalet motif.

Worst idea ever, said Pru.

So they would share the party venue with a bunch of strangers. Only Crease was happy, for it brought up the distinct possibility that he would finally get to see HABAW for a period exceeding that of an elevator ride.

II (N) ii: The following Monday, Crease didn't want to talk to anyone. Rather, he *couldn't* talk to anyone. He'd lost his voice over the weekend. *A weird bug,* he sputtered. There was no pain, just an inability to speak in his normal register. He could produce either a gasp or a very deep monotone, incapable of affect. Both were totally creepy.

He sent e-mails detailing his condition on an almost hourly basis.

I wish I'd taken sign language, he wrote. He remembered a movie in which a guy had gone mute and had to write stuff down on a chalkboard he kept around his neck.

When Pru ran into him in the hall, he tried to speak, but the air caught futilely, a miniature gale welling up in his throat. He went low for one syllable, then switched tracks abruptly. It ended in a disastrous screech. Some of them wanted to comfort him, clap him on the back, but there was the fear of contagion.

II (N) iii: By late Tuesday afternoon his voice was slightly better, but he still avoided talking. He smiled a lot and nodded. He was turning into the Unnamable. On Wednesday his voice had come back. He talked a little too much, mostly about HABAW and what he'd say if—*when*—he saw her the following evening. Everyone weighed in on which lines sounded best. Laars and Lizzie said they'd help out if necessary. Crease insisted he'd be fine. He debated what to wear. He thought a beret might provide a rakish touch, but the others asserted their veto power.

II (N) iv: Grime was keeping a low profile, walking around his desk with his wireless Glottis headset, mumbling away. When Lizzie brought a fax over to him, he raised his eyebrows devilishly but kept muttering, with the unpleasant suggestion that he was dictating hostile little thoughts about her.

Pru thought it might be useful for some of them to distract him while one person snuck onto his computer and looked at what he was saying, but she couldn't find any volunteers for the mission.

II (N) v: Laars claimed to have overheard him say, *So this is what I've learned from Operation JASON.* He tried to linger and listen, but Grime saw him and clammed up.

II (O): Slippery Slope

II (O) i: The holiday party was held at Schüssmeisters. Lizzie and Laars took a cab together straight from the office at 6, figuring they'd get in a few drinks and head home early. No one was in the mood to celebrate, but if they hit the open-bar window, it wouldn't be a total loss. Crease needed to go home and change, as he found his sweater-vest too humdrum, but some suspected it was to pick up his beret. Pru was meeting her date somewhere first and said she'd join them later. Everyone wondered who her date was and suspected she wouldn't show up. Nobody had spoken to Jonah all day but when Lizzie e-mailed he replied he'd come by later. He needed to finish some schoolwork.

I don't want to freak you out, Lizzie was saying to Laars in the cab, *but I was thinking that maybe it's not a good thing that K. was fired.*

How could it be a bad thing? Lizzie could be too forgiving sometimes. It was endearing but exasperating. *K. was the one who fired Jenny,* Laars said. *K. can pretty much rot in hell.*

Yes, but don't you see? They've moved from the Js to the Ks. And there are no other Ks. I think we're next.

Lizzie was like the queen of unwanted information.

<u>II (O) ii:</u> When Lizzie and Laars arrived there was a grand total of four other people milling around. They kept an eye out for Jules. This must have been his new place—the trisyllabic name, the '70s-lodge decor. Ski poles and antlers decorated the walls, and period fondue sets were being set up on the back table. The music was a little off, though: a dour hip-hop number with half the words bleeped out.

They ordered drinks at the bar, or rather the T-Bar, and went over to meet the four people at the center of the room. One of them was the bar's designer, who was holding a pair of goggles and explaining the philosophy behind Schüssmeisters. An accountant from the telemarketing place and her husband feigned interest.

The fourth person was Grime.

Ever since the advent of the swipe cards, Laars had wanted to make Grime confess to his duplicity. But upon seeing him, he couldn't find the words. What was done was done—and if Grime was beginning to call the shots, it was better not to provoke him.

Laars was also reminded of Grime's religious experience. He just wanted to keep as far away as possible.

Lizzie was looking at the ground like she'd lost an earring. The room was filling, the volume level rising by the minute. She wondered if she'd see Jack II or Jill or Jenny, though of course they hadn't been invited.

Laars entertained an absurd five-second fantasy that Maxine would appear and he'd sweep her off her feet, or vice versa. *Laars, I've always thought you were totally hot.* Was that what she would say? He couldn't get the voice right, couldn't hear her in his head anymore. *Laars, I'm so happy you're here.* A little squeal of delight. No. Yes.

He'd ended the vow of chastity a while ago, of course, though in practical terms this did not mean much. He went to the men's room to practice smiling. He popped out his mouth guard. *Oh Laars, I love it when you smile.* There was a restroom attendant, and Laars knew he'd feel obliged to tip him at least a buck, though all he was doing was looking in the mirror. So he washed his hands with a great quantity of soap and accepted not one but two paper towels from the attendant. He patted the mouth guard dry and put it down by the sink. Shockingly, he didn't have any singles in his wallet—just a twenty. He apologized for the lack of small bills and departed without leaving a tip. The attendant didn't say anything—to him, Laars no longer existed.

Laars wondered if he'd soon have to take a job like this one, now that the firing squad had worked through the *J*s and the *K*s. For karma he should have left his twenty but realized he might need it later for a cab.

II (O) iii: Crease and Jonah arrived at the same time. When Crease gave his coat to the girl, he revealed his bravura wardrobe change: a contemporary iteration of an old-fashioned skiing sweater, in red and green, complete with a huge white snowflake knitted on the chest. It was the sartorial equivalent of comfort food—the perfect complement to the Schüssmeisters aesthetic.

Except that *Jonah* was wearing the same thing, the vintage version. He'd been buying stuff from thrift stores lately, checked work shirts, varsity jackets. His beard was amazing.

Crease contemplated cabbing it home and changing to his previous outfit but decided to stand his ground. There was room enough for two '70s-redolent snowflake sweaters. But his confidence was seeping away and his throat started feeling funny again.

The girl brought back his coat-check stub and he could barely gasp a thank you.

II (O) iv: Laars said he was getting déjà vu. He couldn't put his finger on it. Maybe every holiday party recalled holiday parties of yore. Lizzie said she experienced something like déjà vu but not exactly—more like an out-of-body experience in which she saw herself talking and nodding and drinking, and thought that it wasn't real, that it was a dream or even some play that she'd been assigned to review. She had problems with the dialogue and the lighting, but some of the costumes weren't bad. In lieu of her traditional pens, tonight a dark lacquered chopstick held her hair in place.

Was Grime already trashed? He was having volume issues, and slurring issues. They'd never really seen him drunk. He was telling Lizzie and Laars and two random oldsters from the eighth floor that he sometimes got the urge to say things that were entirely inappropriate, just blurt them out for no reason. Sometimes, Grime said, he wondered what it would be like to walk around the office naked, or to talk only in Spanish, or to impersonate a woman.

Normally this would be TMI, but Laars and Lizzie counted themselves as getting off easy. The eighth-floor strangers were nowhere to be seen, having backed away and fled for their lives at some point during the oration.

Everyone was afraid of Grime.

II (O) v: More people entered Schüssmeisters, to persistent sluggish reggae. The Sprout took off his hat and made a bee-line for the T-Bar. They glimpsed Pru shedding her coat and handing it to her date, who took off his fedora and went to check everything in. He was bald, wearing bright red suspenders. He looked friendly and repulsive, like a giant baby. He looked familiar. Laars studied them as they went to fetch drinks, and suddenly it hit him: *Pru's here with the Original Jack!*

Crease brooded at the bar, silently cursing Jonah and the copycat sweater. The Original Jack gave him a bear hug and they talked. From time to time the Original Jack would tilt his face to the ceiling and laugh. Laars observed all this. Crease could be amusing but he was never *that* amusing. Pru wasn't even laughing. She did look unbelievably great, a trick of the light perhaps, but a good trick.

II (O) vi: *Buddy!* said the Original Jack upon seeing Laars, which made Laars suspect that he'd forgotten his name.

Laars received a slap on the back followed by a bear hug. Then the Original Jack gave Lizzie an even bigger bear hug. Lizzie was never a fan of the Original Jack, and she didn't so much return the hug as let it wash over her.

The bad thing about the hug was that the Original Jack's beefy right arm swung too far beyond Lizzie and his college ring hit Laars in the mouth. It made a dreadful noise, like a mug dropped in a sink.

Over the Original Jack's apologies, Laars began to say he was fine. Alas, he couldn't quite formulate the sentence, as part of his tooth had fallen out.

Oh, said Pru. *Oh wow. Oh no.* She gave him her cocktail napkin and went to get a hundred more. Blood trickled down his chin as his upper lip ballooned. He went to the restroom to check out the damage, the bit of tooth still rolling around in his mouth. He secured it to one side with his tongue. Did dentists reattach teeth, or did they just give you a whole new one? Blood dotted the sink. The attendant was in no hurry to help. He was taking his time, groaning at the prospect of significant scrubbing with no promise of a tip.

<u>II (O) vii</u>: *It was good to see that guy but I feel shitty about his tooth*, said the Original Jack. *You know who it would be a blast to see? Maxine. The Maximizer. Where she at?*

She got fired, said Lizzie.

Right.

The same time as Jenny.

Bummer.

And Jack, the other Jack, added Pru.

Question of the evening: Now that Jack II no longer worked with them, could the Original Jack go back to being plain old Jack?

II (O) viii: Crease went to the men's room to inspect his throat, not sure what he was hoping or dreading to see. He was so absorbed in his recurring malady that he didn't see Laars leaving for the night, hand pressed to mouth, his lingering chastity in no immediate danger.

Crease croaked a request for mouthwash to the attendant, who produced a bottle even before he stopped talking. After freshening up, Crease reached in his pocket for a tip, then realized that touching money would compromise the germless state of his freshly scrubbed hands, possibly slowing the healing process.

II (O) ix: Pru spotted Jules mumbling in the corner and waved him over. He was unrecognizable, wearing tinted glasses and a ski hat and chewing nervously on a toothpick. He looked a little like the character who gets killed in the first few minutes of a cop show, to be discovered in the morning by a fresh-faced paralegal on her way to the subway. The Original Jack gave him a minimalist hug. Lizzie shook his hand, which felt weirdly cold and dry. Like Crease, Jules wasn't talking much. He spoke in short sentences, tried to get by with nods and gestures. The Original Jack explained to people that Jules's therapist, the strict Brentian, now wants him to *think* only in French, even when they're not in session.

It's pretty radical, said the Original Jack, clearly impressed.

The whole thing was confusing to Grime, the newcomer, who wandered by, twirling his martini glass by its stem. *You!* he shouted at Jules, who jumped and maneuvered behind the Original Jack's body. Grime laughed and caught Lizzie's eye and began, she thought, to hypnotize her. Was he beckoning her to follow him? Yes. No. Yes. Lizzie was bored, but was she *that* bored? She shifted her weight from one small foot to the other.

II (O) x: *Look*, said Pru to the Original Jack. She pointed to a slender figure.

The pretty one?

I think that's HABAW.

HA-wha?

As Pru explained Crease's obsession, her date clapped a hand to his forehead. He knew her from night school. They'd been in the same advanced statistics class over the summer. *I should totally hook Tracy up with Crease*, said the Original Jack. It would be his good deed going into the new year.

As he went to greet Tracy, the Sprout came over. Pru wanted to follow the Original Jack but thought it would be rude to dash away from her boss.

The Sprout started telling her a story about Jonah, but then stopped.

I feel like we've had this conversation before, he said.

When?

I don't know. Last year.

II (O) xi: *Are you Chris? I'm Tracy.*

Was he dreaming? What was going on?

Your friend Jack said you used to be a teacher? she said, indicating the Original Jack. *I used to teach, too. Never any good at it!* Crease looked back at the Original Jack, who was over by the bar, making enthusiastic head motions and giving Crease the double thumbs-up.

Crease gulped. It hit him. That exquisite British accent—that perfect face! *HABAW!*

Unreal, tingling joy clashed with sheer terror. Here she

was, talking to him. Teacher—what was she saying? She used to be a teacher? Like him? Maybe she said *preacher.* The words were simple, he knew, yet he could not crack their meaning. He took a breath, just managing to fend off a wheezing bout, and called up one of the two dozen perfect opening lines that he'd developed over the past few months. He put down his drink and opened his mouth confidently and said: *HHHHHH-HHHHHhhhHHH!*

<u>II (O) xii:</u> Lizzie returned to where Pru and Jonah were talking.

What's the matter? asked Pru.

I think—I think today was the day.

For what?

For Grime—his—you know.

She stared ahead at nothing, at the lights in the window. *I think he's trying to make me crazy so I'll resign.*

They saw Grime heading to the exit, slowly, even hobbling a little. People gave him a wide berth.

Lizzie said, *I wish this year would end already.*

I think you said that last year, Pru said.

II (P): I Don't Understand

<u>II (P) i:</u> The next morning people got to the office late, some so late that it wasn't even morning. It was a holiday tradition. But this time, for the first time, there was that evil little swipe-card box waiting for them on the wall beside the elevator.

<u>II (P) ii:</u> Laars was able to wake up early and go to the dentist, who put a temporary cap over his broken tooth. He'd left his mouth guard in the restroom at Schüssmeisters, but he wasn't

going to bother trying to get it back. At least his lip was down to its normal size.

II (P) iii: Pru got off the elevator and swiped through, or thought she did. The box was unresponsive as usual. No click, no beep, no sign that the card had left any impression. Out of nowhere she raised her leg and connected with a solid kung fu kick. Her heel hit it from the side, knocking it loose.

Oh shit.

It hung to the wall by a single nail and swung for a sickening second.

Nobody had seen what happened. Pru instinctively slapped the Down button. The elevator opened immediately and she went back in, back to the lobby, and back up to four again, a form of time travel. She would start her day over and everything would be okay.

II (P) iv: Grime was obnoxiously chipper that post-party day, Glottis headset on, great power as he paced. He had his smug face on, his hair in some semblance of order. He tried to talk to Lizzie but Lizzie wasn't talking to him. Every time he came by she was on the phone talking or pretending to talk with Pru or her mom or Liz, the secretary of the Californians.

Grime had the swipe box in his hand, shaking his head. *This was all Russell's bright idea,* he told no one in particular. When Laars made a coffee run at two he saw that the box was back in place.

II (P) v: Crease contemplated loose ends. No one wanted to tell him what had happened, or must have happened, between HABAW and Jonah, who appeared to be absent today—Jonah, his alleged friend.

It didn't matter. Crease could imagine the scene. He'd spied them leaving together while cowering, voiceless and impotent. There had always been something untrustworthy about Jonah.

He passed Pru in the Red Alcove and took a seat among the catalogs and magazines. He drifted asleep as the women talked, inhaling the perfumed ads, his head almost but not quite on Pru's shoulder, then almost but not quite on her lap. Pru went back to her desk as he started to softly snore.

Time melted away. He felt a blanket about his shoulders and wondered, *HABAW*? *Could it be . . . ?*

He struggled to open his eyes, nabbed the foggiest glimpse of someone moving away. Not a woman, no, but the Unnamable, shuffling, mumbling. Crease managed a smile of thanks, tucked the blanket tighter, and sank back to sleep.

II (P) vi: Lizzie was trying to type something as loud as she could so she didn't have to listen to the sound of the Sprout swearing in his office. Something was definitely wrong. Were the Californians on the warpath? Every so often he'd ask her for a phone number, a printout, in a tone he might have used if asking for a new job, a new life. Most of the things he wanted were things she didn't have. She was trying to go through Jenny's old files, both paper and electronic, but it was all an impossible maze. She tried a global search on the network, and her computer said: *I don't understand.*

A little bit later it sounded like he was flinging books across the room, the famous Sprout syllabus, the contents of the most boring bookcase ever stocked. She heard paper ripping, muffled snarls, desperate laughter.

Hoo-hoo. Hoo-hoo.

Now Grime's voice was on the Sprout's speakerphone. The volume was too high and the words got so distorted that Lizzie couldn't even make out his accent.

<u>II (P) vii:</u> Laars tried to do some work for about ten minutes and then decided that the day was shot. He was too restless. He was happy about his repaired tooth. The loss of the mouth guard was liberating. He rewarded his good mood by going online and buying three hundred dollars' worth of assorted gear, and bidding another four hundred on more things he didn't have space for in his apartment.

I totally suck, he said. He took himself down a few pegs on the Ernie scale and canceled all the orders. He hoped he would be outbid on eBay, except maybe on the vintage tracksuit.

As the afternoon dragged on, Laars craved contact, gossip, pointless chat. Wasn't that the one good thing about being in an office? The human connection. It almost always beat being alone, except when everyone got so negative that you wished they would just shut up, which lately turned out to be most of the time.

There wasn't anyone for Laars to talk to at the moment. Jonah was nowhere to be found. *Jonah! With HABAW!* Who knew his beard was so attractive? Laars was seriously impressed. He rubbed his chin and mulled over his own beard potential.

He kept walking through the silent office. He didn't like hearing his footsteps echo.

Lizzie sat at her desk with the phone clamped to her ear, nodding but not saying anything. Crease was deep in slumber.

Laars went to find Pru.

At her cubicle, the Unnamable was making neat piles. There was a blue dumpsterette, half full. A broom and dustpan.

What's going on? Laars asked, forgetting the man's muteness.

Pru's computer was on but the screen was blank—no words, no icons, just a field of gray. A plastic postal-service bin the color of skim milk held a stack of files. An abandoned knitting project had been tossed ignominiously on the trash heap: a glove, brown yarn with a touch of sky blue. Laars noticed that Pru had accidentally knit only three fingers.

Pru, he said to the Unnamable. *The girl who sits here—*

The Unnamable stopped sweeping and shook his head slowly. He slid his thick hand over his heart, and Laars could see, for the first time, that the Unnamable lacked a finger.

The Unnamable made an erasure movement across his mouth, to mark that what followed was secret information. Then he pointed to the end of the corridor. A light burned in the distance. Laars started walking, winding through the labyrinth at the center of which Grime resided.

<u>II (P) viii:</u> Later Laars called Lizzie on her cell. *I don't even understand what just happened*, he said. *I think Grime fired Pru.*

II (Q)–II (Z): DELETED

< *III* >

REVERT

TO

SAVED

FROM: mailer-daemon@jobmilla.com
TO: jonahhh@jonahhh.com
RE: DEAR PRUNE

The following message was received by mailer-daemon at 21:11 on
Fri May 19 and could not be delivered because no username "Prune"
exists.

Tip: Check the address. Make sure you meant "jobmilla.com."

Do not reply to this message.

‹end of automatically generated message›

‹original message follows›

—

Dear Pru—It feels weird writing a letter that's a *letter*, rather than a
drunken 2 AM e-mail (my usual *métier*), all lowercase and punctuation out the window, and doubly weird writing to someone I don't
even write drunken 2 AM e-mails to anymore, but my management
style, I learned at the retreat, is all about following hunches, giving
in to chance, throwing crumpled paper at the wastebasket by the
door and thinking *If this goes in then the answer is yes,* and so I figure
there must be a reason why, after deciding five minutes ago to break
my forbiddingly stringent nondisclosure clause, I typed "Dear Pru"
rather than "Dear Lizzie" or "Dear Crease" or "Dead Laars" (that

should be "Dear"); and though past performance strongly suggests
that I'm not to be trusted, I'm hoping that if this letter ever gets to
you—if, for starters, the words I'm typing now are being preserved
in anything close to legible form, and if I have the balls, once my
ordeal's over, to actually print the thing out and drip it in the mail,
the old-fashioned way (for *drip*, read *drop*, and while we're at it, let's
change *balls* to something less TMI; this is probably a fantastic time
to explain that I can't risk backpedaling and correcting stuff, for fear
of losing my place, because what's been happening is that for the
past three hours—more?—I've been stuck in the elevator, suspended in utter coffin blackness somewhere between the third and
fourth floors—listening to the cables quiver, and every so often
hearing the distant shouts of emergency workers saying, *Hang in
there, buddy!* or what sounds like a very heavy wrench clanking on
assorted beams as it tumbles into the abyss—and even though my
laptop's on, it sheds no light, alas: when the elevator jerked to a
stop, my feet left the ground, and a second after I hit the floor I
heard another thump—the computer had slid out of its case and
was making a disconcerting clicking sound, like it had turned into a
large and talkative insect; it was warm to the touch, so I waited for
the noise and heat to die down—counting out loud, pacing my cell—
and put my mind to more pressing matters, but in the end the thing
was busted: Shortly after I flipped open the screen, cracked my
knuckles, and opted to write a letter to you rather than mull over
whatever appalling spreadsheet Lizzie'd e-mailed this morning, the
document started to dim: I could still make out characters forming
beneath the pixilated fog, but right as I finished typing "Dear Pru,
It's weird to write a letter that's a *letter*," the whole screen went as
dark as the air around me, making it impossible for me to see these
words; luckily, I'm better at this sort of blindwriting than most,

thanks to my regimen: most mornings, after getting to the office early, veins jumping with that good hippie-truck coffee, or a slug of "Sexpresso" from the Bad Starbucks, I'd type with my eyes closed, five minutes of *first thought, best thought*—it focused me, and at the same time re-created a little test my father would give me as a kid, seating me at his impressive, meticulously maintained Shalimar (which was this antique typewriter that gleamed like gold—they show up on eBay once in a blue moon, the Sasquatch of writing machines, the price so high it aggravates my vertigo), on which I'd peck out whatever came into my head—advertising jingles, lines from cop shows, names of presidents—an exquisite corpse for him to pore over and correct, like the teacher he was; and all this Ninja touch-type training is coming back to me here in my metal, or is that mental, cocoon—for example, I know that part of the trick is to establish a rhythm, to imagine the text as a musical score that I simply have to perform, even though it doesn't exist till my fingers touch plastic, and if I have to pause I should count it out like a rest, imagine measures of those black bricks hanging like bats from power lines for as long as I require, and meanwhile find the little nipples on the F and J keys, return my fingers to the home row, and pretend that I'm ten years old again and communing with the Shalimar; it would be useful if I were, say, the sort of savant who automatically keeps track of how many keystrokes he's deployed, registering every letter, space, and comma in some otherwise underutilized fold of the brain, so that he—I—could cleanly zip back via the arrow keys and change *drip* to *drop*, the *Dead* to the *Dear*, switch *balls* to *courage* or *moxie* or that Sprout special, *cojones*, expelled with gruesome south-of-the-border gusto; and while we're discussing keyboard matters, I should mention that last week, after months of touch-and-go performance, the period key on this dilapidated craptop gave out completely, just a few days after the Return button decided to jam, which means that I can end each sentence with an exclamation point!—or a question mark?—but what I'll probably do is just let it all unfurl in one soul-sweeping go, the better to dislodge every memory of this place, every possible bit of evidence in my favor, so that you can see why I had to do what I had to do; and I have the dim realization that this parenthetical account of my current blindness and typographical deficiencies has long ago eclipsed the letter proper—so let's wriggle out of these braces before we do anything else)—I'm hoping, Pru, you'll at least read through to the end and hear me out despite my jumpy style—*Hang in there, buddy!*—because without the prospect of contact my present situation leaves much to be desired: I'm sitting on the rubbery, vaguely canine-redolent elevator carpet, eating the last of my oat bars, forcing myself not to panic, blocking out visions of roaches creeping down the walls, ignoring the phantom whiff of fumes seeping from the shaft—and thus I'm dedicating what's left of the battery (I should have a good two hours, though I have no way of telling the time) to run roughshod over the nondisclosure agreement and fill you in on what's happened since you left, how it all went down with the dreaded unseen Californians, with Operation JASON and Grime and the Sprout, all the latest hair-raising and literally insane developments—not to lure you back but simply to suggest the possibility that I might, in fact, be something other than your garden-variety *backstabbing creep* (as Laars, in the midst of his daily ass kissing, said you once called me, not that I could blame you) or a run-of-the-mill *royal prick* (Crease passed that one along)—and not a day goes by when I don't dream up an alternate sequence of events, one in which I can look into the future, like Henry from HR, and instantly comprehend how all the pieces will interlock, letting me sound the alarm earlier, so that everyone is saved—so

that, for starters, you're no longer *not here*; I can't help thinking that
if I'd been just a *little* bit sharper, and had put two and two together
a few weeks sooner, I could have prevented all the backbiting and
bad-mouthing, the nervous second-guessing as we broke up into
ever-shifting groups of two or three, theorizing with hushed voices
in remote cubicles or outside in the smokers' purgatory, or at the
Good Starbucks, or over one drink too many down the street, basically placing bets on who'd be next to get the shaft, the boot, the ax,
the short end of the stick, the old heave-ho—the gallows humor
reaching the end of its rope as people trotted out the Nazi imagery
(Crease saying Lizzie'd make a good lampshade, Laars pointing to
the ceiling: *This is where they drop the Zyklon-B;* though come to
think of it, did you ever notice how the dividers of the abandoned
four-unit cubicle clusters resemble anorexic swastikas when seen
from above?)—but I should stop telling you what you already know
and tell you something you don't, the story of Grime, which was
weirder than any of you thought (even Lizzie doesn't know the half
of it), and which my legal gag has stopped me from revealing—
I guess I'll start by going back a few months, after we'd come to know
Grime a bit: One night I returned to the office after my class let out
(the class where I was learning how to be an effective manager,
taught by someone who was like a carbon copy of the Sprout, even
down to the soap-clean smell) because I'd forgotten a file—I remember it was Halloween and I just wanted to get home, avoid the horde
of skeleton pirates and Martian reapers and hobo vampires who
were already whooping it up ominously on the sidewalks, in the
streets, spreading out in all directions, as sirens and car alarms rang
out in sympathy, in a demented symphony, but en route to my desk
I heard a curious cross fire of shouts coming from somewhere *inside*
the office, and I went to investigate, treading softly, cupping my

ears to capture every sound, until I was right by the abandoned former conference room around the corner from Grime's lair, the one with the empty propane tanks and furry bundles of computer spaghetti and the single *Psycho* lightbulb: I caught a glimpse of Grime and the Sprout (I'd know that back-of-the-head anywhere) and slid into the shadow of a huge blue trash bin, keeping a sliver of sight line, hunkering down so close to the action that I caught the sickly smell of Sharpies as Grime wrote *Operation JASON* on the dry-erase board and put slashes through the J, A, S, and O, so that only the N remained unmarked, its corners razor-sharp—his handwriting was as cleanly formed as his typing was muddy—and he told the Sprout that the last phase of Operation JASON was about to begin and that he needed his full cooperation in order for it to work; to stumble on the homestretch would be fatal, would erase the progress made in the previous months, to which the Sprout replied, in his most conciliatory voice, that of *course* he'd do everything in his power to ensure the smooth implementation of Operation JASON, which he realized was an important component of the plan, but he didn't know, frankly, if things had to move *quite* as rapidly as Grime required—he knew Grime had his work cut out for him as the CRO (the *what?*), but he felt that there were some things even the most radical, ravenous CROs needed to be aware of: We (*we!*) were down to our last reserves—this wasn't too long after Jill was let go—and it was crucial that no more staff get terminated for the next six months *minimum*, a demand that had the undesired effect of making Grime laugh, with such spite that the Sprout immediately backtracked with *Four months?* and Grime slapped the dry-erase board so hard it rattled and he shot back, in a murderous monotone, *Why don't you do your job, Russell, or I'll do it for you*—at which point the Sprout (so weird to hear him called *Russell*) clarified that he

wasn't trying in any way to interfere with Grime's job (he understood *completely* the gravity of the situation, the delicacy, the need
for discretion—which must have been why they were meeting at
8:30 in the evening) but simply wanted to put a word in for a few
people, a stay of execution for those who most needed sparing; but
when Grime demanded to know *which* people, specifically, required
such treatment, Russell—rather, the Sprout—hedged until Grime
told him to rank us, from most valuable to least: I couldn't see the
half of the board that the Sprout was using, but felt sure he was
placing me either at the very bottom of the roster or at the very top,
so that either way, fingered as the worst or hailed as the best, I
would stick out—too obviously useless, or else too much in the
Sprout's good graces: That reeks of paranoia (or narcissism—it's a
fine line), especially since on the surface the Sprout and I got along
just fine, with both of us always ready with a bit of banter, a level of
friendliness that even survived my weeklong suspension two years
ago (a penalty levied after I protested his suspension of *Crease*,
itself a result of Crease defending *Jules*, after Jules "accidentally" set
Jill's computer on fire, to replay for you the whole sparkling chain of
events)—the weird thing was that the Sprout had opened up to me
in the first place, years ago, because he had inexplicably gotten it
into his head that I had a daughter, and thus assumed I was a family
man like himself, and as time passed it became harder to inform him
that I was in fact not only childless but morbidly single, and it became near impossible to come clean after he confided in me that he
and Sheila had been trying to adopt a second child, a little girl from
China (a companion for their first child, half black like me), but the
paperwork was taking so long—a practically satirical series of lost
files, misaddressed forms, and crucial information mangled on both
sides of the translation—that what had started out as a yearlong

process had now become a three-year nightmare, and though it was awful to admit, they no longer wanted the child they'd picked, the girl they'd gone all the way to China to see, because she was now speaking Mandarin and (on their second visit) displayed only cursory interest in them, if not complete disdain, and additionally had replaced her button nose with an enormous honker and her oyster-like ears with satellite dishes, facial developments so dramatic that they suspected that perhaps this was *not the same baby*; the adoption agency, alas, had quickly caught on to their cold feet and begun barraging them with daily faxes and an impressive array of threatening documents in triplicate, insisting that the Sprout and Mrs Sprout were legally bound to take the child, while at the same time intimating that the actual adoption would not happen any time soon, probably due to their bad Yankee behavior, and as a consequence they would be required to send ever-increasing monthly "maintenance" fees to the agency, in addition to the regular book-keeping charge, and it had occurred to the Sprout that perhaps he and Sheila would simply be raising Ting-Ting this way, remotely and with regularly spaced infusions of cash, for the rest of her life, a perfect child of bureaucracy: So I had this intimacy with the Sprout, based entirely on a misunderstanding, but I'm certain that he thought less of me after my suspension, that I'd become one of *them* forever (his *them* is pretty much a mirror image of our *us*), someone, like a Jules, who would always have an ax to grind—who would, upon finishing the satisfactory grinding of one ax, refuse to relax but instead go back into his cavernous ax storeroom and haul out another one that needed a new edge; and to be fair, I can see why he'd think this about me—that's the brutal thing about his job (which is now, technically, mine): You have no allies, no one you can count on even until the end of the day—definitely not among the people you supersize (that should be *supervise*—I'm starving) and especially not your assistant, who's filing away each of your idiocies, fodder for some future grievance or gossipfest, so that you start thinking maybe it's not such a bad idea to keep your door shut, and keep a bottle of something in your lower-left-hand drawer at all times, an emergency flask, and in the interest of full disclosure I should mention that after lunch—my usual lonely Friday lunch—I visited several establishments, including a liquor store, and since I never made it to my floor, let alone my desk, I've got the booze here in the elevator, and for quality control purposes *only* I've been taking sample nips every so often to wash down the oat bar and give me the courage to finish this letter to you and have it spell out all I want it to spell out, even in this scattershot, parentheses-prone, train-of-thought-jumping manner, but the side effects are that my vertigo is swirling full force, like the whole car is swaying (which maybe it is), and I suspect I will need, *very soon*, to pee—let me retreat from the verge of TMI and just say I think it's going to be a long time before I get sprung from this cage: as I stepped into the elevator a few hours ago, I heard a series of shrieks that only later (as the doors of the carriage walled me in and elevation commenced) did I consider might have been *whistles*, and as I wondered, dimly, if this was the warning for the water-main blasting that they'd promised us months ago (and as I tried to recall if I'd just heard *two* whistles or *three*) a deep rumbling began, so profound it was impossible to determine whether it was coming from below or above, from within the building or without, and a moment later the elevator's ascent halted with such force that I was airborne for a second, then slammed against the back wall, flung forward against the doors, and gently, mockingly placed into a sitting position on the floor (the impact triggering my cell phone to take about fifty pictures of the inside of my pocket, draining the battery from two bars to none), and as an arrhythmic rain of metal and masonry drizzled down on the carriage, my laptop case was ripped out of my hands and pitched to the side; watching the lights above silently go out, I thought, very calmly, *How strange, the building is collapsing*; after a few seconds I opened my eyes only to realize they *were* open, and peered into the dark, calling *Hello?* to make sure I was absolutely alone—that someone very small and very quiet hadn't somehow slipped into the carriage when I did, because a companion would be unbearable in such close quarters as these: the proximity would ratchet up the tension, our reassuring noises to each other would just serve as a nervous prologue to some monumental freak-out involving weeping or fisticuffs, hyperventilation round-robins—not to mention how quickly two people would eat up the available air in these forty square feet (I've paced the perimeter, Pru, put my hands on every surface, punched every button a thousand times)—it's so easy to lose your way in the dark, even when there's nowhere to go: You become all ear, shaping every sound into a clue, and now I'm second-guessing what I heard last Halloween, huddled outside that chamber of horrors: Grime, the CRO, asking the Sprout if he had the slightest idea (*idear*) what the initials stood for, not waiting for a reply: *That they've brought in a Chief Restructuring Officer, Russell, means the structure here is beyond fucked*, it was a *failure* that needed immediate sorting, this last segment of Operation JASON would require cutting one person from the sixth floor and three people from the fourth, he said, and as the Sprout sputtered *But how are you getting these numbers?* Grime launched into a hissing litany of everything wrong with the company, from the shade of the stationery (too bright) to the division of labor (*redundant* came up again and again), a critique somehow ruthless and thorough-

sounding yet oddly abstract at the same time, like this was the nth
minor variation on a speech he gave to all his clients/victims, pep-
pered with constant references to himself and his title—*CRO, CRO,
CRO*, over and over until those initials were beaten into my head,
and I started thinking of Grime as that cleverest of birds, *the Crow*, a
mimicking thing with a fondness for flesh: *I'm here to make sausage,
Russell*, he was saying, *toss all the useless bits into the grinder, so
what comes out the other end'll be halfway palatable*—on and on,
and at last the Sprout stammered that it was hard for him to think
of the office as a butcher shop or a slaughterhouse, because this
place had a *reputation*, a history, an *iden*—— but Grime cut him off:
See, it's not even a slaughterhouse—I'd be ecstatic *if it were, I'd be
over the bloody moon, because then there'd be fresh meat hanging
about, ready for market*—he was thwacking the dry-erase board for
emphasis—*and I wouldn't need to be scrounging for tasty bits, come
back, come back here you insolent—!*—as the Sprout slipped out,
and I drew my limbs in, shrinking to the size of a period, holding my
breath as our depleted leader trudged past, certain he'd see me;
after fifteen seconds, with the Crow cackling acidly to himself, I
started to trail the Sprout, sticking to the walls like a shadow, and
could swear I heard him muttering, as the elevator doors closed on
him: —*fucking dead, I am so*—, a tone of shot nerves and life in sudden flux, and I almost lunged for the button to follow him but instead started formulating a plan, or at least a *structure* for thinking
about what was happening in our office: by the end of the night,
having fled that haunted house and elbowed through the goblin
throngs and picked my way across the vomit-soaked sidewalks, I resolved to keep the Grime episode to myself for a while, and to keep
my distance from you—from Crease, Lizzie, Laars, from all the other
doomed cattle in the slaughterhouse—in order to figure out what

Grime's Crow role was, and the nature of the power he wielded over the Sprout; in the weeks to come I could see that behind Grime's scatterbrained, laid-back, technophobic front, he regarded us as utterly disposable—indeed I began to suspect that he'd wanted us gone from the moment he took roost, which (I later discovered) was *not* after Jill got fired up in Siberia, as most of us assumed, but in fact nearly a year earlier: I know that this chronology will mess with your head, but I'm certain that it's correct—I'll explain how I pieced it all together, but for now just imagine Grime not as we knew him but as *The Crow*, working unobtrusively out of a spare cubicle in Siberia, gathering information about us in monkish silence, not even using the phone or computer, receiving reports from Maxine and the Sprout via the Unnamable, our soft-soled messenger, everything set up to be as quiet as the tomb; I imagine Jill would sometimes see mysterious shadows on the Sheetrock, or hear a footfall, a sigh, a muffled laugh, and imagine she was losing her mind; shortly after Halloween, I began to follow the Crow's movements: Twice a week he would take a cab to a bar in what I assumed was his hotel in midtown, where he'd meet with the Sprout and "K," our mysterious fifth-floor ice-queen overlord, and nurse a club soda while they ordered too much Scotch and revealed more than they should have, encouraged in equal measure by the midtown-hotel-bar, drinking-on-the-clock ambience and sheer psychotic terror, because to them, he was never the chummy, rumpled, winningly incomprehensible Brit who introduced himself with *Call me Grime*, but Gordon G (for *Graham = Grime*) Knott, a fact I deduced because the Sprout would sometimes call him *Gordon*, and "K" would always address him as *Mr Knott*—Gordon Graham Knott, I discovered easily enough, was one of the most notorious CROs in the business, held in awe for his brazen restructuring tactics and bottom-line results, a

man despised not just by the legions of felled employees left floun-
dering in his wake (who surely numbered in the thousands) but by
the more conservative players in his field; aware of his reputation, I
burned some shoe leather tracking the Crow's flight to the midtown
bar, noting the deteriorating mood and the glacial silences and who
picked up the bill (always the Sprout or "K"); occasionally, I'd take
personal days for these stakeouts, watching from a balcony seat as
"K"—shaken and sometimes *sobbing* I think—left the bar for Grand
Central and her train home, and though at first I assumed the Crow
was staying at the hotel, on the company's dime, eventually he'd
make his way back, alone, to the office, never to reemerge, by which
I mean: It became evident that Grime was not one of the hotel's
long-term guests but in fact the inhabitant of a forgotten corner of
Siberia, where he would order in meals, groom (after a fashion) in
the surprisingly spacious janitor's bathroom, have his clothes picked
up and laundered, and sleep on the luxuriously long couch: as far as
I could tell, our office was his home, lending weight to some of the
glowing praise for "Gordon G Knott" that I found online (a "take-no-
prisoners" "workaholic" who "stays obsessed for months on end");
around this time, my burgeoning, dare I say glorious, thickets of
facial hair, begun on a lark, now offered useful protective coloring, a
full-fledged beard joining the serviceable mustache: I was going into
deep cover for this mission, slipping into a new identity, sort of in
the way Grime had masqueraded as a colleague instead of showing
us his full Crow plumage: *I too would become unfamiliar,* so that
gradually in his mind I'd be hard to place, ever strange, anonymous;
some nights, slaving away, I'd take a break, put on a blue work shirt
of my father's, the one I keep on the back of my door, and walk by
Grime's desk, sweeping or spraying, scanning the ground for any tell-
tale detritus, whistling like a loon, looking for all the world like a

blokey member of the custodial staff; I knew my disguise was working when one evening, about a week before the holiday party, he
called out to me as I pushed along my mop and pail, whistling
"YMCA," and asked if I'd mind *nipping out* and *pinching* some *fags*
and beer—I grinned—*and possibly some herb?* he added with an exaggerated drag-sucking sound, if I were the sort who knew how to
come by that sort of thing, and with a friendly wink he peeled off a
crisp C-note, which I proceeded to convert into the requested provisions, and so we drank to each other's health, laying into a Thai
spread he'd had delivered, and I lingered for a while, listening more
than talking, sipping the beer rather than downing it, fake-inhaling
and letting the pot go to work on him (the same way *he'd* drink nothing stronger than club soda at his meetings in the hotel bar); after
comparing English and "Yank" terms for various household items,
controlled substances, and sexual positions, he began telling me the
story of his life, a *real corker,* as he put it, from his beginnings in a
sooty corner of London, son of a traveling ventriloquist, to his big
break as a messenger boy at a barrister's, climbing the ladder, *learning the ropes,* a year of business school, bad drugs, a *tempestuous
marriage* to a British starlet, divorce, rehab, America, *a whopper of a
second chance,* harder drugs, harder rehab, relearning the ropes,
learning altogether *different* ropes, pilgrimage and spiritual awak-
ening on the subcontinent, all culminating in his current runaway
success as a CRO: *What you'd call a freelance hatchet man,* is how he
put it, and spoke of the pleasure he took in breaking things down,
determining what worked and what didn't, amputating, say, what
was to all appearances a company's most successful branch in order
to stimulate activity in the others—*Fear is the greatest administra-
tor,* he said, and *Business is the best art,* like he was giving me, your
humble mop boy, exclusive entrée into the mind of a restructuring

legend; but the odd thing was that most of his insights—even his asides—were ones I was familiar with, right down to the wording (*My only rule is there are no rules* or *In principle I am against principles*), as if every chapter in his gripping life story, indeed every syllable he spoke, had already been quoted or described so many times in the sources I'd read, online and on paper, that it was like encountering in the light of day some artifact first uncovered in dreams; I subtly steered the talk away from twice-told biography and asked him about the actual mechanics of getting an entire company to skip to your tune, even as it's collapsing, and the very *idea* of ye humble broom pusher evincing real curiosity about such rarefied doings delighted him, compelled him to divulge what might be called his aesthetic side, or perhaps his penchant for S & M: *The deep dark impenetrable mystery of it all is that once they hire you, they want to be punished* and *It's as easy as hitting Delete* and *There's a button called Execute for a reason* and *The beauty is that everything goes through someone else*, this last one meaning that his name, crucially, never surfaces in these affairs: The Crow soars high above the fray, and not a single scrap of paper bears his signature, he bragged; he avoids e-mails if at all possible; eccentrically, he always gets paid in cash while his operation is in progress (did I dare ask about Operation JASON?); he never gets identified by his victims as the executioner but instead works through as many of their preexisting nemeses as possible (the Sprout, "K," Maxine), each of whom receives often contradictory information and must, at his insistence, sign off on every demotion and pay cut, carry out every suspension and firing—attend to even the smallest bits of unpleasantness—while he keeps obscure, for as long as possible, any link between himself and the gore; then as soon as he obtains his objective—upon satisfying whoever hired *him*—he takes wing, disappears for months, even a year, with every trace shredded away, until he lands another assignment at another wheezing outfit, giving him a fresh chance to orchestrate the same chaos, to tighten the bottom line; one strategy that he was especially fond of, *a bit of a risk to be honest but well worth it,* involved elevating a low-profile drudge to his second in command—the most dramatic effects, he said, resulted when the worker was someone whom at least 75 percent of the others secretly disliked ("Oh, they hate *me*," I said), and better still if it was someone who'd been with the company for a long time, a lifer whose chances for upward progress had dropped to nil; you get someone who has deep institutional knowledge and harbors deep reserves of pent-up wrath and ambition; at the same moment that this person, this unlikeliest of candidates, was anointed, the Crow would fire whoever was in charge, a maneuver he executed without any malice (he said) but did simply because sometimes a sharp shock is just what's needed, a *major disorientating episode that triggers the adrenaline* (I'd come across these phrases before, in industry reports explicating his philosophy) and forces all the people in the middle to find their bearings and in most cases do their best work in years, which is what he planned to do to our *shambles of an office* (how many other offices, I wondered, had he described as *shambles?*); he said one never feels too bad for the people knocked off the top—they were inevitably *arseholes* anyway and *What goes around comes around, eh?*; we discussed at great stoned length the theory of office karma, and I joked that maybe *I* could be put in charge— after all, I'd been around for nine years!—which made him laugh so hard he spit his drink, and he pounded his desk and said, *Why not? The janitor! Why the bloody hell not?* — — — — — (OK, Pru: I just spaced out for five minutes, maybe closer to ten, sitting here with the computer exhaling hotly and my eyes still drinking in nothing,

fingers tingling with the promise of connection, and now I can't remember the last word I wrote, only that I was describing my lovely
little tête-à-tête with Grime, and that it ended with a question—
so I'm regrouping here, in the safety of these parentheses; even
though I'd intended to get this all down in one single serpentine sentence, *allowances need to be made*, as the Sprout used to say, and so
I'm allowing myself a little breathing room, these parentheses like
little emergency lungs, because it's getting hard to concentrate:
Someone's shouting at me through a megaphone, it's hard to tell
from what distance or direction, and I can make out maybe every
third word—JONAH zzzhhhh ffffff! CAN zzzzhhhh *krrrr?*—but I
don't recognize the voice at all; maybe it's someone from the rescue
team trying to convey the important information that he's going to
pry open the top or drill through the sides or blow the thing up—
Sorry, buddy!—but whenever I call out, there's no response, and
though enough time has passed for me to be reasonably confident
that no catastrophe is imminent—there's ample air, the carriage
hasn't crashed to the ground, the structure has yet to crumble—
I'm still going to race to finish this letter, Pru, and I'm making a
solemn vow right now *not* to drag this document into the trash once
I've escaped this vertical casket and got my craptop screen fixed but
to hit Print and get your snail-mail address from Lizzie or—if you
two *still* aren't talking—the Original Jack, or just look it up (Sharmila
Maternity—you have no idea how many times I've Googled you—
and I've been meaning to ask: So you're designing baby clothes now?
using hemp?) and *send it off* before I have a chance to reflect, recon-
sider, retreat; I don't think I can even risk proofreading it, despite
the errors this sort of eyeless composition inevitably invites, indeed
I fully expect that skeins of scolding red understitching have
wormed their way through this document, courtesy of the MS Word

grammarians—and I would insist that proofreading in general is a sign of *bad faith*, faith being not irrelevant to the situation at hand, for right now the only thing keeping me going, the only thing stopping me from charging at the walls until I knock myself out cold, is faith that you'll read this to the end)—and now it's time to jump out of the parentheses, Pru: Part of the elevator roof *has* come off, I believe, because a cool column of air now penetrates the carriage; my shouts (*Hello?* and *It's Jonah* and *I've been here since three!* and again *Hello?*) still go unanswered, echoing up and down the spine of the building, and I wonder if the maintenance squad has simply decided to take a break until morning; or maybe it's just that the heat gets turned off in the evening—is it evening, now?—which reminds me to tell you how I figured out that Operation JASON had nothing to do with our old friend Jason (by the way I heard from him recently, a random e-mail that said he'd been working in Spain but couldn't stand it and is now working in Philly but can't stand it): I was at home on Christmas, paying an overdue Con Ed bill, thinking about that EB White passage you once showed me, back when you were new here and we used to talk for hours—the swooning bit where he says that it's the native New Yorkers who give the city its stability, and the commuters who give it a daily tidal rhythm or something, but it's those dreamers from elsewhere, the striving poets and wannabe circus performers and so forth, who power it with enough heat and light to dwarf the Consolidated Edison company—I always liked that bit, even though if I think about it for half a second it seems like the purest BS—and I noticed on the bill the small bar graph that shows kilowatt-hours per month, and the first five letters along the bottom were J, A, S, O, N, for July, August, September, October, and November—and I had a eureka moment, as the blood left my face: I flashed back to that mysterious, anxiety-stirring Post-it that Laars

saw on the Sprout's desk, the famous note that ran *JASON—DJ,
FM/AM?* and was signed *—J*, and realized that it hadn't been a cryptic message from some unknown J still among us, but just the
Sprout's idle scratchings, punctuating the initials for the remaining
months (DJ = December, January) with no reason beyond simple distraction, but it dawned on me, looking at the bill, that the kilowatt
bars were high in the summer (reflecting air-conditioning expenses),
then low for a bit, and now that it was winter they would rise again
(heating, more lights)—and I wondered if this corresponded at all to
how many people were being fired here, if every month the number
of folks let go by the Sprout (at the Crow's command) was *somehow
determined by the electricity bill*—and I recalled how the Crow put
slashes through the letters of JASON, on that dry-erase board on
Halloween, and I knew in a flash that my guess was correct, that he
was playing a horrible game with us, that he could have just as easily
rolled a pair of dice, and the Sprout had *no idea* that this was how
Grime was coming up with his figures, he was simply following orders, firing whomever Grime indicated (maybe even submitting "reports" to the Californians on Jack II and Jenny that said they weren't
pulling their weight, feigning shock when they got rid of Maxine);
and of course after J, A, S, O, and N came D, December, and I got thoroughly depressed, thinking for the hundredth time how the last
time I saw you was at the holiday party, a/k/a the night before your
firing, and wondered if it could have played out differently, me in my
incredibly studly sweater with the giant snowflake, as you'll recall,
and you in a green cocktail dress that basically gave me a seizure
whenever I looked your way—whenever I so much as *thought* about
it, and reminded myself that you were there with the Original Jack,
whom I was surprised to see; so demoralizing was his presence, and
what I presumed was your affection for him and his shaved head

that when a buxom elf (there is no other description) interrupted my unseasonable stewing with a jolly *Hey, Snowflake* and asked what I was drinking, I thought she'd asked what I was *thinking*, and so I told her about you, your way with words, your hair and your smile and your purposeful walk, and as her eyes glazed over and she was on the verge of leaving, dissolving back into the crowd, I decided to change course—I became that rarest of creatures, Charming Jonah: what can I say but that I've been living with a default vow of chastity for longer than I care to divulge here, a span that would turn Laars green with envy, then pink with laughter; I guess one of the *major points* I want to get across today (tonight?) is that it took me a while to realize that *this was the girl from the elevator,* Crease's Half Asian British Accent Woman, his "HABAW"!—this somewhat, no, I would say empirically *extremely* attractive (but not Pru-caliber attractive) denizen of the seventh floor whose actual, human name is Tracy, or *Trace*—and all that happened was that, about an hour later, we stumbled into a cab, stumbled into a karaoke bar, where with some of her oddly gnomelike but genial co-workers we stumbled through the repertoires of a half dozen '80s haircut bands and too much treacly Bacharach and an ill-advised foray into Aerosmith, occasionally passing the mike to members of a very good women's volleyball squad from Duluth; then Trace and I stumbled crosstown, stumbled uptown, stumbled to her doorstep, where I learned (as she *tugged my beard*) that Trace was leaving in a week for, my God I can't remember, Prague or Paris (one of those pesky P cities) for a month or a year or forever; and then I, Jonah, incapable of taking a hint, said *So nice meeting you!* and shook her head and then very much *alone* and without so much as a phone number or e-mail address (and basically broke from karaoke) stumbled down into the subway station— did I mention *alone?*—and to think that *this* was the night I last set eyes on you (a glaring, totally pissed off you, no less) still kills me, makes me want to *turn back time* in the manner of the poet Cher, whose vocal stylings were replicated ad nauseam that evening, but instead what happened was this: I took the next day, the Friday, as a personal day, to rewhite my aging bloodshot eyes (my big discovery, possibly the discovery of the century, is that *nobody keeps track of personal days*: before he was fired, Henry from HR sabotaged the program so that these babies get filed differently than vacation days, and basically *never get tabulated*, ever), and when I returned to work late on Monday, you were long gone, and Crease wasn't talking to me because of my HABAW transgression, and Grime was looking awfully satisfied about something, and Lizzie had profound crying-too-much rings around her eyes, and when I finally got the story of your dismissal, I couldn't understand why no one was *doing* anything, why everyone was so quiet; I know in the past we'd write letters of protest when someone was fired or suspended, and for the most part the Sprout would nod and file away these strongly worded beauties or probably just slip them into the shredder, and neither side would speak of the matter again (the civilized thing had been done, points of view had been exchanged, and it was time to move on), but at some point we stopped even this pathetic performance—we didn't do it for Jill, and the Jenny-and-Jack II joint firing (not to mention the elimination of Maxine) had sapped us of all power: When Lizzie told me that *Grime* had fired you, had stepped out of the shadows and swung the ax in person, I knew it was time to build a case against him—to shoot down the Crow, or get shot down trying; I knew I needed an ally, and the kicker of course is that you were the only one I could think of who might pursue this with me till the end; I took a walk around the block, left messages on your cell, pondered my next move: I couldn't confront the Crow just yet—

I needed him to *not know* me for a little while longer, to see me and think *Janitor with Beard*—and so instead I decided to hear what the Sprout had to say; but when I got back to the office and pushed open his door, I found him lying on the carpet, tossing and catching a racquetball with one hand, a lit cigarette in his mouth, with the rest of the pack on his chest and a pencil holder for an ashtray, as the winter air from the open window swept up the smoke and subverted the fire alarm; I sat down in his chair and asked him point-blank if he truly believed that getting rid of you could be construed as a smart move—as anything but a horrible mistake—and he sent up a cone of smoke and stopped the ball tossing and sighed, *Not my idea*, both a confession that he wasn't the one calling the shots and a blanket refusal to answer any more questions, and I figured that the best way to get him to talk was to not say anything—the equivalent of giving him a blank sheet of paper and locking him in a room (or maybe trapping him in a stuck elevator with a laptop and telling him *Type whatever*)—and sure enough, after his cigarette burned out, and the rubber ball lay balanced in his open palm, he said, *I'm going to have to take a hit on this one* and *Let's gut it out for the next few weeks*, he said, *Try to turn it around* and *Need to get on the same page*—and it wasn't clear whether these were things he or I was supposed to do, but I figured this patchwork of vague determination was enough of a welcome mat for me to start asking questions again as he lit a fresh cigarette; *I don't know* was his refrain uttered in a range of tones—prickly, insulting, sympathetic, but mostly just exhausted— as the wind died down and the smoke kept creeping toward the ceiling and the ball was going up and down again, and when I asked if *my* job was on the line—if I was going to be replaced by someone handpicked by the Californians, or if my position was simply going to be erased, the way all the rest had been—he replied, *I can't tell you be-*

cause I don't know—if I knew, I'd tell you, or if I knew and couldn't tell you, I'd tell you that I knew but couldn't tell you, but the truth is that I don't know, and so I honestly can't tell you—it may have even gone on for a few more hairpin turns, an instant Sprout classic, but at that point I realized that the Sprout himself was not long for this office, and strangely enough a little tentacle of grief began working its way through me, and as if hoping at least to salvage his health, I schoolmarmishly suggested he put out the cigarette, advice he didn't heed, instead telling me that it was his first cigarette in nearly a year—he'd stopped because after he fired Jason or maybe it was the Original Jack (*You're all sort of interchangeable*, he said; I laughed), every time he went outside to light up, those already on the sidewalk outside, in the Republic of Smokistan, would be in the process of stuffing their cigarettes into the ash stand, or grinding them out underfoot, barely grunting hello as they made their way back indoors—the first few times this phenomenon didn't register, and when he noticed it he wanted to prove to himself that this avoidance was indeed deliberate, so whenever he'd see a group of us moving toward the elevator (*this* elevator! *this* prison!) to go out for a smoke, he'd take the next one down, and observe how we'd immediately extinguish our freshly unboxed cigarettes and go back upstairs, or just start wandering off in all directions, leaving him stranded by the buoylike receptacle with yards of dead smoke rising from its hole; and after he recounted this heartwarming memory, he seemed to relax, lighting a new cigarette before talking about "your friend Graham"—to get it off his chest, I think, telling me how Mr Gordon Graham Knott had simply appeared one day, like something sprung from nightmare, with his alien accent and rumpled clothes and cold eyes like iron, marching into the Sprout's office to announce that as the CRO, appointed by the Californians to resusci-

tate the company (after the comical brainless *botch* the Sprout and
"K" had made of it), he would essentially be running the show from
now on, and it was up to the Sprout whether he wanted to stay on-
board and help implement the plan or step down immediately—
Grime didn't care which, but he had to decide quickly: And so the
Sprout (*I'm a family man, you of all people know what that's like,
what the responsibilities are*) threw his weight behind this stranger
for survival, but he'd also nurtured, he confessed, a vague hope that
together they would dethrone "K"; unfortunately, as the Sprout was
about to divulge, it seemed, the exact nature of his beef with her—
something we'd all been wondering about for ages (had she screwed
him over? had they just plain screwed?)—the smoke detector went
off, the sprinklers overhead kicked in, and he jumped to his feet in
one gymnast-quality maneuver, throwing his jacket over his computer while barking for Lizzie to call Bill in maintenance (I remember
her shouting above the din, *But Bill's been fired!*), and I escaped with
just a sudden slash of dampness along one arm, like I'd been cut; anyway, after that meeting I think the Sprout *really* began to lose it—
working with the shades down and the lights off, misplacing things,
putting Post-its on his shirt pocket, walking out of his cave and then
spinning on his heel and walking right back in, leaving incredible
messages on his home phone (*Russell, this is Russell! And I seem to
have—forgotten what—I wanted you to remember*), and wearing the
same tie every day to work—the Canada tie, with the red maple
leaves falling against the white background—and the same bright
green coat and those strange blue pants that look like jeans but
aren't, with a black Velcro belt: He looked like something that could
have been drawn with that funky pen I bought in Mexico, the pen
that Grime borrowed from me one night when we were scarfing
down a sausage pizza over at his desk, illustrating a particularly

tricky restructuring concept—those fat pens, did you ever use them
as a kid?—a little awkward to hold, voluptuously stocked with *four*
colors to choose from, giving you the insane flexibility to write in
blue or black or red or green—an instrument that I'd been using regularly and to great advantage: toggling between shades to annotate
with distinction, or suddenly turning a memorandum into a *rainbow*,
cross-referencing, expanding the dimensions of the written word
(didn't you tell me Faulkner wanted to print *The Sound and the Fury*
in four colors? is it weird that I remember pretty much everything
you ever told me?) and this is totally jumping ahead, but not long
after Grime's demise (which I swear I'm going to tell you about, in
gory detail—it'll definitely be worth the wait) I walked by to see if
the pen was still around: I found it underneath his desk, jammed
into the spiral of a beat-up notebook in a plain black cover, which
piqued my curiosity—as far as I could tell, it was some sort of homemade compendium, gathering pearls of wisdom taken from a huge
assortment of business and financial-fitness books, titles you've
never heard of (*Are We Having Money Yet*, *An Inside Man Thinks Outside the Box*, et cetera); my favorite was a passage from *Ernie and
Bert in the Boardroom*, which basically breaks down all of humanity
into fun-loving, chaotic *Ernies* and anal, fussbudget *Berts* (I think I'm
a bit of both—what the author would call an *Ert*—and *this* document, pecked out in the digital dark with a full bladder and too many
ideas, is like Ernie and Bert colliding: Part of me can't wait, needs to
shout out everything I know and feel in one enormous sentence, but
another part is working to keep it all together—navigating the punctuation, making sure that the grammar's well-oiled, that the com-
mas and dashes bear the proper weight, that even though the focus
shifts and the shape gets blurry, I don't just chuck it all and give myself over to the entropy of fragments—because I need to write this

right now or I'll *never* write it, right, and what would be the point of
sending you a hundred disconnected paragraphs, shattered stanzas
of woe and complaint?)—but in truth most of the quotations in that
notebook were insipid, even contradictory, in their advice, and written in a nearly illegible hue of orange pen to boot, like an ink made
out of fruit juices; the *later* entries, curiously, were written using the
cartridges of my Mexican four-color (blue followed by black followed
by red followed by green, in strict, Bert-like rotation), in what was
clearly a different hand altogether, all razory angles; I slowly realized that the final five pages of those business-book gleanings must
have been written by Grime: computer commands (*Revert to saved*)
alternated with the bromides of yesteryear (*The man who buys the
hare gets to make the fur-lined hat*), periodically appended with the
title of a book that kept changing, from *The Plumber's Manual* to
CRO: Memoirs of a British Plumber to *Making Sausage: A Master
Butcher's Five Essential Rules* to *Restructuring* to *Corporate Ventrilo-
quism*, yet seemed basically the same, as if by adding his own
thoughts to those already in the notebook—what I came to think of
as the *Notebook of Power*—the Crow could confirm his legendary
status, or give focus to his own rags-to-riches saga; my thoughts
were interrupted by the Unnamable (who'd become *even stranger*
since you got fired, by the way, his eyes glazed, his humming louder
and sadder and creepier) and in this desolate corner of the office, at
this late hour, he was free from the mute niceties the workday demanded: he *hurtled* toward me, Pru, intent for some reason on grabbing the notebook; when I pulled away from him, the black cover
came off in his hands in crisp staccato, and my vertigo kicked in: I
tripped backward, reeling about the barren cubicle, still clutching
the now-coverless notebook, which I rolled into a tube and tucked
under my arm like a football player as I spun to the right, spun the

desk chair at him, and dashed down the hall, jumping with adrenaline, a '70s cop-show sound track going off in my head as he moaned (*hhhHHH!*), clutching his shin: It was absurd and scary all at once—I heard limping but still rapid footfalls behind me as the Unnamable gave chase, so after gaining a corner, I swung open the stairwell door with as much noise as possible, throwing in a few false steps, of decreasing volume, to lay down the aural evidence that I was zipping up the stairs (though I wonder, in my blindness: Was he *deaf?*); then I tiptoed to the next corner, waiting until he took the bait and slipped, wheezing, through the narrowing gap, before I headed to the elevator with my Mexican four-color pen and the *Notebook of Power,* which I took home and read straight through, and by the time I was done, all the mercenary mantras and leadership one-liners had taken on a soul-crushing weight—I felt short of breath, bitter, unhealable, close to *tears,* Pru, because something so shameful and heartbreaking was swinging into consciousness, cutting through the fog of forced forgetting: On the surface it was simply that part of me—the "successful" part, the part that sees the future as a rosy thing, a/k/a the *false* part—wanted to inscribe two rules of my own onto those pages, two things I rarely articulate to myself but which I simply *know* and abide by, at all times—two rules my father handed down at a tender age: (1) Never let anyone see you yawn; and (2) Never say *I'm sorry;* the first rule is crucial because a yawn tells people that they're boring you—you're essentially broadcasting your indifference, and soon, without quite realizing it, they'll hate you for making them feel dull, and even if they *are* as fascinating as a toothpaste ad, you should never suggest, even in this silent and unconscious manner, that such is the case (in truth I find myself in the impossible position of having to shed another worker next week—and I think it has to be Laars, who exhibits his tonsils rather too freely these days); the second rule, in some ways the opposite (in that you deny rather than appease), was never adequately explained to me, though I now understand it as a tactic to gain an imperceptible psychological edge, finding other socially acceptable phrases to express regret or sympathy without taking on even that small, almost meaningless amount of accountability packaged in those two words, *I'm sorry:* What's weird is that I should have listened to what my father thought at all, or rather that I should have taken these laughably small *life lessons* and internalized them to such a degree (do parents realize that even a stray comment can live inside their kids for years?) and distorted them into *rules to get ahead,* as arbitrary as anything set down in the *Notebook of Power;* my father was intelligent, kind, elegantly educated—but in terms of money he was something of a loser, thinking about it more than he would admit, while entirely lacking even the baseline bloodlust that could help him achieve his modest financial aims: He taught French at a prep school outside Baltimore, a school with an impressive crest and inflated reputation, which I was able to attend because he was on faculty—free tuition was the one significant benefit the teachers had (provided they spawned); the salaries ran shockingly low, and so three times a week I would watch my father dismantle his tie and hang up his blazer at the end of the teaching day and drive over to A Sporting Proposition, where he'd don a bright green polyester bib and transform himself into the twentieth century's least effective sneaker salesman, not really measuring people's feet in the right way, never prodding potential customers into buying footwear, and on several occasions (I would sometimes go with him, ostensibly doing my homework at a price-tag-covered table in the stockroom but actually listening, listening) saying enigmatically cruel things along the lines of *If you think sneakers can change you, then maybe*

sneakers can change you, often proffering, too, a few sentiments
about the sweatshops where said footgear came from—not even to
push a political point, or to deepen the customer's inner life, but because he was so brain-decayingly bored, and humiliated at being so
bored, at having sunk to such mundane depths—nudged by circum-
stance, perhaps, to take on this most anonymous of jobs, but forced
into it only by what he must have seen as a failure in character, lack
of gumption, moxie, balls—a job in which you're constantly in contact with, and have to feign expertise about, the part of the human
body closest to the ground, a site for corns and bunions and odor;
but some days, and then some years, it was too awful to think of him
taking off the old-boy attire he wore to conjugate pouvoir or whatever and putting on that wretched vest-cum-bib, part of his mind,
too, endlessly outlining the book he always wanted to write on
Baudelaire (I catch myself in a protective lie: he wanted to focus on
an acquaintance of Baudelaire, whose name was barely recognized
even among interested scholars, whose name completely escapes
me now), the other part slipping space-age-flavored cross-trainers
onto people's feet—it was a total mind-body split, high and low;
when A Sporting Proposition shut its doors for good (and could it
have been anything other than the gentleman-of-leisure name that
made him apply there in the first place?), the closing happened so
fast that he didn't have time to change out of his vest, and he wore
it home, where it hung on the back of the closet door for ages; every
so often he would say he should get rid of the thing, but somehow
that green vest stayed put; as the years passed he grew ashamed of
his tenure, but also perversely proud to have been, in his words, the
worst salesman in the history of the store, if not in the annals of commercial footwear, and through the school grapevine I knew that he
actually drove a few customers away without even opening his

mouth: Every so often a student would go to buy sneakers only to encounter his French teacher, and the mere thought of discussing soles and arches with someone who'd be grading his vocabulary tests was so unsettling that he'd duck out as invisibly as he could, though some kids of course—real winners, these guys—would sit with smug smiles, gleefully undecided, making my father go into the storeroom for box after box, his armpits darkening with sweat, as my classmates enjoyed the slow social torture they could exact; after A Sporting Proposition went belly-up, he decided, *Now I will write my book,* and turned the basement into his book-writing bunker, taping notes to the concrete walls, gradually moving all the relevant texts from the upstairs rooms to the simple plank shelving belowdecks, carefully polishing the Shalimar, that bright brass tank of a typewriter, stocking up on the machine's peculiar, rose-smelling ribbons, spending what seemed like hours sharpening a quiver of pencils, clearing off his desk in order to concentrate while my mother brought him mugs of tea and one cigarette every two hours, which she'd only let him half-finish; but his day job left him too drained—it wasn't rocket science, as they say, it was teaching high school French, but he was not the kind of man who could give the lessons by rote, and the additional duties every teacher at this rather fancy school, this school with seemingly baronial ambitions, had to take on—from overseeing a table of students at lunch to monitoring study halls to advising the recalcitrant to coaching sports teams (or in his case, *managing* them, whatever that meant— filling water bottles?)—all had a deleterious effect on his ability to focus on his book, this book about some forgotten friend or half friend or half-hour acquaintance of Baudelaire, this nonentity whose name my father (I remember now) wouldn't even tell me, as if to protect me from the curse it had placed him under (though I wonder, was she or he perhaps a prostitute?), and I remember in those months after he lost the shoe-selling job, he would say, *I just need to make it to the summer,* meaning he just had to keep working on the book until the long summer break (J—J—A, in Con Ed speak), when he would have the energy to *attack* the project from morning till night, or through the night and into the wee hours, whatever schedule worked best from day to day—but the summer turned out to be the hottest on record, and lethargy set in as the electric fans spun, and by Thanksgiving he had lost all hope; the writing had been going terribly—had barely been going at all; the only thing that he had to show for it was his gaunt face and seething mood, a new potbelly, a consumptive cough; just as bad, or worse, was that the money from teaching alone was being stretched thin—even I could tell that my clothes were looking shabby, and though I knew I shouldn't complain, I did, first to my mother, then to my father, in a shouting manner that came out of nowhere, completely surprising me and my parents—the shock couldn't have been greater had I produced a handgun and shot out, one by one, the windows in the house across the street; that Saturday, I went to the basement to say good morning, and to apologize, expecting to see him shuffling his notes and sharpening his pencils, and I noticed there was no paper on the walls, just a neat stack on the desk, about twenty pages trapped under an old brick, a threadbare handkerchief shrouding the typewriter; I didn't dare read what he'd written, outlandishly imagining it would be a list of my sins and shortcomings; when I emerged upstairs my mother explained that he had gone back to A Sporting Proposition, or rather to the business that had taken over the space—an endlessly aisled, blindingly illuminated drugstore—and had found a job there, a higher-paying one than the shoe-selling gig; at first I had the insane notion that he had secretly been training to be a pharmacist, squeezing in extra classes between teaching and shoe selling and book writing; but alas, he was the janitor, the *janitor,* which meant that he had to work Saturday and Sunday mornings, and on weekdays he'd come home from school and watch the news while he ate dinner and then grade papers for an hour before my mother would drive him to the store at 9, as the last customer was being turned out, and he'd wash the floors and scour the toilets and bag the trash until nearly midnight, when she'd pick him up and bring him home; on that first day he brought me a present from the 99-cent store that inhabited the same plaza with the drugstore: a mug with my name on it—except it wasn't my name because, he explained, they were all out of *Jonah,* and he knew I didn't like it when people misspoke or miswrote my name as *John,* so he picked *Joan,* which made me laugh, and I forgot momentarily about his new job, and his new, nauseating smell, a marinade of mop water and sweat, and instead I poured some orange juice into my hilarious new cup and silently vowed, smiling all the while, that I would never follow this path, his path—I would resist all temptation to *help people* or *promote understanding,* I would never teach anyone anything, reject entirely the little sad life my father had carved out for himself, one in which my mother and I were embedded: We would not think of criticizing him, and at the same time we had to bear his agonies, his genteel desperation, and that was something which just had to *stop*—yet still, still, I remember not to yawn, and I never, ever say *I'm sorry,* and it so happens that these ironclad points of conduct *have* served me well (though perhaps I give them too much credit, out of a sentimental need)—this is all a roundabout way of saying that when circumstances dictate, I can be a machine, even a monster— and here we get to the main event, Pru: The day I discovered you'd been fired—that Grime had *deleted* you—I resolved to look deeper, punch lower, rethink everything that had happened in the office over the past year; on my personal days, I wouldn't stay home but would come in early and sit at my desk, my door shut and my lights off, nursing a flowerpot-size coffee and penciling intricate diagrams, sometimes so hard that the point would break, spending most of the rest of the winter this way; on one of these I'm-here-but-I'm-not-here days, immersed in pointless activity and wasted motion, I shouted to/at myself, *SHAPE UP, JONAH!* and after a deep hum a document opened up on the screen of my computer, and *CHEZ PAJAMA!* materialized in 18-point Times New Roman; it took me a full dumb minute to realize that my craptop was still equipped with an old version of that voice-recognition software, Glottis, which Bernhard (the IT guy right before Big Sal, for about twenty seconds) had installed for me, at the peak of my carpal tunnel distress, back in the daze (sorry, *days*) when my wrists would tighten angrily even before I opened the door to my office, and though I'd never had the patience to "train" it—my words always emerged garbled (*Jonah* was regularly rendered as *Joan, ahh* and *Joaner* and occasionally *sho nuff*)—I never bothered to have the program removed; in my post-Pru haste that morning I must have accidentally tapped one of the mystical "function" buttons at the top of the keyboard, just north of Delete, and activated Glottis, which interpreted my cri de coeur, *SHAPE UP, JONAH!* as the cuddlier *CHEZ PAJAMA!*—this, of course, led to hours of experimentation, a welcome (if too early) respite from my plotting; my vertigo would wax as my statements triggered reams of Dada-ready sentences, leading to all sorts of glum *pensées* about the inadequacy of words, the impossibility of communication, and the like, but I prattled on, talking up a storm, and when I made a remark about someone (well, *you*) having a penchant for *cute clothes*, it must have registered as EXECUTE CLOSE, because a dialogue box popped up and asked, rather smarmily, *Do you want to save the document "Chez Pajama"?* the document's default title derived from its first two words—thinking back on it, had I clicked *No*, my life would be different now: After choosing to preserve my file of nonsense, I saw it transform into a little icon inside a vast folder on the server entitled GLOTTIS, to which my laptop was somehow connected and which now lay open on my screen; I proceeded to study its contents, not really sure what I was trying to find—maybe just my earlier, long-forgotten attempts at spoken-word composition, stabs at correspondence that had rapidly derailed—and as I scanned the names of the various files, a strange feeling came over me: Surely I hadn't written, or dictated, *this* many documents, during my brief Glottis phase; about a third of the names resembled the masking gibberish with which spam salesmen infiltrate your in-box (*django heartbreak liter* and *steakhouse wurlitzer divot*), and the rest were simply dates—dates which didn't correspond to my previous Glottis usage, nor to Jules's earlier stint (that is, they were all fairly recent, created within the past three or four months)—and then it hit me: These documents were the work of Grime, the only person in the office currently using the voiceware—Big Sal in IT had never bothered to set up a private folder for him, not thinking that anyone else used Glottis; and while I had no moral compunction about reading Grime's private documents, I worried that Grime might try to access one of his files and learn that it was in use by someone else in the office, so instead I opened up a doc entitled PERSONAL DAZE—what I imagined was a draft of Jules's screenplay, the one he wrote by dictation; but as I double-clicked, it struck me as unlike him to leave any Julesian traces behind (after every lunch he'd make sure all crumbs were neatly swept into a napkin, all spills were sopped up—once I even saw him picking crumbs off the *floor*), and when the document opened it was immediately clear that this was something entirely different, something that didn't originate from Jules's hand (or mouth), a massive block of insanity-inducing text that began (I have the first sentence by heart—I wish I could just copy and paste the whole thing for you): *Personal Daze here, in the vinyl face of a Parisian chastened, with everything going accordion too bland*—now what you have to do is read *final phase* for "vinyl face," *Operation JASON* for "a Parisian chastened," *according to plan* for "accordion too bland": this gives you a sense of what I had to go through, decoding pages' worth of misrecognized words; it was obvious, right from that first sentence, that I wasn't looking at Jules's screenplay at all, but a sort of diary in code, a war journal, kept by Grime, our resident Crow; the title of the file came from the first two words, *his real name*, which Glottis misheard as "Personal Daze"—and it was this discovery that shook me: Jules had said, months ago at his restaurant, that he came by his screenplay title, *Personal Daze*, because it was the mangled moniker of someone he knew, which meant— didn't it?—that he knew Grime, that he had somehow met him before, knew him by another name—as you know, Jules is very difficult to talk to these days, running his various eateries, uttering only the bare minimum of words, but that night I tracked him down at one of his establishments—Demagogue, the politically themed bar, up on Sixty-ninth—and sat him down in the back room, blocking the door with a chair, refusing to let him out until he told me Grime's real name (how had it transformed into "Personal Daze"?), thrusting a printout of Grime's Glottis document; Jules didn't look like he was going to spill the beans, and I worried that we'd be there for hours, staring ferally at each other, and that I'd have to start slapping him with the manila folder that was resting on the table; finally I said, "Jules, come on—this is for Pru," and after he asked what you were doing ("Maternity wear? You mean she's a seamstress?"), he began to unfold the story: During his last months at the office, after having been hit with a huge pay cut, Jules looked on that Jobmilla website (remember that weird commercial?) for some extra cash to make ends meet—it was the most depressing thing, he said, because he realized he had no skills beyond typing thirty not-very-reliable words per minute; still, he needed money, and found a gig moonlighting as a restroom attendant at a nightclub, in which role he proved so popular that the owner transferred him, with a big bump in salary, to Vlad's, an adult-themed space on Eleventh Avenue, where Jules did triple duty as a valet, tout, and (his newfound talent, he supposed) restroom attendant; also a few times a night he peered into the private rooms, where strategic gyrations and heavy petting were part of the menu but more intense contact, in danger of breaking state and local laws, needed to be dispelled by a rap on the jamb, a warning tattoo that had to be instantly recognizable as such—Jules's rapidly expanding new skill set included a sharp roll of the knuckles that would make the sensation-drunk client pay heed without wrenching him too far from his fantasy world: This was of course not the most pleasant aspect of the job, and in some cases the violator would ignore him, requiring further, louder warning raps and, if noncompliance continued, the quick summoning of one of the beefy security guards, who got pissy if you took them away from their sudoku; every so often chaos, even minor melees, would ensue, but Jules was never in any danger, and after a few weeks began to warm to other aspects of his job: the women were sweet, for the most part; the patrons tipped generously when he handed out towels and mouthwash; as a valet, he got to know some of them well when they came out for their frequent smoking breaks, shooting the breeze as the northbound traffic whizzed past, men of

all ages, some of them fresh out of business school, others leathery
vets, white-haired wiseguys—and before too long a few of these reg-
ulars, over cigarettes, encouraged him to start his own business, and
would eventually invest in his first venture, that toaster-oven
restaurant (Balustrade? Cellophane? Tenement?)—this was all very
interesting, but I needed him to focus: With a big sigh he said, *So this
is for Pru,* and went back to telling me about those private pleasure
chambers, and what went on there—most of it you can imagine, but
every so often—*Well, there was this guy,* middle-aged, who drove a
well-maintained but very *close*-smelling SUV, which you got a lung-
ful of when you had to park it, and Jules's boss (a melancholy barrel-
chested man called Duke, who called everyone Ace or Commander),
told him, *Keep an eye on this one, Ace—usually he's fine but sometimes he's not*—the guy had been coming into Vlad's two or three
nights a week for over a year, didn't drink anything stronger than
7UP, didn't appear high, usually just watched the main stage, but
every couple months he'd get a room, and something would happen,
something different every time—Duke had been on the verge of bar-
ring him but hoped he'd learned his lesson; then one night when
Jules was making the rounds he had to deliver his patented warning
rap, not because of any overly lewd contact but because—there was
this guy *choking* a girl; and then two nights later, it was a different
girl—*choking the guy;* Duke came around, threatening to bar him
from the premises; the next week, the man and yet another girl were
choking each other simultaneously—all of these permutations necessarily arranged in cash beforehand: this time they were gasping,
locked in a horrible death embrace, eyes bulging like grapes, bodies
flailing, the scant room accents knocked to the ground and getting
smashed by their uncontrollable stampings—and Jules barged in,
trying to pull the man off the girl (Vera, someone he'd been dating,

against Duke's advice); as two guys from security detached her (she was weeping and even in the bad mood lighting he could tell her color was off) and sat on the guy's legs, Jules went to find the man's SUV, which he'd had the displeasure of parking earlier, and left a long key mark across one side, then the other, then all across the hood, not letting the key leave the surface, even as it traveled across glass, and then jogged around the lot to let off steam, throwing punches in the air; ten minutes later, the guy came out of Vlad's for a smoke, looking calmer and a shade less ruddy, and offered Jules a cigar and a No hard feelings? which Jules, surprising himself, accepted, realizing as soon as the stogie was lit that the valet on duty must have been on break, because he was all alone in the parking lot with the man whom he'd just grappled with, the man who'd been engaging in a little mutual asphyxiation society with his semi-girlfriend (Vera was a dead ringer, Jules also said, for Maxine), and though the guy wasn't a weight lifter, he had shown impressive energy, a boundless will to try to relieve his aggressors of their facial features; self-preservation kicked in, there on the desolate pavement, and Jules introduced himself and shook his hand, at which the man said, The name's Percival Davis, call me Percy if you like; Percy asked how he got hooked up with the strip-club gig, and Jules explained how he wasn't making enough money at his office job, and so he'd found work at a nightclub through Jobmilla-dot-com (I sounded like I was in an ad, Jules told me), and all the rest, and Percy didn't know what he meant until he remembered Jobmilla's motto—humming the jingle till he found the words, What goes around comes around! (laughter); but when Jules asked Percy what he did for a living, he grew silent, and time dragged uncomfortably until the cigars were done; Percy said it was just about time for him to head out, and apologized for the fisticuffs; since the other valet hadn't shown, Jules nervously fetched the freshly vandalized vehicle and said good night, really, really wishing he hadn't scraped it up, listening to Percy whistle the Jobmilla jingle again as he drove off, and for the next few days he waited for the other shoe to drop, his appetite vanishing, notes for his last will and testament breaking into his thoughts with alarming frequency; just when he thought he was in the clear, and that he might have a future on this earth, he was greeted at the club by the news that a "Mister Davis" had stopped by earlier and left a note: The gist was that he knew what Jules had done to his car, and that the next time he saw Jules, he would choke *him*—Jules quit the gig that night, figured he'd find something else on the Jobmilla site, or through the temp agency he'd hooked up with when he first came to the city, and in the meantime keep polishing his screenplay—dictating new dialogue, revising an important heist scene—and when he found he needed a name for a villain, Percival Davis came to mind, which Glottis instantly turned into "Personal Daze," a perfect title: More than anything, Jules was relieved to be away from Vlad's, amazed that he'd even done the job for as long as he had—he was certain he'd gone briefly insane, really, and resolved to get his act together, stop drinking (especially in the mornings), work up a serious business plan for the toaster-oven restaurant he'd always wanted to run, go to the gym a little more (or even *once*)—he had faith in himself, faith in his future; so it happened that one Friday not long after his escape from clubland, while heading for the elevator up on the sixth floor, Jules saw a figure moving in the opposite direction, and his blood froze: *Percival Davis*—!!—the face was the same, a little paler, the eyebrows pruned perhaps, the hair cut short—and Jules began throbbing with the fight-or-flight impulse; in a daze he coughed to get Davis's attention, but when the man turned around, he just said *Cheers*, in a friendly

British accent (at first Jules thought he'd said Chairs), and Jules sputtered what must have sounded like a bizarre pickup line (Don't I
know you from somewhere?), losing his grip on reality, for although
this new resident of Siberia looked like Percival Davis, he smoothly
gave his name as Graham: But as he walked away, he was whistling
the Jobmilla tune, What goes around comes around, that catchy
paean to the zero-sum nature of employment and unemployment
(which strictly speaking didn't make a whole lot of sense but which
presumably tapped into people's latent belief in karma), a melody
that looped in Jules's head all weekend and into the following Monday, when he toured Siberia in terror, looking for Percy/Graham,
finding in one brightly lit cubicle things that he could have sworn
weren't there before, a mound of crumpled paper garnished with
fresh red rubber bands, a coffee cup bearing thin stains in progres-
sively wider-spaced rings, like a tree trunk, which he studied as if it
could offer clues as to when a human had last drunk from it, some
time frame to work with; but there was no one around, the Firings
had claimed so many victims up there, and the floor remained empty
all afternoon, and so he sat at his desk, anxiously awaiting a burst of
violence, a gunshot, a sudden scissor blade to the heart; over the
coming weeks he became a wreck, even less capable of work than
before—something even Jules would have deemed impossible—and
when the Sprout abruptly fired him a month later, he was secretly relieved; Jules finished his tale by saying that at first he was sure Percy
had tracked him down to the office, but now wonders if it was all a
coincidence—if during a drive in his mobile home, that scratchitti'd
SUV, he recognized our building from its starring role in that old Jobmilla commercial (all the unemployed slobs on the conveyor belt)
and decided to get a job here; his motivation remained mysterious
to Jules until I told him how Grime (as we know him) had pretended

to be one of us, an illusion sustained for all save me, ever since that October night when I discovered he was working as an outside consultant, as the CRO (Jules nodded, fully in the know, comfortable with business-world acronyms) hired by the Californians to slash away at budgets, firing people behind a protective screen consisting of the Sprout, Maxine, and "K"; but having pursued Gordon Graham Knott for several months, I was starting to wonder who Grime really was—if he was not even *Knott*, the famed chief restructuring officer, the hungry Crow, but someone else entirely; I told Jules how, when I inadvertently opened Grime's Glottis document, *Personal Daze*, I knew, instantly, that he was someone else, someone whose name *sounded* like "Personal Daze": But now that I knew he was Percival Davis, the mystery deepened—who *was* Percival Davis, and why had he taken on the character of Gordon Graham Knott (a bona fide CRO, whose name regularly crops up in the industry rags)?: Though Jules was busy with his various restaurants and bars, he agreed to help me gather information on our slippery interloper, even going back to Vlad's and quizzing the dancers and bouncers, getting the license plate number from the valet's log; what we discovered was as sad as it was shocking, and I waited for the right time to blow the whistle, but it's harder than you think—there's the question, first of all, of who to trust: even though I'd wanted to go to the Sprout with my newfound knowledge, he was deep in exit mode and visibly disturbed—every time I came to his door it looked like he'd been crying or drinking, or *punched* really, and what he said was barely coherent: half aphorisms and repetitions on a good day, but mostly mumbling, an unprovoked *Hoo-hoo!*, his eyes darting from my head to my feet like he was sizing me up for a little pick-up aikido session; I noticed that all his personal effects were gone, his bookshelves bare, his plants dead; the only thing on his desk was a large-screen computer with a tiny laptop hooked up next to it in such a way that anything that happened on the large screen happened simultaneously on the small one, and I'd watch documents blossom in duplicate, hear beeps chime in near stereo, the purpose of it all completely hidden; my fear was that if I *did* bring all my information to the Sprout, he simply might not believe me, and instead see the opportunity to get back into Grime's good graces (let's keep calling him Grime for now) by dismissing me on the spot, a preemptive action that would be perfectly legitimate since it never came from the Crow at all: But if it was difficult figuring out what to do, every day also brought new information, another piece of the puzzle, and I used more personal days to make fact-finding trips, sometimes with Jules; finally I was forced into action when, about two months after you left, Grime pulled his most dangerous stunt yet—telling the Sprout to contact a headhunter to *replace himself*: His capacity for self-debasement finally exhausted, the Sprout tendered his resignation to the Californians the next week, and the Crow perched at last, alone, in the vacated office, calling Crease and Laars and Lizzie in for interminable, hectoring meetings, either individually or ensemble, and when one of them wondered aloud (innocently? not?) why *I* wasn't there, the Crow got confused—*Who's Jonah?*—and, muttering that he thought I'd been fired months ago, he picked up the phone in front of everyone and called my extension, and I caught up with his rage on voice mail: I was to meet him at nine o'clock sharp the next morning, the tone suggesting a fatal dressing-down; things were coming down to the wire and I didn't bother to swipe out, breathing deeply as the elevator made its sluggish way up to meet me, eyeing the swipe box crazily and wondering, *What if*—and gently plucking the box from the wall, as light as a box of tissues, and in the elevator (*this* elevator!) I saw that there was *nothing in the box*, no wiring at all, no strip reader, just a few cubic inches of air, and I marveled at the sheer sadistic psychology behind the routine (I know Grime had started telling people that swiping in was the Sprout's idea, but we all knew that it wasn't): For months we'd been fretting about our hours, fitting a card into a slot so that the Californians could keep tabs on us, but it turns out we were swiping just to swipe, the whole contraption never even registering our moves—then the elevator opened and I was free: On the way home I threw out my janitor's shirt, got my beard and mustache removed by a barber in the subway station, and bought new shoes, fresh clothes, strong cologne, and a box of contact lenses, so that when I met Grime the next day I had the advantage of confusion—I could sense him wondering if he'd seen me before; as he talked, distractedly, about the terrible job the Sprout had done all these years, how a new age was about to begin, I caught a change in his thinking: though he'd never really talked to me while sober (we'd had a half dozen late-night boozefests), there was *something* about me that was familiar, and he knew that not only had I been operating under false colors but I was circling around his secret; after the meeting fizzled to a close without incident (his parting words, believe it or not, were *Keep me in the loop!*), I rushed back to my desk to call Lizzie: *Don't say anything,* I warned, *just pretend I'm a friend, pretend I'm Pru, just calling from Sharmila Maternity for a chat,* and I asked her if she could very quickly, very subtly e-mail me the contact information for whichever one of the Californians the Sprout used to talk to the most—I'd explain it all to her and Laars and Crease later; my heart was going triple time as I punched the numbers; my Californian took my call—as it happened, he was in a meeting with the others, so they put me on speakerphone, and listened, rapt, as I gave the streamlined version of what I thought was going on with

Grime/Graham/Percy, and when I was done there was pure silence—
you could have heard a pin drop anywhere between us, you could
have heard an eyelash fall in Nebraska—and then the Californians
confirmed what I had so recently figured out: They'd never hired a
CRO, it wasn't their style, they were still planning on coming to New
York and giving us the ax themselves (laughter)—and as the chuck-
les faded I got the nervous feeling that the Crow might be making
his way toward my office, so I dashed out the back stairway and in
two hours, miraculously, I was on a flight to what the Californians
determined to be the halfway point: Bozeman, Montana, where we
convened in a sub-rosa club room near the Northwest terminal, sipping a Shiraz that smelled like an expensive shoe and eating tender
venison sandwiches, juice dripping down our chins, as I told them
everything Jules and I had dug up about the man who wasn't Grime
or Graham or anyone even vaguely resembling Gordon Graham
Knott (president of GGK Restructuring)—a name that, in any case,
did not immediately register with the Californians—but the phantom of a phantom, someone with the odd name of Percival Davis,
age 42, a former midlevel management consultant who was ulti-
mately fired by a consultant, visiting from a different firm—an experience that must have made him feel like he was stuck in some
Möbius strip, or looking into a mirror and seeing his back with a
knife wedged in it, with a hand much like his own gripping the handle: on that day, three years ago, when he lost his job, it touched a
nerve, indeed his entire nervous system, and Davis snapped, walking
out on his wife and kids in New Jersey, never to return, wandering
the streets in a fugue state until repeated attempts to float in assorted fountains across the city led to a stay at Bellevue (where
I imagine him muttering CRO, CRO, CRO, ad infinitum), and once I
sniffed out the company he used to work for, a midtown outfit no

longer in existence, it only took a few minutes of online searching
to discover that it had been the *real* Gordon Knott, a silver-haired
CRO (living in splendid contentment in Greenwich) who'd filleted
Percy's former employer in ingenious ways, *turning it around* by
bleeding it dry, getting rid of Percy's whole team (a year later, after
Knott had split, the company would suddenly and utterly disappear); after Bellevue, Percy—or Grime, or whatever you want to call
him—essentially lived on the road, in his SUV, eluding his family,
working through his savings, until he decided to infiltrate our office,
concocting an accent, impersonating the very villain, the maverick
CRO, who had *deleted* his previous life—the initial aim being, I think,
to run a company aground so disastrously that the *real* Gordon
Knott's name would be dragged through the mud, though in truth
I think he simply thrived on the destruction he discovered he could
do: having bonded with our born-again security guard by pretending
to be a Holy Roller, the newly christened *Grime* coolly installed his
revamped self on the barren sixth floor, then briefly on the fifth, and
eventually the fourth, ingratiating himself with all as the affable,
floppy-haired "Grime"; smoothly convincing IT to set him up with the
necessary phone and computer accoutrements and IDs and pass-
words; commandeering the staff to do his bidding; abusing Maxine;
issuing increasingly bizarre directives to the Sprout (or as I reminded myself to say, *Russell*) and suggesting to him that by pre-
senting these decisions as his own, he'd win the Californians'
approval, and be in a strong position to displace "K"; engineering
spurious data, which he'd then present to the Sprout as justification
for eliminating employees; harassing Lizzie with scatological mus-
ings; sleeping (I think) with Maxine; driving "K" to total meltdown by
telling her to do things like *Write the program that makes you obsolete*; carefully misspelling nearly every word he typed—on and on my

tale unwound, some of it based on educated guesses, most of it entirely provable: the sum, in any case, being greater than the parts, so
that three things quickly became clear to the Californians: (1) There
was a criminal in the New York office, who needed to be removed as
soon, and with as little noise, as possible; (2) Given that I knew the
most about the situation, I would also be the one to oversee his re-
moval; (3) If I was successful, I would immediately become the new
head of operations (the new Sprout—or was it the new Crow?), re-
porting directly to the Californians: all of which made my head spin,
my dizziness hitting me even way out there under the huge hinter-
land sky with the enormous moon chalked in and the stars coming
out; it was all so confusing, because I'd *hated* the Californians, despised them with a passion, but for now I needed to compartmental-
ize, put that anger aside—so I nodded, shook some hands, received
multiple thumps between the shoulder blades, and flew back to kick
off Operation Fallen Crow, Mission Eradicate Grime, The "Personal"
Affair: In a cab from La Guardia to the office, I called the police and
explained that there was an unauthorized person in the building,
providing them with a foolproof description, and by the time my
taxi arrived on the scene the last squad car was pulling out, a captured Crow limp in the backseat, eyes shut, wings clipped; afterward
I walked aimlessly, dazed by the bloodless coup and by the warm
night, moving north and then east and then west and then north,
east and then south, west and then north again, as though circling
something that wasn't there anymore, and I was transported to a
warm night last spring, the end to a grueling day packed with aller-
gens and dread, a day on which someone was fired (it's terrible but I
can't recall who, exactly—*you're all interchangeable*): The situation
demanded that we survivors go out for early drinks, in order to ana-
lyze the murky dynamics of it all, the usual futile dissection, and the

talk drifted to other topics, Maxine's wardrobe (specifically, did she wear a thong?), the Sprout's sex life, a softball team of all things; and too many drinks later I walked you to your subway stop even though it wasn't the same as mine—I came up with some story that I was going uptown to see a friend, though of course I have no friends—and as we waited to cross the street there came a soft clattering rush: the sound of thousands of those small white petals which fill the city for about two weeks, and now a whole army of them trundled across the pavement in the wake of the gypsy cabs and a crosstown bus, a vast carpet moving in one direction, like the tail of some immense creature whose body had already dissolved into the night, trailing delicate bits of skeleton that would reassemble in another dimension, and as the light changed the petals were still marching along, their ranks cut into parts by the Third Avenue traffic and sent whirling into eddies, and this, Pru, this was the evening when my dizziness started, my inconsolable vertigo, because as we crossed you touched my arm and pointed at the sky and without a word we watched a hundred more petals fall, from some point lost in the dark roof of the night, like confetti at a parade commemorating the Unknown Worker, the petals taking time to wander through the air, and when my eyes returned to street level the whole world was rubber: cars bent like taffy, the ground beneath me shuddered like a gangplank, traffic lights wobbled and smeared, even the architecture appeared to expand and contract at once, and you'd forgotten your fingers were still on my arm; I'm hoping that, now that I've told you this, set down my confession at last, I'll be cured, but what I'm getting instead is a slow, cranky whir coming from beneath my overheated wrists, a sound I know well: it means that this craptop's battery is about to go out—I've got three hundred seconds and counting!—here we go!—so I'm hitting Control-S one more time, to save this last stretch of immortal prose—I feel so strange now, like the top of my head has just floated away, or maybe it floated away hours ago and I'm only just realizing it; and now a fine mist is coating my face and hands, and I don't know if that's a voice I hear in the distance through the opening in the roof or a complicated wheezing, like the Unnamable has sprouted wings and is hovering somewhere above me, my unexpected guardian angel, maybe reaching down to pull me up—OK, I just tried standing and grabbing at the air above but I don't think I'm tall enough, or else his arms aren't long enough—obviously I'm losing my mind—and sitting back down has suddenly made me very, very tired—and maybe the computer has completely shut down already, but I'll keep writing anyway, because I'm a little light on activities here, and in a few seconds I'll save this one last time, shut the craptop for good, and lie on top of it to protect it from the soft but steady spray of what I hope is just water, maybe slap on a Post-it saying PLEASE PRINT OUT FOR PRU! in case I don't make it out of here—but how can I be sure my handwriting won't be completely unreadable?—oh! *oh!*—actually this just occurred to me, a genius solution: *I can send this to you as an e-mail,* even though I can't see the screen, because (a) the wireless in this building, which we were stealing from the ad agency on the seventh floor, probably still works, and (b) Glottis understands spoken commands, provided they're well-articulated, so when I'm all done writing I'm going to hit the function key to open Glottis, and put my mouth two inches from the mike and utter, in my clearest voice, *Select all text* and *Copy,* and then *New e-mail* and *To Pru at Sharmila dot com* and *Paste* and finally *Send*—leaving two seconds after each command, like the manual says—and the idea that you'll get this message soon, sooner than tomorrow—that there's a chance you'll read this *tonight,* maybe before I'm finally released (*if* I'm released)—is incredibly comforting: The air's getting kind of terrible now, like eggs and ammonia and gasoline, so I need to wrap things up and—*I'm sorry*, Pru, sorry I couldn't say all that I wanted to, tonight, but in truth it was as much about imagining I was saying something to you as it was about actually saying anything: You said yourself, once, waiting for stuff by the asthmatic printer, that the office generates at least one book, no, one *novel* every day, in the form of correspondence and memos and reports, all the reams of numbers, hundreds of sentences, thousands of words, *but no one has the mind to understand it*, no one has the eyes to take it all in, all these potential epics, *War and Peace* lying in between the lines; so maybe just think of this letter as one such novel, one such book, cobbled from the data all around me, and I'm trusting that at worst you'll ignore the NEW E-MAIL flashing in your in-box, bothering your screen, but at least you'll be conscious of it, as you sit at your desk or your worktable with the sewing machine, over there at Sharmila Maternity Wear, and slowly the unread message will invade your thoughts, and curiosity will get the better of you, as you wonder what I could possibly have to say to you after all this time, and why I remain,—Your friend,—JONAH

< *ACKNOWLEDGMENTS* >

I'm grateful to Maureen Howard and James Browning, for years of encouragement; my eagle-eyed sister, Aileen Park; Jenny Davidson and Eugene Cho, esteemed structural and re-structural advisors on this project; Julia Cheiffetz and PJ Mark and Julia once again. I'd like to salute all at *The Believer*, Team Dizzies, and the Poetry Foundation; friends from *Voice* days, especially constant interlocutor Dennis Lim; Ros Porter, Alex Bowler, and Jynne Martin; early readers and listeners, including Benjamin Strong, Nicole Bond, Rachel Aviv, and Aimee Kelley. Many thanks to my father and mother and the delightful Duncan, to friends who've been waiting forever, and to all my family on both coasts, other continents.

This book goes out with all my love to my wife, Sandra—not just the beauty but also the brains of the whole operation.

Photo: © 2008 Sylvia Plachy

Ed Park was born in 1970 in Buffalo, New York. He is a founding editor of *The Believer*, the former editor of the *Voice Literary Supplement*, and an editor at the Poetry Foundation. His articles have appeared in *The New York Times Book Review*, *Modern Painters*, the *Los Angeles Times Book Review*, and elsewhere. He lives with his family in Manhattan, where he publishes *The New-York Ghost*. Visit him online at ed-park.com.

Printed in the United States
by Baker & Taylor Publisher Services